THE CARETAKER

THE CARETAKER

DAVID BADURINA

This book is a work of fiction. Any references to real events, real people, and real places are used fictitiously. Names, characters, places, and incidents are a product of the Author's weird imagination. Any resemblance to persons, living or dead, actual events, organizations or locations is coincidental. Maybe.

All rights reserved. No part of this book may be reproduced or transmitted in any form or by any means, including but NOT limited to: Graphic, Analog, Electronic, Mechanical, Telepathy, Beat Poetry, Interpretive Dance or Modern-Day Bard Song. Reproduction or transmission via photocopy, recording, taping, cave drawings or by any information storage recording or retrieval is expressly prohibited without direct written permission by the Author. References to artistic media or works are the property of their respective creators and copyright holders. Don't steal.

© 2020 David Badurina

All Rights Reserved

ISBN: 9798672088426

Printed in the United States of America

DEDICATION

To Joseph. My hero, my friend, my brother. The day you passed, my heart was irreparably broken. In our last voice conversation, you asked all about this project, barely a thousand words old.

Well, here it is. 32 chapters for #32.

I hope somehow, some way, in some time or alternate reality I can hand it to you, and we can celebrate this accomplishment together. Your loss made me realize that the time to dream big and follow your heart is today. I hope whoever is reading this is inspired to do just that.

I will forever be your little brother.

CHAPTER 1

THE HOLE IN MY HEART

With a little luck, I'd be dead in exactly twenty-three minutes.

This part was the most nerve-wracking. I was twelve miles from a deserted warehouse off a country road in the middle of nowhere, ready to meet some kid for the first time. His job was to deliver an unopened package to my hands.

I'd spent the past six months tracking down the contents of that parcel. My contacts in the antiquities and connections throughout a network of black market artifact dealers had led me here. I owed too many favors now and had an abundance of cash to replenish, so I was hoping my efforts would pay off tonight.

I'd been down this road twice before a few years ago, after being robbed of my responsibility. Recovering a one-of-a-kind artifact was always difficult, yet easier than you'd think. Prized items produced an abundance of talking and hushed whispers within a secretive circle. Most of them had known I was coming for it, so it didn't get too far before I was able to arrange to have it back in my hands, where it belonged.

I had three things on my to-do list for the night.

First, I had to meet someone I'd never seen before in a random, desolate location, then lie about why. I needed to make sure it was safe and secluded, and hoped they hadn't posted their evening plans on social media.

Second, I had to assure them I didn't show up to murder them. That was the toughest part. From their perspective, they'd had someone arrange a no-questions-asked package delivery for a decent payday. That sounded shady, because it was.

Third, I'd kill myself.

Tonight I'd have an audience of one. I had to do it in front of them in hopes they could follow simple instructions while I bled out at their feet. I'd always been happy to pay someone for following directions.

Sometimes I'd catch myself wondering hard if this life was something worth my gratitude. Though I'd miss the excitement if I were just, I don't know, dead. I never thought I'd become an adult and have to spell out things such as, "Please don't throw up on me," or, "Don't call the police." In my experience, they almost always called the police, and it almost always became super complicated after that.

All I knew was that this time I was meeting a teenager looking for quick cash. Another short-term acquaintance in a lifetime littered with them, I was sure.

I'd developed the habit of not getting too attached to people—that's what endless disappointment had gotten me. I hoped whatever kid was delivering this thing wouldn't freak out like the last one. I'd been two weeks dead in shallow weeds behind a gas station in Hoboken. Were it not for that inebriated homeless guy bringing me back to life, I'd still be there.

I'd smelled worse than he did when I came back.

The radio had produced only static for the last forty miles. I could barely see the road. I'd been watching massive farm insects smashing into my windshield all evening. If nothing else, it was a constant reminder that life could be brief, and could end in the most unceremonious of ways. Time was becoming a factor. If I ended up even a minute late, all kinds of things could go sideways. I was already trying to make up lost time because of a flat tire just outside Omaha.

The dark country road I'd been on for countless hours looked bathed in artificial light up ahead. The warehouse. It was nice looking at something other than massive stalks of corn and a starry sky. It was a crumbling old building with a crappy Honda in the parking lot, yet still a welcome sight.

So far, so good; I had five minutes to die. I backed into the parking lot a few spots from the other car and noticed something: it had a Starfleet Academy window sticker.

Perfect. A nerd.

I always faced my car out toward the road just in case I had to run later. After turning my car off, I stashed the keys and my wallet in the glove box. It was time to get into the abandoned warehouse and meet my delivery person.

I pulled hard on the heavy door and squealing, rusted hinges announced my entrance. A frightened young man stood there, nearly soiling himself at my abrupt entrance. We stared at each other across a large lobby with a grimy waiting room.

"Wh-who are you?"

I considered him for a moment. He had on ripped jeans and a ratty old John Deere T-shirt. Big blue eyes stared at me through a mop of disheveled golden hair hanging just below his eyebrows. While unkempt, my gut instincts considered him harmless, so I figured he could get the condensed version of what was about to happen without too much hand-holding. I snatched the package from him and my frantic hands began unwinding the twine.

"How old are you, kid?"

"Seventeen."

"Great. This'll sound super weird, but I need you to help me by following precise directions."

"Okay, but, who are you?"

I sighed. Every one of them played the get-to-know-you game. After dealing in artifacts for as long as I had, I'd developed the habit of avoiding personal information.

"You can call me William," I said. "The first rule is don't ask me another damn question until I'm done talking." I spared a moment to check my watch: 9:38 p.m. Damn it all, I was already one minute late. Unraveling what seemed like three miles of twine wasn't helping.

"Do *not* call the police," I continued. "I won't hurt you. Something has to happen tonight that has the potential to mess you up unless you do as I say. So just stay calm, and when it's over I'll explain everything, I'll get you paid as promised, and you can be on your way. Got it?"

"I-is this a drug thing?"

"No, no drugs. Also, no, your cash isn't in my pockets. You can't take it and run when you feel you can make a getaway without me putting up a fight."

"I-I wasn't gonna—"

"Shush. I need to focus right now."

The poor kid seemed terrified, and we were just getting set up. I unwrapped the last bit of twine into a heap beside my feet.

"Now clear out an area where I can lie down."

He looked a little more than flustered. "Mister, I'm not gonna do, you know, sex stuff."

"Kid, don't flatter yourself. Please just shut up and do it." I started unfolding the canvas wrapped in twine, eager to see if the object was what I expected. If it wasn't? Thankfully that'd never happened, and I couldn't imagine how I'd react if it ever did.

9:39 p.m. I was two minutes late. The balancing act of hurrying my ass off while also making sure everything went nice and smooth was always the most challenging aspect of my job.

"Young man, what's your name?"

"Harvey."

He'd just finished clearing a small space in the broken old lobby. There were a few busted chairs, and one of those 1960s-looking standing ashtrays next to a polyester loveseat. Paint had been peeling from the walls for decades. There was a filth-covered coffeemaker with a cracked carafe perched on a small side table. A yellow rotary phone dangled off a warped wooden shelf beside a puke-green metal door leading to the rest of this expansive old warehouse. Thick layers of dust and peeled paint lay gentle across the entire room. It was serene, like a layer of fresh-fallen snow blanketing a long-forgotten wood.

Ages had passed since anyone has waited in this old lobby. The place smelled moldy from the damp floor, and there were rat droppings along the wall.

A perfect space for death.

"Okay Harvey, here's how this will shake out." I held the folded canvas in one hand and placed my other over it, devoting full attention to eye contact with this scared young man as I spoke. "There's a knife in this fabric unlike anything you've ever laid your little virgin eyes on. I'll take it out of here, kneel in that clearing you so graciously created for me, and drive it into my heart."

This was typically the point where someone would tell me they were ready to vomit. I studied him as he took a step back and placed his hands against a rusty old desk, grounding himself. "I-I think I'm gonna get sick."

There it was.

"Please don't throw up on me. Relax. I'll be fine. I've done this before," I reassured him. "You just have to do two things for me."

"Wh-what?"

Harvey was panicked, but I thought he was doing well so far.

"First, don't call the police; it'll complicate things. Second, when I've bled out completely, pull the knife out. Set it down on the canvas, and in moments I'll wake up and explain what the hell is happening."

"Wait, blood? What—"

"Do. Not. Touch. The. Blade."

With a flourish I moved the canvas over and exposed the knife to his eyes.

I'd done this more times than I could count, yet it left me in wonder every time.

Bathed in the soft light of the musty old office, nestled within the worn, stained fabric was the knife I'd hoped to see. The first thing my eyes always noticed was the single green emerald fitted into the pommel. My gaze drifted up the hilt, adorned in pearl and veined with black opal, to the golden rim affixing the blade to the handle.

Harvey's jaw dropped as he leaned forward, clutching his chest with his hand. "Holy . . . I can't . . . I can't breathe."

I didn't acknowledge him. It was the blade. It was always the blade. A honed edge so sharp it could've been a single atom in width. A shade so dark a human brain couldn't comprehend it. It looked like an illusion, even though it was right in front of us. I tried to focus on the blade, but it was so black that no matter how hard I concentrated, my eyes slid off it. It wasn't even a color so much as the absence of reality.

Harvey kept looking back and forth, from the knife to my face. "What—" He swallowed, his breathing as labored and ragged as my own. "What is that?"

I grabbed the hilt and took two knees on the ground. Blood was pounding through my body, and my face was hot. Good. Adrenaline coursing through my veins always helped me bleed out faster.

I couldn't keep my eyes off it as I spoke. "A blade as black as the void," I whispered. "Adorned with a single emerald by mortal man. It's not of this world. Forged outside all life and time, it will outlast all creation. She is the First and The Last. Harvey, meet Death."

"What the fu—" he stammered. "Death? What's happening?"

Our surroundings were changing. The walls had tinted shades darker, and the room now chilled me to the bone. It was unnerving what this blade could do to its surroundings. Harvey was full-on freaking out, grasping for whatever object he could hang on to, so he could connect with reality. I'd been there.

When you light a candle in a dark room, the soft glow of light illuminates everything. Delicate flame highlights shadows and gives you a better picture of the material world that surrounds you. Warmth and life come into focus with the smallest ember.

This ancient blade did the opposite of flame. It would always be the ultimate extinguisher of life. Impenetrable darkness radiated from it just as light shined from a lit candle. Light became dark, life faded, warmth disappeared, and cutting through me like an ice-cold wind was a sense of loneliness and emptiness. Everything pulsed—as if breathing—and with each meticulously paced breath it drew, darkness intensified for a moment. Death's heartbeat drained life from its presence.

By this time, I knew what to expect during one of these special evenings. It was still terrifying, sure, but I was always prepared. Harvey wasn't, but I didn't have time to hold his hand and tell him everything would be okay.

It was time.

"See you in a few minutes, kid."

Harvey's eyes were frantic. He began waving his hands around. "Wait, mister! No! No, don't do that!"

My knuckles were stark white as I grasped the hilt, and with one motion, I slid the blade slowly and steadily into my heart. I hated to admit it, but every time this happened, I was reminded of how good it felt. A moment of panic and a sting of pain gave way to sweet and terrible relief. It was what an addict might experience, horrified and embarrassed that a needle was slipping in one more time. I supposed that shot of pain was a reminder that something felt so good. I couldn't help but wince as it tore a hole in the center of my heart. With a slight twist, my warm, sticky blood soaked my shirt and streamed out over my hand into a growing pool on the floor. Every time my heart pulsed, it jetted out, and I heard it slap and splatter against the concrete.

I collapsed.

Harvey was in shock. He may have been throwing up in the corner. It didn't matter. Death was embracing me. Warm, terrifying, blissful.

The knife was insatiable. The darkness intensified and pulsed around me. I felt the tip deep in my heart, draining my life faster and faster. Its preternatural enthusiasm overpowered my will to stay alive.

I closed my eyes.

For a moment, everything went white. Whatever ambient noise was in that office quieted. Harvey's frantic panting and the echo of my blood tapping the concrete floor as it spilled out began to fade away. It was like listening to the world underwater. Senses faded as I drifted faster and faster into the deep unknown.

I opened my eyes.

My hands went from being coated in jets of blood on a damp concrete floor to resting in cool blades of grass. Somewhere atop a small hill on a perfect day, a warm breeze touched my face. Beautiful cherry blossom trees surrounded me. The sky above looked as if Monet himself had painted it on the atmosphere. Then I heard her.

"Tsk, tsk, William," she cooed. "You're six minutes late."

CHAPTER 2

A Date with Destiny

I shook my head, looked around, and attempted to orient myself. Blooms of white, pink, and red were flittering to the surrounding ground. The colors reflecting in my eyes were vibrant and intense. A whispering breeze carried the cheerful song of black-capped chickadees perched in the surrounding cherry blossom trees.

The blade I'd felt draining my life just moments ago rested snugly in its sheath against my hip. That sweet warmth of the morning sun bathed me in comfort, and a deep breath offered an opportunity to settle my nerves. I stood up and turned around, facing a well-worn gravel path through the feathery green grass ending by a small porch in front of a tiny yellow farmhouse.

There she was, sitting on a porch swing for two, her delicate hand patting the seat beside her. I smiled at my tardiness and walked up to the porch. If I'd been a dog at this moment, my tail would've been between my legs.

"Sorry I'm late. It was a rough trip."

She was so beautiful swinging back and forth. Her thin summer dress caressed her curves and highlighted her sun-kissed skin. Her bare feet dangled a few inches from the porch floor. Wavy hair as rich as decadent dark chocolate cascaded past her shoulders.

Her brown eyes met mine. I always found her eyes stunning. Staring into Dee's eyes was an experience. It was as if standing outside a mountain, looking into a deep cave full of unknown mystery and epic adventures.

"How are you, my sweet William?"

I sat beside her. The chain suspending the swing creaked and we rocked back and forth, lazy and calm. I soaked in her voice. I'd missed it so much. Feeling her soft fingers rest on my hand as she looked to me for an answer made me melt. This was the fourteenth time I'd visited Dee, and the fourteenth time I wanted the impossible: to stay here forever.

I sighed. "Lost and lonely, if I'm being honest."

She cocked her head to the side and a slight frown drew across her face. Even saddened, she was beautiful.

I shrugged. "Hey, you asked."

Dee turned to face me on the porch swing, extending her legs over my lap and crossing them as she brought her hand to rest on my shoulder. She perched her chin atop her hand, her perfect lips grazing my ear. I could feel her warm breath against my neck and never wanted it to end. I closed my eyes, trying with all my might to remember every touch, every sensation, every sight and sound, and every feeling during my time with her. It helped me when in my darkest moments to recall the sense of safety and comfort she'd always given me.

"Do you think about the past, William?"

"No, I don't." That was a lie, and she knew it. I don't know why I bothered. I was consumed by thoughts about my history.

"Such a crooked past," she whispered.

"It doesn't matter."

She leaned forward and nuzzled my neck with her nose. I wanted to turn my head and kiss her. She knew it too, but I was apprehensive. Nervous.

"Do you know why I let you visit me, William?"

"Because of my job," I answered. I thought backing off and being more professional was the right move.

"Because I know you," she whispered. "I know everything about you. I know your grace."

She walked her fingers up my chest, resting their delicate tips at the base of my throat.

"I know the words you leave unsaid," she whispered, her voice as melodic as the surrounding birds. Her finger slid down my chest, resting over my heart. "I know every hole in that big heart of yours. I know how many more scars you'll collect. I know the pain. We're both so lonely now."

I shrugged. "That's because nobody can run from you. They all try."

"And fail," she added. "You cannot avoid the path you're on."

We sat in silence. Dee rested her head against my chest and we swayed on the porch swing, drenched in warm light while enjoying a soft breeze. This moment felt normal. We could've been a couple living out a dream in a farmhouse underneath a perfect blue sky. It was hard not to feel overwhelmed with sadness that we would never live that dream.

"I know what's in your heart, William."

"Of course you do. I still don't know why you wanted to see me, though."

"Show her to me?" Dee asked.

I leaned forward and reached to my back, unsnapping the sheath from my waist. Dee moved her legs off my lap and folded them under herself as she readjusted beside me. It was as if we were just two kids and I was about to show her something mundane, like a coin collection. I held the sheathed blade in my lap and she put her hand on it, closed her eyes, and drew a slow breath.

"She needs you, William."

"Yeah, I know."

"Do you ever wish she was different? More like me?"

"Every day," I answered. "Being her Caretaker is lonely. It's just an object. Why am I even continuing to take care of it?"

"William, that's not fair. She can't touch you. That doesn't mean she doesn't care. You've been together for so long. She appreciates you, more than you could imagine, and chose you for a reason."

I stayed silent, wishing and dreaming.

"William, there's a reason I wanted you to see me. There's something you need to know."

That was never good. I turned to her, and the comfort and joy I'd felt just a moment ago disappeared. I was sure she saw my concern.

"There are secrets and whispers."

"What whispers?" I asked.

"Threats," she whispered.

"Dee, is someone threatening you? Who?"

"I can't."

"Dee, tell me. I'll erase them, I swear. You know I can."

She allowed herself a slight smile and caressed my cheek with her warm hand. "The tide is rising, William, and if you aren't careful, it will take you just as it will take me."

Intense emotion boiled to the surface. I felt like a jealous boyfriend. If I had to annihilate every being in the universe to protect her, I would.

"Dee, I will destroy whatever threatens you, just tell me what's going on!"

She shook her head. "Something will take me."

She had to be mistaken. "Take you? You're untouchable. Never. It can't happen!"

Dee pressed her hand to my chest and looked into my eyes, and everything came into focus. There was no happy ending here. All this comfort was my projection. It fooled me every time because that was my wish. This would never be normal and I could never have her, no matter how hard I wanted it. But her being taken away? After what I'd been through and what we'd shared? She was all I'd ever had. I didn't understand.

"She will need you, William. We all will. I wanted you here tonight because even though I shouldn't, I had to warn you."

"Enough with the riddles! Who the hell is it? Tell me!"

"I told you not to be late, William. I knew you'd be. It's okay. It's not your fault."

She gestured toward my lap. My eyes shifted downward and to my horror, the blade had disappeared. Something had happened. Something with Harvey, and the blade, and my body. The timing was wrong. I should've still had the blade.

Dee stood up and held on to my wrists to help me stand in front of her. She rose to her toes to come closer to my height. She wrapped her arms around me, resting her body against mine. Her lips grazed against my ear once again as she held me close. I breathed deep, breathing her in, letting her sweet scent fill my lungs as I felt her body pressing against me. I knew I had only seconds left. I tried to memorize how she felt against my fingertips, how her voice filled my ears, how her sweet scent filled my lungs. I didn't want to leave.

"Get the blade back," she whispered. I could sense it upset her. Her voice wavered with the nuance of shielded emotions. "Find her where love is, William. She will help you."

"Find her? Who? Th-the blade?"

Dee pulled back. "We'll see each other again, my sweet man. I promise."

Her hands drifted from my shoulders to caress my face as we lost ourselves in each other's eyes. She leaned forward and pressed her lips against mine, soft, slow, warm, and sweet. I let go of my doubts and fears and let myself drift through this moment like that warm breeze around us. She had my heart, I was hers, and everything felt very, very complicated. I just didn't care.

As first kisses go, it was perfection. It felt as if we'd kissed a thousand times before.

In an instant, everything ended.

I opened my eyes.

Coming into focus was a bloody concrete floor in an abandoned warehouse lobby. Sights and sounds returned. I felt numb. Frozen.

I looked to Harvey as I gagged on chunks of coagulated blood, spitting it out to clear my mouth. A deep, wheezing breath echoed from my lungs. My chest felt like fire, and intense pain vibrated through every cell in my body. I sensed broken ribs.

He was sitting beside me on a rusty old filing cabinet, eyes wide and hands covering his mouth.

My eyes met his and I gasped enough breath through my blood-choked throat to ask the only question on my mind.

"Harvey, what the hell just happened?"

CHAPTER 3

CUT

I couldn't imagine the confusion Harvey was experiencing. Some guy stormed into an abandoned warehouse with him and committed suicide, then stayed dead for, well, nobody knows how long. You can't tell time through blood-covered watches, and I was too weak to do anything but breathe again. If I lifted a hand off the damp concrete floor, my face would hit in its place.

My wits were returning and my frustration dissipating. I needed answers. Harvey watched in horror as I came to. I was blood-soaked head to toe but propped myself up. I wiped dried blood off my watch face. It was 2:35 a.m. Five hours dead.

I should have known. That late arrival had cost me. Again.

"Mister, I-I'm so sorry. It just all happened so fast."

Harvey had moved a decrepit old filing cabinet to my side, perching himself there as if keeping watch over me. I looked around. The warehouse door was off its hinges.

Debris littered the floor. There were bloody footsteps everywhere. In the parking lot, my car was a smoldering wreck. Soft orange light from the remaining embers of the vehicle streamed through the grimy windows, highlighting the foulness of our surroundings.

What I thought would be a peaceful, albeit temporary, grave was wrecked. Knowing my surroundings had been upended in such a boorish manner offended me. It was obvious none of this was Harvey's doing.

I got straight to the point. "Look, kid, just tell me what happened."

"They just busted through the door. They knew you'd be here. One of them took the blade out of you, and the others started shoving me and kicking me, hitting me, laughing. You were lying there and you stopped breathing, so I sat here and waited. I froze, there was so much blood. I didn't want to just leave."

"How long ago did this happen?"

"A few hours, I guess. They tore off east in a big blue pickup. What the hell is going on? I tried to stop them and they laughed, roughed me up, took it, and sped off."

"The car?"

"One of them threw a Molotov at it. I-I'm so sorry, mister. I can pay for—"

"How many, Harvey?"

"Three. I-I stayed here and waited for you to come to, like you said. What was I supposed to do? I thought I was dead. I'm sorry!"

This picture was coming into focus. I sensed my heart beating at a reasonable pace. Sore chest, sure, but the wound had already healed, and I had color coming back into my skin. Regenerating fifteen pints of blood is never easy, regardless of what supernatural entity is keeping you alive.

Death nights weren't supposed to be like this. Chasing after anyone now would be pointless. Whoever took that blade had too much of a head start, and my car had melted, anyway. We wouldn't be making up hours of lost time in Harvey's piece of shit on wheels.

All that effort, and now I'd made it back to square one—having to track the blade down through connections, black market contacts, and cash. For a moment I considered letting it all go. It seemed so meaningless and lonely unless I visited Dee. It would be easier, but I still had a responsibility to uphold. Dee's words kept echoing in my head. Even if I wanted to, I couldn't quit now. I couldn't protect her if I did.

"Well kid, I'm sorry, but it looks like your cash is ash right now. I'll get you paid another time."

"Forget the cash, mister. Can you tell me what the fuck is going on? I don't understand."

He deserved answers at this point. It wasn't my policy to give too many details unless I wanted to see someone ranting in a padded room for the rest of their life, but I figured I could humor him, at least a little.

"All right, Harvey," I said, propping myself up and making my way to an overturned chair, straightening it out to take a seat and catch my breath. "We have a few minutes. I need to recover anyway. Ask a few questions. I'll answer them, and we'll leave. Go ahead."

"Um, okay." I was sure he had a hundred questions, and nothing was making any sense. He might forget tonight, and his psyche might protect him by convincing him it was all a terrible dream.

Harvey needed some prodding to get the conversation started. "Go on, kid. Ask a question. I won't live forever."

That was a poor choice of words considering the events of the last few hours.

Harvey relaxed a little, settling in his seat. He cradled himself in his arms like a self-hug. It didn't take a body language expert to realize the last few hours had been traumatic for him.

His voice was soft. "You were dead. Now you're not. Are you, I don't know, immortal or something?"

That was the best place to begin. It would help him understand what had just happened.

"No, not immortal. I'm just favored, I guess."

"Favored? Mister, what the hell are you mixed up in?"

"Harvey, in my, um, industry, people have one of three different jobs. I'm what's called a Caretaker. Caretakers are people who take care of objects imbued with certain properties. We call those properties Concepts. Other than Caretakers, there are Stewards—they're the most common. Stewards are people who are eyes and ears for powerful Concepts who prefer to remain hidden. I'd wager you've met a few of them, even in your short life. Then there are Guardians—you don't mess with them. Ever. My guess is a few of them were here tonight and snatched the blade before they beat the shit out of you. The point is, I'm a Caretaker, and that blade is my responsibility. I need to get it back."

"Concepts?" Harvey asked.

"Yeah. Concepts are actual, real beings, not abstract things. Surprise, I guess."

"I don't understand."

"Almost every Concept you can think of—Destiny, Hope, Death—they exist. I've met many of them. They're actual beings, and I help one of them. Some are in the form of objects, some are walking among us, some silent and exerting influence from shadows. When I killed myself hours ago, I was visiting Destiny."

Harvey was trying to wrap his head around it all.

"So you killed yourself to visit Destiny," he confirmed.

"Yes."

"Which Concept do you work for?"

"Death. I'm Death's Caretaker. We kind of go way back, though we've never met. It's complicated. That blade I drove into my heart, that was Death. On Earth, we call that knife the Blackwood Blade because we need a name."

"Is that why you came back?"

"It is. I've died many, many times and have come back many, many times. A long time ago something happened to me, and on that day Death took a liking to me, I guess. Traveling to visit those other places and other beings involves nights like tonight. I have to die to do it. I try not to do it too often."

"Why not?" Harvey asked.

"It hurts."

Harvey looked down at the floor, still hugging himself. Poor kid, his trauma was far worse than I thought. My body began to relax a little. I tried to sit up straight, then reached into my coat pocket and pulled out two butterscotch candies in blood-soaked crinkling plastic and offered one to him.

He shook his head. "No thanks."

"Suit yourself, kid." I unwrapped one and popped it into my mouth. Feeling a little saliva return was pleasant. People didn't realize how fast you dried out when you were dead for more than a few minutes.

"So no Grim Reaper or anything?" Harvey asked.

I'd seen my share of Hollywood movies. They depicted death as some guy in a long black cloak carrying around a scythe, harvesting souls and all that nonsense. It was hard to undo all those preconceptions.

"Okay, Grim Reaper is a cliché. Death isn't a skeleton in a cloak walking around and harvesting people with a farm tool like we're all a bunch of fat, stupid potatoes."

He nodded. "So if that blade ends up destroyed, nobody would die?"

"It can't be destroyed, but it can be used for nefarious purposes. I need to get it back."

I realized the blade always ended up in my hands because that was where she wanted to be. But stolen? And someone knew I was here? My gut churned at the thought. Some entity was working hard to circumvent me and cover their tracks. I had some ideas.

I looked outside. The flame on my car had died down. Harvey's ride was shit but seemed decent enough and should run. There were no sirens in the distance. We were safe now.

From my experience, only Guardians could have done this. Knowing who they were working on behalf of was impossible without more information. I wasn't in the mood for a mystery; there were more significant tasks ahead. I had to get Harvey in a better mental state and find some fresh clothes, as my charred suitcase was useless. Harvey could be more than another disposable helper. He now knew what he was dealing with and hadn't run screaming yet.

He'd survived a trial by fire. That was more than most.

I didn't like to keep people close. I dealt with too much death, and they all left. Whenever I got to this stage with someone, I ended up feeling conflicted. Should I have them along for the ride if they didn't have the benefit of being favored by Death? She always found them. Still, it had been a long time since I'd had any kind of companion, and Harvey seemed to be a decent kid.

I still couldn't get over the fact that just a few hours ago I'd been sitting on a porch swing in Destiny's arms. I'd have liked to be right back there instead of in this demolished lobby covered in sticky blood not knowing who'd taken the blade.

"William!" Harvey shouted.

I'd been so lost in thought I hadn't realized Harvey was trying to ask me something else. He may have said my name a few times.

"Sorry. What is it?"

"How old are you?"

This question. I had to be careful with my answer.

"The first time I died was in 1915. I was twenty-six years old. Then I died again in 1923. Then again a few years later. Again, and again, and again. And now here I am. Death was with me every time. You'd think being twenty-six forever would be incredible. It isn't. Looks aren't everything, kid. Doing what I do takes its toll in unseen ways. It's ironic, I suppose, that the one thing keeping me alive is Death."

"I guess so," Harvey replied. "How did you die?"

And there was the boundary I wouldn't let him cross. It was a logical question. The first death was always the hardest. He could never understand, and I wasn't in the mood to attempt explaining what I didn't fully understand, either.

"I'm sorry, I'm not answering that."

Harvey stayed silent. Thousands of chittering insects in the endless moonlit cornfields made the only music accompanying us. I felt terrible and wanted to explain, but sometimes the truth was worse than whatever your brain could conjure up.

It was time to go, and I needed a ride.

"Harvey," I said softly, "can you get me to Sioux Falls tonight? It's an hour away."

He sat balled up, holding his arms. "I-I'm not sure."

"Come on, man. I'm sorry for tonight and throwing that on you. It's hard to wrap your head around all of this. I need some rest, and I need the blade. We should get cleaned up—"

"No, it's not that," he interrupted, not making eye contact with me. He was staring straight at the floor.

The hair on my neck stood on end. Something was wrong. Something had happened. What was Harvey hiding, and how the hell did I miss it?

"Kid, what is it?"

He let out a pained wince as he rolled up his sleeve and looked at me.

The motion drew my eyes from his face to his arm. There was a deep gash just above his hand. The outer edge was turning his skin a light shade of gray.

They'd cut him. My stomach dropped. I held my breath as I stared at his wound.

"When they came in, I-I tried to stop them. Tried to hold the door closed. I tried to protect you lyin' there, I swear. My arm's numb now. I think when they were beating on me, one of them had the knife in his hand. The cut's hurting. Maybe I should go to a hospital?"

"Harvey," I said calmly, "are you certain they cut you with the Blackwood Blade?"

"Yeah," he replied.

That poor kid.

CHAPTER 4

LOOK BOTH WAYS

I regretted every single thing that had happened tonight. This poor kid got mixed up in something he couldn't wrap his head around, and now I had to explain what was going to happen to him. Tonight shouldn't be his last night.

"Harvey, I want you to listen to me. You're marked."

"Marked?" His breathing was fast and ragged and there was clear panic in his eyes. My hair was standing on end watching him go through this. Damn, that poor kid.

"I can help you, but I need you to not move right now. Just stay right there and don't move a muscle, okay?"

Harvey swayed like he was going to pass out. He shuffled toward the door with his feet dragging. I expected him to throw up, but he'd already emptied it all out when I killed myself in front of him.

"Harvey, don't move!" I shouted.

"What do you mean marked? A-am I going to die?"

This was all my fault. All those decisions I'd made in the last twenty-four hours—the fast-food drive-through meal I'd had, that extra bathroom break, not driving a few miles an hour faster—had contributed little seconds here or there, adding up to six minutes late, and now Harvey was hanging on to his life by the thinnest of threads. Sometimes normal people thought about these things. When you've had a car accident, you always think, "If I got ready a little faster, I would've missed the collision," or "If only we'd gotten there sooner, we could've saved him." I'd had those thoughts more times than I could count.

"Kid, there's a reason I tell people not to touch the blade. Anything can happen to you right now. Hand me your keys. Let's get you in the car. I'll drive. We'll get to civilization, and I'll get answers. We'll get this fixed. Until then, you're in a lot of danger. I can help you."

Somewhere, Dee was looking at me and she knew. She knew I was thinking about her, and she knew what was happening to Harvey. I didn't know what Destiny had in store for him. I just had to do my best for the kid to make sure he lasted longer than the next few hours.

"Make it stop!" he shouted. "You work for Death! Just tell them to stop!"

I watched as Fear tightened his grip around Harvey.

"Harvey, I don't control Death. Haven't you been listening? Just calm the fuck down, you'll have a heart attack!" I tried, but I couldn't settle the poor kid. If a meteor flew into the atmosphere and struck his head that instant, it wouldn't have surprised me. To live, he'd have to do what I said.

I watched him stumble through the doorway, then take off running through the parking lot toward the cornfield across the road. I took off after him as fast as I could run. There was no telling what could happen to a poor kid lost in a Nebraska cornfield in the dark after being marked by the Blackwood Blade. Every second that passed was more dangerous than the last.

"Harvey, stop!"

He looked back at me as he ran full speed to the road. The moment his feet hit the pavement, a rusty old car with its headlights off sped out of nowhere, plowed into him, and launched his lifeless body high into the air. I stopped in my tracks as I watched the horror unfold in front of me. The sound of shattering glass and snapping bone filled the air as the tires screeched and the car flipped into the cornfield. It rolled multiple times before coming to a stop upside down, engine dead, with no sign of life or sound. It was something I would've walked away from, broken and dazed but alive.

She came to him, and She took him. I hated it, but I knew it would happen. Whoever had taken the blade while I was with Dee knew it too. Harvey's cut looked deliberate. It wasn't a self-defense wound; it was made by someone who knew I'd have to deal with the marked kid. It was intentional, and it was beyond cruel. Why not just leave him be?

Harvey's twisted body lay lifeless by the side of the road a few yards away. I walked over to him.

Blood had soaked through his green John Deere T-shirt. One of his shoes had landed upright in the center of the road. The collision had torn his flesh open, and too much bone was visible. His neck had likely snapped, as his head rested at an impossible degree from his shoulders. One eye was still open, but his spark was long gone. Unlike my experience bleeding out earlier this evening, Harvey wasn't visiting anyone at this moment. If there was a soul, it was living somewhere I'd never been. There was no porch swing for the young man, no beautiful eyes, no sweet whispers or caresses. I didn't know what was out there for him. It wasn't Dee, though.

This was the fate she crafted for him, his last moments tied up and twisted with my path.

I searched through his pockets and snagged his wallet, a metal flip lighter, and the keys to his car, then took a short walk through shattered glass and random debris into the cornfield to view the wreck left behind from Death's hand. The driver of the rusty old car was just as mangled and lifeless as Harvey. Whoever they were, they were now unrecognizable as once being an intact human. This was someone who up until a few short moments ago was living their full life. A pair of fuzzy dice, spotted with blood, were twisted around the rearview mirror. This was someone's child once upon a time. Someone's best friend.

As Death's Caretaker, I was used to seeing life disappear in the blink of an eye.

In the back seat of the car and covered in shattered glass and corn husk, I spotted laundry in a busted laundry basket. It would have to do. Combing through the driver's pockets yielded a small wad of cash, and I found a pair of jeans and a clean black T-shirt in the scattered laundry. My best bet was to change right here in the field and then mix my bloody clothes in with the laundry in the back seat. This accident scene was too much of a disaster for there to be questions about blood-soaked clothes by authorities.

I took out Harvey's lighter, lit the clothes on fire, and tossed them into the broken heap of an automobile in the cornfield. It should cover any tracks I'd leave behind. The car wasn't mine, so I had no concern about being tracked down.

There was too much death hanging in the air tonight, and I had to focus, which wasn't easy. There was no time to mourn Harvey, no time to call the police or his parents. Dee had warned me, and now I understood why. Something big was happening, and I was a Caretaker without the object I was supposed to take care of. I'd just have to keep moving with ninety-three dollars and clean clothes. Thinking back to my other terrible nights, this wasn't the worst start I'd ever had.

So with a little cash and someone else's clothes on, I started Harvey's car, pulled out of the parking lot, and left the wreckage of the night behind, my only soundtrack for the ride north being the constant chirping of insects in the fields. I was on my way to Sioux Falls, South Dakota.

As the hum of the car engine drowned everything out, I kept thinking back to my visit with Dee. I missed her hand on mine. That sweet, warm breeze and the gentle swaying of the porch swing.

That kiss.

The first few times I'd visited her, I kept believing I was just dreaming. It took a few deaths to understand that it was real, just not in the reality I thought I knew. I wanted to return to her. I wanted to stay there with her, forget natural laws.

Her words kept echoing in my head. "Find her where love is."

I didn't know what she meant, but I had a hunch too strong to ignore. First, I had to get to civilization. I was about an hour from Sioux Falls, and Harvey had been nice enough to leave me with a full tank of gas. After a few hours of rest and a meal, I'd need to move.

My next stop?

LOVE Park in Philadelphia, Pennsylvania.

CHAPTER 5

WHEREFORE ART THOU

It had been about two days since the night both Harvey and I had died. In those two days, I'd made it through Iowa, Illinois, Indiana, Ohio, and Pennsylvania. It was a long, boring ride in a noisy car without a working radio, working air-conditioning, or working heat.

Once I made it across the border into Pennsylvania, Harvey's car sputtered and died in a much more muted fashion than Harvey himself. I was fortunate enough to not have a lot of stuff with me. I packed the small bag I'd gotten hold of in Iowa and relaxed at a rest stop for a few minutes. Many people were coming and going. I waited for my opportunity, then stole the most mundane-looking black sedan I could get my hands on. The woman who'd been driving it was having what I could only imagine was an awful bathroom visit. She'd most likely packed down some rest stop fast-food sitting under a warming light for the last nine hours. That would do it.

It was time to leave any trace of Harvey, and his car, behind.

I still felt awful for what he'd gone through in his last moments, but there was a time to mourn, and a time to get to work. It was time to focus. I ended up scoring some additional clothing by stealing from various laundromats. Stealing cash from unsuspecting travelers at various rest stops from South Dakota to here also had to happen.

I wasn't proud of the criminal activity I had to take part in, but when it came down to it, Death was missing. Actual Death. Dee was right, Death needed me, and she'd chosen me—for whatever reason—to be her Caretaker. If someone had to buy an additional pair of pants because the fabric of life and death was at risk of being out of balance, well, so be it. I tried to never take more than I needed. That was a rule I'd developed a long time ago. I never took too much from any single source. The truth of my reality was that it'd given me something that was both a curse and a gift. It was a responsibility.

I had to uphold that responsibility. I'd admit though, it was hard. It was just a knife to me. I was lonely and had grown tired of fighting for something inanimate.

I couldn't slow down as Death's Caretaker. I couldn't have a happy little family in a condo somewhere in San Diego with a dog and two kids. My life, since my death, was comprised of constant movement and constant action borne from tuned intuition. Coming back to life all those years ago was the one thing that prevented me from living a normal life. More irony.

There were millions of people dying now or dying soon that wouldn't come back, and I understood that.

There were families ripped apart by death, consumed by pain at the loss of kind loved ones.

I came back.

I supposed, while burdened with this grand purpose, I shouldn't steal twenty bucks out of someone's wallet when I only needed five.

Sometimes, though, you just have to swipe a car.

I'd slept in my stolen wheels last night in a parking garage a few blocks from LOVE Park in Philly. If I was being technical, it was John F. Kennedy Plaza, but tourists flocked there for the iconic statue. I'd been here once before, many years ago, but only because some nasty business brought me through the town. That night had been awful. Another death for me, a visit with Perseverance, who ended up being a great guy, and a lot of blood spilled by others. I'd scored a fantastic cheesesteak before leaving town.

There were worse things than cheesesteaks to reminisce about on nights I'd died.

With a stretch and a yawn, I got out of the car and made my way to the trunk. I was used to living in weird places or out of vehicles, so I set up whatever car I was driving around to have a trunk bedroom. Sticking a mirror on the inside of the trunk let me see how terrible I looked. Small compartments of clothes in cardboard boxes helped keep the place organized.

Everything stolen from laundromats.

I also always kept a bag of snacks and water—just because I couldn't starve to death didn't mean I wanted to try. Besides that, I kept necessities like a toothbrush, deodorant, and baby wipes.

When I wasn't around showers too often, baby wipes were priceless consumer items.

I had a long stare at myself in the trunk mirror. The reflection staring back looked like a dead guy with insomnia. It took my best effort to tame my tussled brown hair and give myself a quick shave. After some deodorant and a quick toothbrushing, I'd head into the city.

Cities, though, made me nervous.

Doing what I did, suspicion was necessary. In a city with millions of people walking around, it was easy to run into a Steward or worse, a Guardian. As Death's Caretaker, I'd been a target since day one. I was one person with a unique job for a unique object, and it attracted others to that power.

I'd seen one dramatic death start or stop wars, and a single death blossom into a love to last all time. Quiet deaths—undramatic to the last moment—could change the course of human history through their impact.

I'd been an active part in many of those moments. Alone. Not as an assassin, but as someone chosen to carry out the will of the Concept that favored him. I'd thrown the Blackwood Blade on the passenger seat of whatever car I'd been in before, traveling across the country. I'd had full-on conversations, but I didn't think a knife could listen.

Funny, I ended up having lots of time talking to an inanimate object when I couldn't hop on a plane with it. I couldn't imagine having it taken away by police. "Please, Mister Security Person, I promise I'm harmless. I'm just trying to bring literal Death on your airline. Will there be snacks?"

That wouldn't work, and I'd rather stay in the shadows, anyway.

I always kept a low profile since any person walking around, no matter their class or associations, could be a fellow Caretaker, Steward, or Guardian for any Concept. It was almost impossible to spot them at a glance, so I always opted for caution. Sometimes I got that feeling that someone near me was in the same line of work, but it was rare.

For instance, I remembered meeting a woman named Anastasia in New York City at CBGB in 1975. We'd run into each other during a classic set by Blondie, and we just knew. She'd been Steward for Satisfaction, and let me tell you, that was a great night right there. At least what I could remember was great. Let's just say that when Mick Jagger sang "I can't get no satisfaction" back in 1965, it was obvious he'd never met Anastasia.

I finished my out-of-trunk bedroom routine and made my way to the street to start the short walk to LOVE Park. It was Friday, and the city was bustling with commuters and people living their day to day, grabbing coffee and breakfast and heading to their jobs.

As I made my way toward the park, I went over questions in my mind. Find her where love is? Would I meet anyone? Was I in the right place? Was this a fool's errand? Where the hell was the Blackwood Blade right now? Was Destiny okay?

I quickstepped my way down the street, weaving in and out of pedestrians. I made a quick turn around the corner toward the park and tripped over a tiny dog, landing hard on the concrete.

People said things like, "Oh my God, are you okay?" and "Is that dog okay?"

"I'm fine," I reassured them, looking up from my concrete close-up and placing my hands on the ground to get back to my feet. That was embarrassing.

I'd stopped paying attention to any of those onlookers, though. In the distance was the iconic Love statue. Right in front of my face was a wheezing, slobber-covered pug, looking at me with its head cocked to the side.

Dangling off its collar was a small charm in the shape of a heart with a name etched in the center.

"Well, good morning, Romeo," I said through a smile.

He gave my face a lick. I knew it. I was in the right place.

CHAPTER 6

CRAZY LITTLE THING CALLED LOVE

I stood up from my unlucky parkour pug fail and dusted off my jeans, uncovering a small rip in the knee. I'd scuffed up my brand new Converse All Stars too, which was disappointing. I didn't often treat myself to something new and did my best to keep things neat and clean for as long as I was able.

It would eventually be blood-soaked, anyway. Or worse.

Romeo, the pug, was staring up at me. He had a leash a few feet long resting on the ground and was waiting for me to do something.

I looked around, and it didn't seem as if there was an owner nearby. There were a few couples around the park taking selfies in front of the Love statue, and a few kids skateboarding around the opposite side of the park. Some commuters were walking around in their business clothes, ready for a Friday of work and a happy hour a little later this afternoon. A few chuckles had happened right after I fell, but otherwise, everybody just kept moving along with their day.

I leaned over and picked up Romeo's leash. As soon as I had a handle on it, he turned and began walking. Being led through LOVE Park by a pug named Romeo was one of those events I never thought could happen, but here I was. Being walked. This was the best lead I had at the moment—literally and figuratively.

We made our way past the statue and toward a street musician with an acoustic guitar singing "Can't Help Falling in Love."

Romeo stopped and looked up at me. I stayed there for a moment enjoying the guy's music. He was good. I'd seen Elvis live in Las Vegas; nothing beat the King. But an inspired rendition of this song? I'd take it any day. It was nice to at least remember older times. The music was filling the air, and I could feel it in my heart. I was right where I needed to be, I just didn't know what to do next.

Romeo waddled a few steps forward and sat beside the empty guitar case the guy had set out for tips, then stared at me.

"Okay, buddy," I said to him. "I'll play."

I took a dollar out of my wallet and tossed it into the case, getting a nod from the young guitarist who then thanked the dog. With that complete, my new pug friend began walking again, pulling me across the park to a large shady tree.

There was a distinguished-looking man sitting in the shade. He was on a well-worn red quilt with his back against a large oak, smiling at us as we approached. He had short salt-and-pepper hair and a matching shortened beard.

I noticed he was a big guy with serious muscle on him. I had a solid physique. I'd learned that if you're Death's Caretaker, you'll get mixed into things from time to time. I'd spent decades on flexibility, kickboxing, and self-defense. This guy looked like he could hurl me over the Love statue without stressing his cardio.

Romeo began pulling hard on the leash, so I let go and he ran the rest of the way toward the red quilt, turning around a few times until resting with his head on his paws. I smiled and walked up to the quilt.

"Looks like Romeo found his way back. Nice companion you've got there."

The man smiled and patted the relaxed pug, then motioned to a space on the blanket. This was all part of the game. Whoever this man was, he knew I was involved in the same life he was. We sat there and enjoyed the guitar playing and singing for a few moments. I wasn't in any kind of hurry. True, my Blackwood Blade was missing, but I'd be able to find that easy enough. I'd been in this predicament before.

Through all the things I'd experienced, Love and I had never had a reason to meet. I'd always wanted to say hi, and I had plenty of questions, but I'd not had an important enough reason to visit. I was jumping the gun just a little, anyway. I still wasn't sure who I was sitting next to, apart from what felt like the smartest pug on Earth and his handsome owner, who must be one hell of a dog trainer. We sat there listening and watching the musician finish "Can't Help Falling in Love."

I turned to the man next to me. He was clean-cut and seemed to have a constant smile. He appeared to be a few years older than me—by the standard of appearance. I doubted he was over 130 years old, though. To anyone's eye, he looked like a well-taken-care-of man in his mid-fifties. He had on a spotless pair of leather dress shoes, a wrinkle-free pair of khakis, and a button-up white shirt—no tie—with small silver earrings in the shape of hearts.

"Lovely Day," I remarked.

"Bill Withers," he replied. "1977. A classic, but I love rock and roll."

We both stared forward as the young man with the guitar took a short break, had a drink of water, and got ready to play his next song.

"Joan Jett & the Blackhearts," I replied. "1980."

He turned and smiled as he corrected me. "1981."

I'd been testing him. I smiled back. We both turned to face the guitarist again as he started into Jack White's "Love Interruption."

"You know," I said, speaking toward him but keeping my eyes on the street musician. "I don't think I'd want love to change my friends to enemies."

"And show you how it's all your fault?" He laughed.

"Exactly."

"That ain't love," he said.

"Well," I answered, "I want to know what love is."

He smiled. He didn't have to say the next line of the song, but we both knew he said it in his head, and we didn't have to play games anymore. I showed my hand, and he showed his hand. He turned to me and put his hand on my shoulder.

"You must be William St. Denis."

That surprised me. I'd used hundreds of fake names during my life, and I remembered most every face I'd seen. This man knew who I was, but we'd never met—I would've remembered him. Something was at work here, and it was an interesting mystery.

"It's okay," he continued, petting Romeo and looking back out at the street musician as the music filled the air and the sounds of the city surrounded us in the background. "I can see the love in your eyes, William."

"I don't know your name. If we'll be here talking about the power of love, maybe you can at least offer me that?"

He closed his eyes and shook his head. "I'm so sorry, my friend," he replied, offering his hand out for what ended up being a very firm handshake. "Emmanuel. Emmanuel Love."

I laughed, shaking his hand. "So I detect a hint of an accent. Where are you from, Emmanuel?"

"Haiti, but I've been everywhere. These days I hang out here. It's quiet in this park. I could spend all of my days watching sweet old couples dancing and young lovers taking selfies."

It was time to break the ice further. I didn't do too much dancing around when there was an obvious unsaid question hanging in the air. Not that I didn't have the time for it, I did, but right now my curiosity about my new friend Emmanuel was at an all-time high.

"Steward?" I asked. Straight to the point.

He nodded and looked back out over the park, resting his hand on Romeo and giving him a good scratch behind the ears. The guitarist had broken into a rendition of

"Lovesong" by The Cure, and I watched as Emmanuel closed his eyes, listening to the slow cover song.

"Beautiful," he whispered. "The lyrics are perfect."

I stayed quiet. One of my most valuable skills was knowing when to shut up.

"Yes," Emmanuel continued, "Steward. You're wondering how I knew you'd be here?"

"Indeed I am."

"I know who you are, Caretaker," he continued. "Your blade is missing. I know why you're here, and I have been tasked to help you."

This mystery was unraveling at a furious pace, and each time I thought I pulled the thread that would give me the answer, it produced more threads. Who had told him about me, who was talking, and what was going on? How did he know?

I stared at the guitarist for a moment, listening to his singing. My favorite lyric to the song was always, "However far away, I will always love you."

It gave me a hint.

"Dee?" I asked.

Emmanuel smiled and nodded. "They talk," he said, "the one I work for and your friend Dee. They're very intertwined. They have to be. Often, who you love is part of your destiny, isn't it? We can't control who it is we end up loving, but it's always meant to be."

He was right. In another time years ago, it was the one thing I'd struggled most with. I'd been part of so many relationships. There was a pile of broken dreams, broken hearts, and hard-fought love that ended up dissolving into complacency and sadness. I'd never met Love, and I wanted to ask questions, but I guessed something larger was at work here, not my curiosity about an ex from 1953.

I took a deep breath. This environment, the park, it was intoxicating. The music and singing of the guitarist, the comfort of a quilt in a lovely patch of grass, the sounds of the city speeding by as we slowed down and enjoyed the moment. Even Romeo's steady breathing contributed to one of the most beautiful mornings I'd ever felt. As incredible as this experience was, however, I needed answers.

"Emmanuel?"

"Yes, William?"

"I'm missing something very important to me. I'd appreciate any help you could offer. A cryptic message led me here, and I don't understand what's going on."

He sighed. "It must be hard to be a Caretaker. I imagine it's lonely and hard to find that love and happiness."

"Well, what about Love?" I countered. "Have you ever met?"

Emmanuel smiled, looked down at Romeo, then gave me a sly wink.

I looked down at the wheezing, fat little pug. "No way," I whispered. "You can't be serious."

He nodded and smiled. "Just for today," he said. "He wanted to meet the real you, not the one you represent when you visit. He'll leave tonight, back where he's safe."

There I was in a park in the middle of Philadelphia, hanging out and listening to a street musician, chilling on a blanket with Love's Steward, Emmanuel, and Love himself in the form of Romeo, the pug. Once he revealed that, I tried to pick out the Guardians who were most likely among us. To unknowing eyes this was any day at the park, but just below that bustling surface was more. This was the unquestionable territory of Love himself.

I looked down at Romeo and he looked up at me, slurping at his snot-covered nose and wheezing as he breathed.

"It's, um, it's nice to meet you."

Romeo turned away, rested his chin on his paws, farted, and went to sleep. Emmanuel laughed.

This was an interesting development, but I couldn't stop thinking about Dee's words when we'd last spoke. "Find her where love is." Love was right next to me in the form of a malodorous pug named Romeo. And I was hanging with Love's Steward. Neither of these beings were Death, and they sure wouldn't have the Blackwood Blade.

"So, what now?" I asked.

He leaned away from me, reaching back by the tree he was resting against and into a picnic basket. He pulled out a canvas shopping bag, a small bottle of a caramel-colored liquid with no label, and a smaller bottle filled with some kind of crystallized powder.

"I will give you a gift," he said as he mixed the powder into the small bottle, corked it, and swirled it to mix it together, looking at it in the sunlight to be sure it was dissipating.

"Is that scotch?" I asked.

He handed me the bottle and the small bag. "Drink this tonight, all at once. But maybe be somewhere private when you do. Yes, it's a 21-year PortWood Balvenie. Single malt. That's pricy scotch, William. I have connections, though. That's the power of love."

"I hate scotch," I protested, staring at the bottle as I took it from him. "It tastes like barbecued hand sanitizer."

Emmanuel laughed. "Well you will hate it more after you polish this one off, my friend."

"Fair enough. What did you put in it?"

The street musician began playing "Need a Little Taste of Love" by the Doobie Brothers. Romeo's ears perked up when the song changed.

Emmanuel shrugged. "Let's just call it Love Potion Number Nine."

I studied the bottle. A single malt scotch with something added. "Number Nine?" I asked.

"Well, strychnine," he replied, matter-of-fact.

Strychnine. Fuck that.

I'd never ingested that poison but from everything I knew, it was a wretched way to die. You experienced horrific seizures while the poison attacked your nervous system. There was a reason it was so good at killing vermin. The cruelty of this poison was the fact that as you succumbed to it, you had full awareness. You got to experience the joy of watching yourself convulse while you asphyxiated to death.

It had all the subtlety of a shotgun blast to the face. Strychnine's wickedness was unmatched, and my hangover would be unmatched too.

I looked down at Romeo, then back to Emmanuel. "Are you sure it's the only way?"

Emmanuel scratched behind Romeo's ears. "It is the way he wishes. He wants to see how well you hold your liquor. It is unlucky to have to travel like you do, but sometimes, Love stinks."

"Yeah, yeah," I replied, standing up and stretching my legs. I slipped the small bottle of poisonous scotch into its accompanying bag and held my hand toward my new friend.

Emmanuel smiled a brilliant smile at me. "Tonight," he said, "after midnight, when that full moon is big and bright. You'll have about fifteen minutes of a rough ride before getting there, so be wise. You may be noisy. Oh, and stop by that newsstand over there, pick up a paper."

"A paper?"

"Yes, my friend. A newspaper," he said. "Get in some light reading before you take your trip tonight. I like you, William. I can see the love in your eyes."

"Thanks, I guess. I hope to see you again," I replied, shaking his hand. "I guess I've got a lot to learn about love."

"Always remember," he said, petting Romeo and looking back at the street performer, "Love will find a way."

"Yes," I replied. "Big Generator. 1986?"

"1987," he replied.

I smiled and waved a quick goodbye to Romeo the pug, who wanted me poisoned to death in the most excruciating way imaginable. If all went well, I'd be visiting Romeo in a different form after midnight tonight. I turned and made my way toward a small newsstand on the street corner, the sounds of song drowning in the background as the sounds of the city intensified around me.

There was a kind-looking woman in the small stand, surrounded by newspapers, packaged snacks, and drinks. I looked over what she had for energy drinks, pointed to the cheapest, and took out my wallet. It was two dollars. I pulled out a five to hand to her and dropped a loose dollar bill on the stack of papers at the stand. She turned to get me change and the drink as I reached down to pick up the dollar bill and the paper it was resting on, and there it was, staring me in the face.

The newspaper had a small headline on the right-hand side under the category "Weird News in New Jersey."

It said, "Trenton Librarian Thwarts Robbery, Only to Be Crushed By Falling Piano From The Sky."

"There it is," I thought to myself. There were no coincidences with the Blackwood Blade. Death was in Trenton, New Jersey. I would have to go there tomorrow and get her back. Tonight I'd be drinking poison, visiting Love, and getting answers. I had twelve hours to get myself a cheesesteak and do some light reading.

CHAPTER 7

SPLIT IT WITH YOU

I looked to the sky as dusk hit Philadelphia, and the shadows cast by the tall buildings felt like creeping tendrils wrapped around pulsing city streets. The anticipation of death drifted by with the cool fall breeze and I was feeling very unsettled by it. I had a newspaper under one arm and a perfectly warm cheesesteak in my hand. To an outside observer hanging out in the city, I probably looked like any evening commuter. I could be someone's brother, friend, or coworker heading home after a long day in an office, except I had a small bag with a bottle of very expensive poisoned scotch. Soon enough, I'd be drinking down that terrible concoction and embracing death in the silent solitude of the witching hour.

The things I'd do for Love.

I kept thinking about the plan and worrying about one little detail: the unknown of how long that poison would work for. The Blackwood Blade was easy—it was as if we knew each other. Death by any other means could get tricky. The time I put a .45-caliber round through my heart, my body began healing much faster than I'd expected, so I'd ended up being pulled into the world sooner than I'd wished. Thankfully, Perseverance had come through. I also learned that the next time I opted for firearm travel, I'd use a hollow point or just go straight to three-inch slugs.

Tonight I'd have to drink poison if I wanted to get some answers. Not only was I not looking forward to being poisoned to death, but I didn't know how long it would last before it started the inevitable purge from my system. I supposed there was a first time for everything, but the unknown was unsettling. Had Emmanuel put in too much strychnine? Not enough?

I didn't want to lie there on the outskirts of death, suffering for hours. From what I knew of the stuff, I was looking at a fifteen-minute window before mercifully slipping away.

I made my way up the parking garage stairs and swung the door open when I reached my floor. I looked out across the parking spaces and the few cars that were there. There was a young woman resting a few yards from my car, leaning against one of the structural supports.

Maybe it was my apprehension about the evening, but I took slow, deliberate steps as I walked toward my car. She looked to be in her early twenties. She had a nearly empty bottle of water, a pair of well-worn shoes, beat-up jeans, and a large backpack. Her wavy blond hair was tied back in a ponytail, and I spotted a few tattoos I couldn't make out. She looked tired.

Still, I could never be too sure. Some crazy things had happened the past few days. Any random encounter had the potential to be a category 5 drama hurricane. She could be a Steward for a wicked Concept. Even worse, she may not have any idea. That was a dangerous set of circumstances for a Caretaker.

"Evening," I said, walking up to my car, putting the paper down on the roof, and hunting for the keys.

"Hey."

"You okay? Just hanging out in a parking garage?"

She reached a hand around her backpack and pulled it close to her body. "Something like that, yeah."

I opened the car door, tossing the paper, the cheesesteak, and the small bottle of spiked scotch onto the back seat. "I'm sorry," I said. "Just having a conversation, not trying to freak you out or anything. You have a home, or are you just on vacation in a dark parking garage on a Friday night in Philly?"

She smiled. "Just passing through. I'm on my way to Boston. Parking garages are quiet. It beats breaking my back on a park bench."

"So you break your back on a concrete floor instead?

"Something like that."

I nodded, leaning against the back bumper of the car as I chatted with her. I wasn't getting any kind of feeling. She just seemed like a young lady who was probably having some hard times. I'd spent a fair amount of time in homeless tent camps and shelters. She struck me as a transient, drifting through a temporary time and situation on her way to something else, hopeful for a better life.

I knew the feeling well. There was a lot of solitude when you left home—whether or not you wanted it.

"Boston." I smiled. "Fun town. Long way from here. I'm heading up toward Trenton."

"Not a fun town." She smiled back.

I was usually pretty in tune to my gut feelings, and right now my gut was telling me to stop what I was doing and spend a few minutes with this person. There was never harm in a brief human connection. Connections filled life with special moments that flittered away in a thousand different directions, like blowing on dandelion seeds in a steady spring breeze. You never knew which small interaction may sprout into something far-reaching.

"My name's William."

"I'm Elise."

"Nice to meet you, Elise. So, are you hungry?" I asked.

"I guess," she said. "I, um, I didn't really have lunch."

I reached back into the car and took out my wrapped sandwich. "I just scored a huge cheesesteak, and I won't eat the whole thing. We could split it? Break bread with a stranger?"

She looked at the car then looked me over for a moment. It was the body language someone exhibited when they had trust issues or had a hard time accepting help.

It was like looking into a mirror.

"Sure. I'd like that," she said. "Thank you."

Splitting the food was perfect. I didn't want to eat too much a few hours before drinking down that scotch. The emptier my stomach, the faster the poison would metabolize, and I'd rather spend less time doubled over in pain.

Elise moved over and switched her bag to the other side of her legs. I sat beside her, unwrapped a perfectly gooey, greasy cheesesteak covered in Cheez Whiz and grilled onions, and split the two halves. In Philadelphia, it was typically referred to as a "Wiz Wit." Whiz, with onions. I ordered it this way to fit in, to be honest. Get one with Swiss cheese and mayo and locals scoffed. The less I did to stand out, the better.

"So, how old are you?"

"Twenty-three," she said. "You?"

"About a hundred and thirty." I smiled.

Elise covered her mouth and smiled as she chewed. She let out a quick laugh and took a sip of her water, looking me up and down. "I'm guessing about a century less than that."

"Spot on. Twenty-six," I lied.

"What's your story?" she asked.

"It's a long one," I sighed. "I'm heading to Trenton to recover something I lost."

"Oh? What's her name?"

"Nice," I replied. "Nothing like that, just an object that's important to me. What about you? What's waiting for you in Boston?"

She shrugged. "A friend."

"Oh? What's his name?"

Her smile faded. Mine faded to match. I'd struck a nerve, apparently.

"I'm sorry, I—"

She shook her head and looked to my eyes apologetically. "No, it's fine. I'm an open book. Man, it's been a hard few weeks. I have a friend in Boston who I might be able to stay with for a while. Until I get back on my feet, I guess."

"I've been in your shoes," I told her. "Maybe not the same experiences, but I know what it's like to drift for a while. We're both adrift."

Elise looked at the car and then back to me. "Nice car to drift around in."

I shrugged. She'd caught me on that one. I didn't look adrift in a spotless stolen sedan.

"Let's talk about something else," I offered. "Favorite type of music? What do you listen to?"

Elise lit back up. "Probably stuff you wouldn't listen to, being a hundred and thirty and all." She winked at me.

"Try me," I replied. "I've got good taste for an old man."

"My favorites are Al Green, Aretha Franklin, Marvin Gaye, and Bill Withers."

My jaw almost hit the floor. "Aren't you surprising," I said. "That's some serious taste in music. Classics."

Elise laughed. "I grew up on the stuff. It's all my dad listened to when I was a kid. He'd always play Motown as he made dinner for me and my sister. It brings back some memories and makes me feel good. We used to dance in the kitchen together."

"Hell yeah," I said. "The first thirty seconds of 'Love and Happiness' is absolute musical perfection."

"Hmm, you're probably right. Sam Cooke comes close though."

"Yeah he does," I replied. "Just like the river I've been running ever since."

Elise looked down at the ground. A long pause filled the air. The thoughtful expression in her eyes turned sad once more. "Sometimes it sure feels that way."

It wasn't clear to her I'd lived through those golden years of music. Hell, most of those recordings were from before she was born, and I'd seen Al Green perform in person in the early '70s. Still, this was a crazy coincidence, and in just the few moments we'd been hanging out on the floor of a parking garage, she was feeling like a friend.

"So, can I ask what brought you through Philly?"

Elise finished her last big bite of cheesesteak and washed it down with the rest of her water. "It's a long story. My dad and sister died about twelve years ago. Drunk driver. Then it was just me. I should have been in the car but I was at a friend's birthday party."

I reached out and placed my hand on her shoulder. "I'm sorry. I've seen a lot of death. I know how hard it can be."

Elise nodded and stayed quiet.

"It's probably been tough since then."

"Constantly moving, living with relatives but always feeling like a burden, yeah." She reached into her bag and pulled out a small pack of chewing gum. She offered a piece to me and I accepted. We leaned against the pillar next to each other and looked out over the quiet, sparse parking lot, both lost in thought for a moment.

"I was in Arizona a couple months ago," she continued. "I had an apartment, a good job, and a girlfriend."

"Girlfriend?"

"Yeah. Cassie. You love who you love, you know?"

"Believe me, I do."

"We're not together anymore. I looked past a lot to be with her. Things were good. One night I came home from work and she was on the floor beside the sofa. Overdosing. She'd promised she would stop using just days before. She was full of promises. I rushed her to the hospital. They saved her, and I left the next day."

"Why?" I asked.

She turned and looked me straight in the eyes. "I don't think I can make it through another death or another broken heart."

I understood that. Elise had been through some pain and she'd handled it better than most people her age. I admired her strength. "Listen, we're both heading north. Travel with me? I promise I'm not a creep."

She looked me over, processing my offer.

"I've got some work to do," I continued, "and you're good company. Plus, it's nice to travel with someone who has the same fantastic taste in music."

It looked as though I'd single-handedly lifted a massive weight from her shoulders. Traveling alone was hard—I knew that. A friendly gesture when you were at a low point could breathe life into you like little else could. As lonely as it could be as Death's Caretaker, deep down I supposed I was just wired to fix broken people.

"Are you sure?" she asked.

"One hundred percent. I've got a few bucks. Maybe we can crash in a motel or something? Nothing fancy, but better than a concrete floor or sleeping in my car. If we can find one cheap enough, I can spring for two rooms."

"No," she said. "Your car would be plenty comfy for me."

I shook my head. "We shared a meal and some great conversation. It's my thanks to you for making my journey a little less lonely. It's getting chilly, anyway. Please?"

My mind was all conflict. I had to visit Love tonight. I had a bottle of poisoned single malt scotch I had to swallow down and had to get answers to big questions. On one hand, that kind of thing would be impossible while spending time with someone I'd only just met. While it shouldn't be a repeat of Harvey, all kinds of things could go sideways. I'd managed an actual human connection to a genuinely nice person. Sure, I'd rather her not be hanging out while I'm poisoning myself to death, but I'd like to at least continue our connection a little longer.

Elise looked at me, and I got the sense she was trying hard to find a reason to decline my offer. She smiled. "Okay. As long as you aren't a murderer or a creep, we can do some traveling together."

I smiled back. "Not at all."

I wasn't a creep, but any normal person seeing what I did with the Blackwood Blade would have a hard time absorbing the nuanced difference between being a murderer and carrying out Death's will as her Caretaker.

I stood up and dusted off my jeans, then held out a hand and helped Elise up off the hard concrete. She threw her bag in the back and made herself comfy in the passenger seat.

"Do you want to crash in Trenton?" she asked.

"Probably somewhere close to there. It's getting late, but let's at least make it out of the city and up through some of Jersey. This area is a little out of my price range."

We pulled out of the parking garage and a few minutes later we were comfortably cruising on I-95 alongside the Delaware River. I had to find a place to sleep and pay a visit to Love, but I didn't know how the next couple of hours would go. Now I had someone riding with me, which complicated matters. I would have to figure out how to break off on my own after Elise fell asleep later.

Trenton wasn't far, so I had a half hour to figure out sleeping arrangements, kill myself, and determine how to manage the morning. It was 10:15 p.m. In two hours, I needed to be dead.

"Hey, you got any tissues?" Elise asked, interrupting my deep thought.

"Sorry, I was just lost in thought there. Maybe check the glove box?"

Elise started rummaging through the glove compartment as I kept my eyes on the road. "Nah," she said, latching the small door closed. "Nothing."

"Sorry," I replied.

"So, what's your story?" she said, reaching across her seat to turn the radio down. "Married? Divorced? Girlfriend? Boyfriend? You make a habit of picking up girls in parking garages?"

I chuckled. "Nah. I have a lot of responsibilities for the work I do, so it's better to stay unattached. Plus I usually have to travel a lot."

"My last name's Campbell. How about yours?" she asked.

"St. Denis," I replied. "My father's side was originally from Canada, but I don't think there's a lot of French blood left in my body."

Considering how many times I'd bled out over the last century or so, I thought it was a funny comment. Sometimes it sucked not being able to share a joke like that with someone who would appreciate it.

Elise nodded and looked out the window for a moment before turning back to me. I sensed a question hanging in the air. The car felt awkward all of a sudden.

"What?" I asked.

"Well," she said, leaning back in her seat and putting her well-worn sneakers on the dash. "The car registration in your glove box says this fine automobile belongs to someone named Katherine Wells. There was also makeup. It wasn't the right shade for your complexion."

"Oh," I managed.

"Right. You need cooler tones. So let's talk. Who the fuck are you, what do you actually do, are we in a stolen car, and why Trenton?"

"You weren't looking for tissues, were you?"

"No sir," she said with a smile and a hint of victory in her voice. "I was not."

I'd never been a decent chess player, but from what I remembered, this was exactly what checkmate felt like. I let out a long, resigned sigh. That was a savvy move and there was nothing I could do other than appreciate her cleverness in silence.

"Touché, Elise," I thought to myself.

"Okay," I said, reaching to the radio and turning it off. "Let me explain."

CHAPTER 8

TRUST ISSUES

I pulled into a parking spot at the Four-Leaf Clover Motel just outside of Trenton, New Jersey. It was seedy, the kind of neon-lit backstreet beacon that drew adulterers and illicit activity like horny little meth-addicted moths to the most alluring of flames. There was a crooked sign in the motel office window that said, "Get Lucky at The Four-Leaf Clover." I wasn't sure if Class was a Concept, but if it was, it sure as hell wouldn't be caught dead here.

This motel rented rooms by the half hour, but for a single night, it would work. I would die here—no sense in messing up a nice hotel or paying for a continental breakfast that I wouldn't be eating on account of being poisoned to death.

Hotel eggs were always gross, anyway.

I looked to the passenger seat. Elise was staring at me. I'd spent the last fifteen minutes spinning a web of lies to this poor girl, and I was certain she'd bought it. I'd had more than a hundred years of practicing little lies, and aside from carrying out Death's will, it was my greatest talent.

"So, you stole the car in Pittsburgh?" she asked.

"I did. Check the registration."

"I did. It said Independence."

"You already checked?" I asked.

"Of course I did. I couldn't verify your story otherwise. Do you think I'm an idiot?"

I shook my head. "Hell no. I admit I underestimated your cleverness, but I won't do that again."

"And you aren't a drug dealer?"

"No, I'm not. I promise. I'm not looking to hurt anyone. I just have something I need to get back."

"And it's not a human trafficking thing?" Elise continued.

"Absolutely not. Those people deserve all the bad karma they earn."

Elise was looking at me as if she was peering through a microscope. I wouldn't underestimate this girl again. She'd earned some respect for how devoted she was to verifying everything was on the up-and-up. I didn't jump right into the whole thing about working for Death, though I didn't think she would've blinked if I had.

Still, I felt like I needed to be cautious with her. Maybe it was apprehension and distrust—she could be a spy for another Concept, or just hired and paid to monitor me. She was clever enough. Hell, if I needed someone to spy on a Steward or Guardian, I'd hire Elise in a heartbeat.

Or maybe I was being careful for some other psychological reason. I didn't know why, and I didn't have the luxury of psychoanalyzing myself.

"Look, I was in the Midwest, South Dakota. Someone stole something of mine, and I need it back. I tracked it down to Trenton through a friend."

Nothing I'd just said was a lie. I'd been in the Midwest killing myself with the Blackwood Blade. I'd been in South Dakota. Someone had stolen the blade out from under me. Emmanuel was a friend, even though he'd given me a bottle of poisoned scotch, assuming I'd use it to kill myself this evening.

All of that was truth-telling. At least, that's what I told myself.

"Okay," Elise said, narrowing her eyes at me. "You told me you weren't after a girl, so what is this thing you're tracking down?"

"An antique."

"That's too broad a definition. Be more specific. That could be your grandmother's silver locket or a fucking teak armoire."

"Okay, it's an ancient artifact. A knife. Collectors call it the Blackwood Blade."

She scoffed. "The Blackwood Blade? That sounds dumb."

"Whatever, it's just a knife then. A stupid knife that has caused me a lot of trouble for a long time, and I just need the damn thing back, if you must know. It's worth a lot. Priceless."

Elise held up her hands and gave me a smile. Even though her manner was blunt, she'd shown herself to be quite intelligent. Underneath that cynical exterior, she was quite charming.

"This is about money, then?" she asked.

"No," I answered, checking my watch. Eleven o'clock. Time was becoming a factor.

"It's not about money, but you said it's priceless?"

"Do you interrogate everyone like this?"

"No," she answered, looking around as if what she was about to say was the most obvious observation known to humankind. "Just fucking car thieves."

"Fine. It's a family heirloom. Listen, it's time to get a room, chill out, and get some sleep. I can get you your own room. I promised. We don't have to travel together tomorrow if you don't want to."

Elise looked down at her lap, likely processing everything that had happened in the past couple of hours. I was thinking about the same things. It felt good bonding with someone, but trust became an issue. It was difficult for her, and it was difficult for me. I was sure if she stuck around for more than a day or so she might end up like Harvey.

This life had been hard. I wanted to help people. I'd always had this ingrained desire to fix the broken, the forgotten, and the pained. But no matter how hard I tried to fix people, I just ended up bringing more death to them. Harvey was a perfect example. He'd handled himself pretty well a few nights ago. I'd tried to bring him in, to see if he could handle the world I lived in. Maybe we could've been friends. He'd tried to protect me, and he owed me nothing. The kid had a good heart. Moments later, he was dead in pieces on a deserted road in the middle of nowhere.

Elise didn't deserve that kind of end, too.

"Fine," I blurted out, interrupting both of our thought processes. "Okay. I'll get a room for me, a room for you, and we just don't—"

"Let's stay together," Elise interrupted.

"I understand—wait, what?"

"Look, you seem decent, and you were trying not to freak me out, and I appreciate that. You shared your dinner with me and we like the same things. You could've just said to fuck off, but you didn't."

I nodded. "Okay."

"Plus," she continued, "nobody could come up with something as dumb as 'the Blackwood Blade' on the spot, so you're not lying."

We shared a laugh.

"Can you just do me a favor?" she asked.

"Anything."

"No more hiding things. No lies," she said. "I've dealt with a lot of liars. I just can't anymore."

That was a gut punch. I wanted to be open and honest with her, but for some reason I couldn't. I needed to do my job tonight and move forward after getting answers from Love. If I broke this young woman's trust in retrieving Death and fulfilling my role as a Caretaker, so be it. It was more important.

"You got it, Elise."

We gave each other a fist bump as a pact-sealing gesture of truthfulness from here on out, and I left her in the car and entered the front office of the motel. I paid for a single room from the seedy-looking creature running the place, and with a key in hand, went back to the car to retrieve a few items. I took some clothes and my toothbrush out of the trunk, then grabbed a newspaper and the small bottle of poisoned scotch, which I hid within my clothes. Elise had her backpack, and we headed toward Room 22.

The motel was your typical type of temporary stop. Two floors, a large parking area, and all the doors were individual outside entrances facing the road in a questionable neighborhood. We were fortunate enough to have a room on the second floor, close to the end of the building and far away from the main office. There were a few people staying here this late Friday night, and most of them were likely men and women staying together for sex dates while their spouses were home, unaware of the infidelities.

I unlocked the door and walked in as I turned on the light.

"Well," Elise remarked as she stepped into the room, "maybe don't turn on a black light." She seemed afraid to touch anything.

She was right. The room wasn't cozy. It had artificial light—one of those bulbs that makes every zit you've ever had during all of puberty show up in the clearest detail on your face. The matted shag carpet looked oily—they should've replaced it in the 1970s. There was a queen bed nestled between dated light fixtures mounted to shiny wood paneling. To the opposite side of the room was a small sofa that looked like a red burlap sack.

"Okay." I sighed. "How about we just head back to the parking garage?"

Elise laughed.

"Call it. Bed or sofa?" I asked. "It doesn't matter to me."

"It doesn't matter to me either," she replied.

"That's not a choice."

"Fine." She smiled. "I'll take the sofa."

"No you won't. I'll take the sofa. I'd rather couch surf."

"Ugh, we're so annoying," she said, flopping her backpack on the bed and taking some clothes and personal effects out of it. "Both of us are living this weird temporary life, neither of us comfortable on something so homelike as a bed. I guess I'm exhausted enough that it doesn't matter."

She wasn't wrong. It was past eleven, and I shifted my attention to figuring out how I'd drink scotch and kill myself in this room without Elise waking up. If I waited for her to crash and brought a blanket into the bathroom to pad the tub while my muscles twitched and locked, I could do it there. I should wake before she got up tomorrow morning, and I could come up with some excuse for being locked in the bathroom in the morning with a blanket.

That was my plan.

I brushed my teeth and changed into a pair of shorts and a T-shirt, then parked myself on the sofa. Beside me was a scratchy blanket I'd swiped from the small closet. Elise spent a few minutes in the bathroom and walked out in a pair of boxers and a long, loose T-shirt.

She was sweet, and she looked out of place in a gross motel room. This was a bright young woman who, through a set of terrible circumstances, had ended up in a sketchy motel. Her roommate for the night was a guy who'd spent the last couple of hours dancing around the truth.

Plus, I was about to kill myself while she slept.

Her sleep shirt should be an oversized pajama shirt she'd stolen from her girlfriend's wardrobe. She should be in her own place, with her own furniture, loved by people, family, and friends. She should be snuggled up on a sofa after a day of work at a great job, watching movies and falling asleep in her partner's arms.

Elise deserved better.

"Good night," I said as I switched off the light. I pulled the blanket up, a hidden bottle of scotch by my side.

Elise settled under the covers of the bed across the room and everything fell quiet.

"William?"

"Yeah?" I pretended to settle into the sofa.

"Can I ask you something?"

"Of course," I replied.

"Is your name really William?"

"William St. Denis, yes."

There was a pause in the air. I could tell she was thinking through something.

"Good night, William," she whispered.

"Good night, Elise," I whispered back.

I sat there and stared at the ceiling, eyes wide open, for what seemed like an eternity. Between cars outside and the random noise of the heater kicking on and off every few minutes, it was difficult to tell if Elise had fallen asleep. In the brief moments of total silence, I could hear her breathing, deep and rhythmic.

I inched my hand out from under the blanket and looked at my watch. It was 12:04 a.m. I slid the blanket off, wrapped it up under my arm, and stood up, scotch in hand.

The amber light from the parking lot streamed through the curtains, setting a soft glow to Elise's golden hair. Under the covers, her body rose and fell with each breath. She looked peaceful.

I hoped she was dreaming the sweetest dreams as I turned to the bathroom and let out a steady breath.

The witching hour had arrived.

It was time to die.

I picked up a small notepad and pen sitting on a side table by the sofa and tiptoed my way into the bathroom. Placing the blanket on the floor, I set the scotch on top of it and turned to close and lock the bathroom door, careful to not make any noise.

Using my illuminated watch face as a temporary nightlight, I uncapped the pen and wrote a note I hoped my new friend would never read.

Elise,

If you're reading this, please know that I'm not dead or overdosed. I probably look pretty messed up but I promise I'll be fine by morning. I tried to do this quietly to not freak you out. I had to take some weird medicine and I need to sleep it off. I AM NOT DEAD. Just leave me be. If this is too intense for you, I'm so sorry. You can leave if you want. Take the car. If you read this and stick around, I'll explain.

I'm so sorry you had to see me this way. I like you. Please don't be upset.

-William

I tried to convince myself that I wasn't lying.

I put my watch back on and uncapped the bottle of scotch. I took a deep breath and drank the entire thing in one shot. My eyes watered as I choked it down.

It was a poisonous event horizon. Now ingested, there was no turning back.

It felt like I'd drank lava. Scotch was nasty. I'd always hated the stuff. The strychnine gave it a bitter taste on top of the awfulness of that peaty charcoal flavor. I did my best to hold my mouth closed and not make a sound, but I had an urge to scream and coat the walls in fire-vomit.

Through tear-filled eyes, I checked my watch. 12:10 a.m.

I knew I had about ten minutes before feeling strong effects from the poison. On an empty stomach, it would hit fast. I spread the blanket out in the tub, folding it over once for some extra padding. I placed the empty bottle in the trash as quietly as I could and put the note to Elise on the bath mat with the pen clipped to it. If she opened the door, it would draw her attention, and the weight of the pen attached to it should weight it down enough so it wouldn't move.

I stepped into the tub, lay down on the blanket, and tried to relax.

It felt like an eternity slipped by and I did my best to not stare at my watch. Within a few minutes, I started sweating. My heart began pounding in my chest.

The strychnine was in my bloodstream and attacking my nervous system. I could see it coming, feel it in the air, and braced for it. It didn't matter. Death was on the horizon, and she was coming for me.

I began sweating and could feel my heart beating a little faster. I anticipated Death's arrival very soon. I only had to withstand a few minutes of suffering and should then be visiting Love.

I was so very wrong.

It felt like somebody had fed me lightning. In an instant, my muscles tightened like a massive, twisted steel cable, ready to snap. I heard my legs thump against the edge of the bathtub and my back arched. The only thing touching the tub were my feet and the back of my head as my spine arched. I wished my neck had snapped.

The pain was excruciating. Every muscle tightened to a point where ligaments were ready to rip away from bone and coil underneath my flesh. My jaw bit down like a vice, hard enough that I felt my teeth grinding. I thought the pressure might shatter my molars. The soft light through the grimy bathroom window looked like a spotlight. My heart pounded like gunshots.

My chest tightened. Breathing was impossible. Every second felt like an eternity. My knuckles cracked, white and stressed. All of my senses were overloaded.

Time didn't matter. My breathing ceased. I let loose with a series of violent convulsions.

I felt my body stretch, twist, and tighten. I thought Elise might pound on the bathroom door. I couldn't tell if I was quiet.

Exhaustion was setting in. My lungs compressed.
I slipped toward unconsciousness.
Breathing stopped.
The light faded.
The pain faded.
She had come for me.
My eyes closed.

CHAPTER 9

STIFF DRINK

I opened my eyes.

I was facedown on a piece of wood. I felt it against my cheek and I saw a small, empty glass in front of me. Where had I ended up?

A voice called out, chipper and enthusiastic, "Good day, William St. Denis! Welcome! At last we meet!"

The ambient noise of the room filled my ears. There was chatter and music. The sweet aroma of fresh ground mint permeated the air.

I was in a bar.

I dragged my hands up to the wooden bar top to help lift my weary head and look around, desperate to focus. Everything was fuzzy and my head was pounding. Either I had the worst hangover known to humankind or had just died from strychnine poisoning. I couldn't tell the difference.

"You know, I have something for whatever it is you're experiencing. Allow me to fix you up, my friend!"

I kept blinking, trying to fight through the blurriness. I focused enough to spot a jukebox against a wall and an empty set of tables. There was a massive expanse of glass shelves with every manner of bottle I'd ever seen placed along its length.

"Where? Who is that?" I listened to my own slurred words. That trip had messed me up.

The jukebox was playing "L-O-V-E" by Nat King Cole. There was an old couple on the small dance floor, holding each other close as they swayed. The lights were dim and the air warm.

"Focus, my friend! I cannot drink it for you! You must lift your own glass!"

I shifted my attention to behind the bar. Standing before me was an unassuming middle-aged man with both hands resting against the bar. He had a genuine smile under a manicured handlebar mustache and wore a dark pair of sunglasses. Atop his head was a red velvet bowler with a fresh piece of holly tucked into the band.

"I-I'm trying," I managed.

"Ah! There he is!" he proclaimed to nobody in particular.

The cheerful man leaned back from the bar, running his thumbs under his suspenders then straightening the bright red bow tie affixed to the collar of his spotless white button-up dress shirt. He pointed to the empty tumbler on the bar in front of me.

I stared at the glass, then back up to my chipper barkeep, confused. "It's empty."

"Oh, my apologies!" He snapped his fingers and in an instant it was a full glass with bright green liquid, perfect ice cubes, and a magnificent garnish featuring a bloomed red rose.

"What is it?" I asked.

"I call it the Immodest Aphrodite," he said.

"The contents, I mean."

"Oh, something for that headache of yours, of course! Absinthe with crushed mint and basil, a twist of lime, and a generous measure of maple syrup! Just the libation for you on this fine day!"

"All out of poison?" I asked.

He waved his hand and dismissed my rhetorical passive-aggressiveness. "Oh come now, this is a time for celebration and introduction! New friends! Together for the very first time! Sarcasm is unbecoming during such a grand event!"

I couldn't help but notice that he never looked at me, but just over my shoulder. That explained the sunglasses.

Love was blind.

I reached out and picked up my drink, taking a slow sip. My head stopped pounding the instant it hit my tongue.

"So," I said between long sips, "Love, I presume?"

The bartender held out his arms and bowed in grand fashion. "At your service, Caretaker! Congratulations on finally finding love! Please call me Romeo. Love is so mundane, I've not used it in an age."

I looked around the small bar. Apart from the older couple dancing, there were a few people hanging out in small groups and a lovely young gay couple taking selfies. Above the shimmering bar shelves was a large neon sign in the shape of a bow and drawn arrow, casting a warm red glow throughout the bar. Emblazoned above it was the name of the establishment.

"Cupid's?" I asked. "Isn't that kind of cliché?"

"Well, the clientele typically want sweet love in a marketable package, and who am I to deny the desires of my clients?" he replied.

"I suppose I'm not one of your clients, then?"

"Touché, William," he replied with a smile. "Technically, no. You aren't. Not since you died in that horrible manner all those years ago. I'm not quite sure you have a soul, to be truthful."

Love's disfavor annoyed me. I missed Dee. She was what I wanted, but she was a Concept. I'd drifted in and out of many relationships in the last century. Almost all of them had been distractions, doomed to failure. Romeo was right. I was nothing more than a dead guy. I had no right to tell him that I deserved more.

It was time to get my answers.

"Romeo, I'm looking for an object and someone pointed me in your direction for answers."

"You mean Dee." He smiled.

"Yes," I replied, "Fucking Dee, who I'd much rather be with right now. You know, you're super shitty for Love."

Romeo wiped the spotless bar top in front of me as a smirk crept across his lips underneath that perfect mustache. He placed an elbow down and leaned in close.

"William," he said, "love isn't all roses and chocolate. It's not forever. Sometimes it hurts. The deep longing of knowing there is something you cannot have puts love into focus, does it not? Longing is the ultimate amplifier, my friend. That is the experience of loving."

I finished my drink.

"After all," he said, "there's a reason I'm such great friends with Pain and Death!"

I'd just killed myself, and now I was being lectured by Love. It would take a lot to consider this trip a success.

"Have you ever heard of Cinderella?" he asked.

"Are you telling me you want me to throw on some glass slippers and do your fucking dishes?"

Romeo threw his head back and laughed. He snapped his fingers, producing another drink right in front of me. "Ladies and gentlemen, the uncanny William St. Denis! Now I know why she adores you so much. I meant Cinderella, the glam metal band. They have a song called 'Don't Know What You've Got 'Til It's Gone.' That's an important lesson."

"The knife?" I asked.

Romeo waved his hands around. "Oh right, I'm sorry. Let us talk about your missing friend."

"Friend?"

"But of course!" he replied.

"It's a knife," I explained, "nothing more. I just need to find it so I can be on my way."

Romeo sighed. "William, you lack perspective. Look at your life right now. What do you see?"

"I have to chase a knife all over Earth," I answered. "I don't have a home or a family or a life. I drift and die, and I can't be with the one person I feel most comfortable with."

"If you are referring to Destiny, it would be wise to remember that your dearest Dee isn't a person," he countered, "even if she does exhibit such affection for the broken William St. Denis."

It was a fair point. Dee was Destiny, not a person. There would be no going to the movies or taking a vacation. She couldn't be a girlfriend. We would never do something as simple and joyous as texting emojis to one another.

"Fine," I said. "But at least Dee isn't just a knife."

"Nobody is just a knife," he corrected. "Death is real, and she has grown very attached to you."

I took another sip of my drink. Romeo had me feeling depressed.

"William," Romeo started, "I have known her from the beginning. She is the first and the last. Death was here before nearly all of us. She was wonderful. She still is. Why do you think she takes that form? An inanimate object? What could she possibly be experiencing that makes being a blade easier?"

"Because she enjoys stabbing people," I said, finishing my second drink.

Romeo shook his head. "Oh, stop it, my dear friend. This drowning-your-sorrows nonsense does not suit you. The answer is, because she is too powerful and too misunderstood. She sees you, and she can hear you. Trust me."

I shrugged.

"Imagine having to justify your actions and your purpose for the whole of existence. Being conflated with evil. Drawing sadness out of the simple task of being you.

Imagine being feared and reviled by every creature capable of emotional thought. Used as the scorecard for the toll taken in every war. That will mess anyone up. This may sound strange, but Death has feelings, too."

"So she makes me suffer with her? Carry out her wishes?" I asked.

"She leans on you because you understand feeling misunderstood. Out of place. Alien. Perhaps she hopes you will come to understand her as she understands you. Maybe she's waiting on you to be the friend she'd hoped you would be, William. She isn't Evil. Evil is an asshole." Romeo laughed.

I laughed with him. He had a point, and he was giving me a perspective I hadn't considered. I realized I had a lot of disappointment reserved for myself in how I carried out my duties as a Caretaker.

"Romeo?"

"Yes, my friend?"

"I've lost her. And if I'm being honest, I suppose I've lost my way."

"I know." I watched as he reached out and touched a small analog clock hanging on the wall.

"Last call?" I asked.

He nodded. "Soon. That poison won't last forever, but my, did you have quite a bit. I want to help you, William, truly I do. I can't go back to your world though, not as a pug, or in any physical form. If someone is brazen enough to steal Death out from under William St. Denis, there's no telling what they would do to someone less capable. It's too dangerous. Thank goodness for Emmanuel. He can be a friend to you, if you need."

"Who took the blade?" I asked.

Romeo let out a long sigh, looking around the bar then leaning in close once more, his elbow resting on the bar top so he could be within whispering distance.

"I can tell you who, but I need a favor."

I shook my head. "You fucking Concepts. There's always a catch."

"This is no catch, my new friend. Learn to love again, without my help. That's all I ask."

"I don't know if I can do that," I said.

"You're cursed, William. Capable of so much love, yet you offer it only to whom you cannot have. To the detriment of everything else, in fact."

I stayed silent, feeling the tiniest tug beginning to drag me back into my reality. I only had moments left with Romeo, and I feared leaving with no answers.

"Have you ever stopped to consider why you are so unlucky in love, my friend?"

"No, Romeo. I haven't. I just blame you. I feel myself slipping. Would you just give me a straight answer already?"

"Haven't you been listening? I gave you a direct answer." He smiled.

I stared at him, confused.

"One more thing before you go, William."

"What? Wait!"

"Everything you need is staring you right in the face. I love you, my friend," he said, smiling.

"You didn't tell me anything!" I slammed my hand on the bar top. The music in the bar came to an abrupt halt as everyone stared. The neon lights darkened. I blinked and the gleaming shelves had disappeared, revealing only a bare brick wall. I blinked again and there was no bar.

I was alone, sitting on a barstool in a dark, empty room.

Everything faded to black.

I closed my eyes.

CHAPTER 10

THE MOON IS DEAD

I opened my eyes.

Every muscle in my body ached. My face was pressed against a crunchy shag carpet on a motel floor. My body was crushed.

Someone had stuffed me under a bed.

In a different room.

I heard frantic pounding on the motel room door. I blinked and saw Elise's trembling jaw and tear-streaked face inches from my own, her hand holding up the bed skirt. We were nose-to-nose.

I opened my mouth, attempting to communicate. My throat felt like someone had ripped it out and my lungs clicked and let out a faint wheeze as I began drawing my first breath. My skin was ice-cold, and I was too paralyzed and pained to move.

"If you can hear me," she said through clenched teeth, "don't you make a fucking sound until I drag your ass out of there."

I noticed my crumpled note to her resting a few inches from my head.

At least she hadn't left.

She dropped the bed skirt and stood. I saw her bare feet on the carpet floor walking toward the motel room door. She was still wearing the oversized sleep shirt.

It was still night. The light of a full moon peeked through the curtains.

Elise stood in front of the door. I saw up to her waist. Just behind her back she held a cocked semiautomatic pistol that I'd never seen. Her finger rested on the trigger guard. She kept it hidden as she swung the motel room door open.

There was a tall man in the doorway wearing a tailored three-piece suit with a tie sporting an oversized graphic of a king of diamonds playing card. There was a pocket watch chain dangling from his vest and a black, wide-brimmed fedora obscured his face. He was flashing a stack of cash in one hand and rolling a poker chip along the top of his knuckles with the other.

I held my breath.

"Hello there," he said to Elise, his voice deep and smooth. "I'm looking for a friend of mine. Have you seen him?"

"It's four in the fucking morning. Go away, I'm trying to sleep," Elise said.

He ignored her response. "About six foot. Shaggy brown hair. Brown eyes. Lean."

"Go away," Elise demanded.

"Broken-in charcoal canvas jacket," he continued. "Scars. Always going on about emotional nonsense. Ring a bell?"

He had me pegged.

"I said go away," she replied.

"Calls himself 'William' these days, I believe."

That bastard. As if trust wasn't enough of an issue. I watched him lean forward and whisper quiet words through pursed lips.

Elise looked down and shook her head.

He held the cash out to her.

"I don't want your fucking money. I have no idea what you're talking about. Leave or I'm calling the police," she said, firm and loud.

His lips peeled back over perfect white teeth as he let out a laugh that chilled me. I knew in an instant he was a Guardian. Only someone favored by a Concept would laugh so wickedly when threatened.

I moved my hand, slow and steady, toward the bed skirt.

I'd caught Elise up in something far beyond her limited understanding. An image of Harvey's twisted dead body flashed in my head. She didn't deserve that fate. I didn't want to see her eyes lifeless and her spark gone as I had Harvey.

I had to reveal myself.

It was the right thing to do. If I died, I'd come back. Death ensured that. Elise couldn't.

With a slow, steady motion, I peeled the bed skirt up enough to glimpse his face. He had a slender, chiseled jaw and the predatory gaze of a crow—black eyes, steady and unblinking. The man used his hand to push his suit jacket aside. He tucked the cash into his pocket. I spotted an ivory-handled straight razor tucked into his belt. The spine of the razor glinted like bright polished chrome. It looked surgical.

That wasn't a weapon, it was a threat. He wore it with such honor.

With the dexterity of a magician, he flipped the poker chip into his palm and extended his hand to Elise.

Her quivering thumb slid the safety off on her pistol. In an instant she could jam the barrel of that gun under his chin and attempt to pull the trigger. If she did, it would be her last act. He would cut her down long before the scent of gunpowder permeated the air. She took the chip from his hand. He tipped his hat toward her and strolled away across the second floor walkway toward the parking lot below.

Elise closed the door with a gentle touch, locked it, and pressed her back against it. Her breath was rapid and ragged. Her knees gave out and she slid down into an awkward heap on the floor. She held the gun in one hand and covered her face with the other.

I didn't want to move. I watched as her slender frame shook through erratic breaths. Her eyes told terror as they darted back and forth. I was certain the trauma she'd just experienced burst through her conscious mind like a massive wave of pain and betrayal. Past experiences pulled her under and dragged her without mercy into an unforgiving sea of emotion.

I stayed silent as eternity ticked by. With every breath she drew, I blinked, ready for the tortured symphony of choked sobs that followed. I watched as she drowned amidst the pieces of her life and the shattered remains of her oft-broken heart.

This was all my fault.

It was time to attempt fixing this. I needed to move after being poisoned to death then having my body contorted under a bed. I lifted the bed skirt up and put my hand down on the floor, beginning to drag myself out from under it.

I felt like a dead man, buried alive by mistake, crawling out of his grave.

She raised the gun to my face. Her hand shook. She'd never hit me with a round while shaking like that, even from just a few feet away. Still, if she got lucky and did, it would hurt like hell. I didn't want to get shot.

"Elise," I said quietly.

"Shut the fuck up," she growled, sobbing. She brought both hands to the gun and steadied it, pointing the barrel at my forehead.

"Look, I-I'm so sorry this happened," I said. "Please put that down and talk to me."

She stood. It occurred to me that every time I moved farther out from the bed, she moved to be above me. She always took high ground. Even in distress, her instinct was right. I made it out from under the bed and kneeled beside it, staying low to allow her to be in control.

"There's a lot going on, you're confu—"

"You were dead. You *are* dead. Dead in that fucking bathtub. What are you?"

Slowly and carefully, I moved to sit on the floor. My legs were aching and my body fought through shivers, trying to warm back up to normal temperature. Elise used her arm to wipe her tears while staring at me from down the sights of that handgun.

There was no way around it at this point.

"Elise, I work for Death herself, and because of that, I can't die."

Her eyes narrowed.

"That Blackwood Blade I told you about, that blade is Death incarnate, and it's my job to keep her in my care, protect her, and carry out her will if I have to."

Elise stepped forward, her jaw tightened, and she pressed the hard steel barrel of the gun to my forehead, pushing my head back and pinning it down to the mattress. I didn't fight.

"It'll hurt me like hell if you pull that trigger, but do it if it'll make you feel better."

"I swear I'll fucking do it," she said, pressing the barrel harder against my forehead.

"I believe you. I won't like it, but I'll come back. I always come back."

We stared at each other for a moment. She was considering a trigger pull. She had a white-knuckled grip on the gun. Our eyes locked, hers looking down the sights, mine looking up from the wrong end. There would be no missed shot from this distance. She kept my head pinned against the mattress, the steel barrel pressing into the center of my forehead, right between my eyes.

Tears rolled down her cheek as she stood there considering blowing my brains out. I felt them drop to my face, warm little taps on my cheeks. We were in a standoff. She would either shoot, or leave. I didn't want her to go.

Not like this. Not with another piece broken from her heart, launched into a world made more cold, desperate, and confusing by our intersecting paths.

Romeo told me everything I needed was staring me in the face. I'd woken up, and there she was. I'd been a Caretaker for Death for more than a century. For whatever reason, our paths had crossed. This had to happen. Maybe it was my path to take care of Elise too, or maybe her role was to take care of me.

I knew what I had to do. I blocked out everything I felt in that moment and summoned a memory.

"Elise, it's a full moon tonight," I said.

"What the fuck of it?"

"You used to believe the full moon was magic. Do you remember?" I asked.

Her eyes widened, her grip loosened, and her shoulders slumped. She backed up a step and sat down on the floor in front of me, the gun falling beside her. She brought both of her hands to her mouth and began sobbing as she stared at me.

"You remember."

"You can't know that," she whispered, tears flowing from her wide, innocent eyes as she looked to me in disbelief. "How?"

"I'll explain, but tell me the story first. I want to hear."

She turned her head and looked toward the window, then back to her hands in her lap. Her messy hair obscured her face. I waited for her to compose herself.

She took a big, unsteady breath. "It was my dad."

"What about him?"

"When I was a kid, he used to tell me the full moon was magic. He'd put me and my sister to bed. She always fell asleep right away. I needed more time with him. Like, a story or something."

"What did he tell you?"

She smiled. "Full moon nights were always my favorite."

I could tell that at this moment she was looking at him in her own memory. A sweet little girl lay curled up in a warm, safe bed with her father's hand stroking her cheek slow and sweet. He was her hero. She swallowed and let out a sigh. "He told me that anything I ever wished for could come true over a full moon night. He said to make a wish and then put a quarter on the windowsill."

"A quarter?" I asked.

She nodded, wiping tears from her eyes. "When I woke up the next morning, there were always two quarters on the windowsill. He said it was the moon's magic. Proof that it listened to me. We did it every full moon. For years."

"Elise?"

She looked into my eyes.

"Do you still believe?"

She shook her head. "No. I-I wished for him to come back. So many times."

I nodded.

"For years," she whispered, "every full moon. I cried and wished so hard. I just wanted him to come back. I always placed a quarter in the moonlight. I always found the same quarter when I woke up."

"I am so, so sorry."

"The moon's magic died when my dad died."

She sat there crying, reaching her hands to mine. Through a memory, I had reached into that unforgiving sea, sought her pained heart, and pulled her to the surface. Pain that had been buried deep was laid out before the both of us in the soft glow of a full moon's light streaming through the curtains.

I reached my arms around her and pulled her close. Her hair tickled my face and I held her tight. She wrapped her arms around me and let the tears flow. Maybe I couldn't piece her back together, but I could be there for her.

I could be more than Death's Caretaker. I could understand, and I could help her heal in whatever small way I was able.

"How did you know?" she whispered. "I never told anyone."

We settled into each other's embrace. It was the most comfort I'd had in a long time. Tonight was a disaster. There had been danger, death, lies, and threats. Beyond that, it was cathartic.

"I'm Death's Caretaker. I'm tuned to her. When people die, I can recall memories. They're out here, like the air you breathe. When Death is intense, I can pull them in. It looks like wavy heat reflecting off a road. I just have to concentrate to find them."

She held me tighter. "Did you see him?"

"No," I answered, "but I believe Death spoke to us both tonight, and I believe she gave me that memory as a gift, so I could give it to you."

We held each other. Her tears subsided, and we were both able to breathe a little easier. We released our caress and gave each other awkward smiles.

Dawn was approaching, and it would be time to collect ourselves and go, leaving a night of death, memories, and pain behind us. Elise rummaged through her backpack, finding a pair of jeans to wear. We traded a few minutes in the bathroom and packed.

"Elise?" I asked.

"Yeah?"

"You pulled me out of that tub and dragged me here, right?"

"I did," she said, zippering her backpack up and hoisting it on her shoulder. "That guy showed up with a few others. I heard noise. When I looked out the window, I saw them starting to search rooms. I figured it involved you. I thought if the manager told them where you were, it was best to move."

"The gun?"

She nodded and flashed a big smile. "It was in the glove box of your stolen car. I lifted it when I peeked at the registration. You should pay closer attention."

I smiled at her.

"I don't understand what's happening, or why," she said, tying her hair up in a messy ponytail. "This all seems insane."

"I'll explain it. I mean, if we're traveling together, that is."

Elise looked at her shoes and chewed on her lip. She shrugged. "I mean, we can. If you still want me to. I was going to blow a hole in your skull not that long ago. I'm sorry. I have nowhere go."

"Boston?" I asked.

She shook her head. "That was just me hoping. You're way more interesting than anything else I'd have ahead of me. Do me a favor though?"

"Of course."

"Give me a heads-up the next time you kill yourself so I know to keep watch."

"I'd like that. Can I see that poker chip?"

She handed it to me. It was a weighted red poker chip. On one side, in tiny black letters, there was a printed name, "Dolos Casino and Resort."

"What is it?" she prodded.

"How about a ride to Atlantic City?" I asked.

"Sure," she said, "as long as that's enough time for you to explain what the hell is happening."

CHAPTER 11

SLEIGHT OF HAND

The ninety-minute ride from Trenton to Atlantic City, New Jersey was one of the more enjoyable experiences of my long life. I'd known Elise for twenty-four hours. In that small span of time she'd saved me from a Guardian when I was at my most vulnerable, and I'd given her hope that there's more purpose to existence than jumping from one terrible opportunity to the next.

Elise was a broken young woman, but she was beyond sharp. I thought maybe her experiences and trials had hardened her in the same way mine had hardened me. We'd both lived through tragedy.

She asked smart, pointed questions about what it was I did and how my existence worked. We rode in silence for the last ten minutes. I found that Elise needed moments to process and analyze the answers I was providing.

She broke our silence.

"So, can I ask you something?"

"What's that?"

"How many Concepts have you met?"

"Seventeen," I answered.

"That sounds like a lot."

"It isn't. There are hundreds, at the very least."

"Are they ones you had to die to visit?"

I nodded. "Traveled to and visited, yes. Some more than once. I've also met a few in human form in this reality. I've met many Guardians and too many Stewards to count."

"Other Caretakers?" she asked.

"Just a couple. We hide, and it's rare that a Concept takes inanimate physical form. There's only ever one Caretaker for a Concept. I'm not sure why."

Elise turned and looked out the window, likely thinking about her follow-up question. We would park in Atlantic City in just a few moments. This wasn't my first visit to the New Jersey Boardwalk or the giant casinos stacked up against the Atlantic Ocean.

Driving toward the city, we traveled through trees and marshy swampland until this gleaming stretch of concrete and glass appeared on the landscape with the expanse of the ocean right behind it. Before we reached the glitz and lights of the Boardwalk and those giant casinos, we had to make it through neighborhoods of all kinds. All of this existed separate from the surrounding life. It was a strange place.

Las Vegas was much the same. It was as if the emotions, thoughts, and intensity of feelings around these people and massive structures drained the existence from what surrounded it. I didn't feel safe here. Gambling mixed with alcohol, drugs, and debauchery was too alluring for

Concepts that wished to surround themselves with such influences.

Peace and Hope were not welcome here. Greed and Anger were everywhere.

Elise rolled up her sleeves and flipped down the visor, checking herself in the mirror. "Ugh, I look like shit."

"You look fine."

"Says the guy who was dead in a bathtub a few hours ago, thanks."

I laughed.

"So," she continued, "do you have any favorite Concepts? Nice ones?"

"No," I lied. "Some are okay, I guess."

She didn't need to know. I wasn't ready to talk to Elise about Dee and my feelings toward her. I felt like I should at some point, but not now. We'd only been together for a day, and if last night's motel visitor was any sign, today would get weird.

"What about awful ones?"

I nodded. "There are some I dislike to visit and dislike being around when I do."

Elise's eyes lit up and she smiled wide. "Oh, now that sounds like juicy gossip, Mister Caretaker. Tell me more."

I smiled back, winding my way through the back neighborhoods of Atlantic City and looking for a place to park. "Well," I said, wanting to offer her some information but not get into too many details. "Trust is awful."

"Trust?"

"Yes, I know that seems weird, but I never liked it."

"It?" she asked.

I pulled into a parking spot and turned the car off, turning to Elise and looking her straight in the eyes. "Sometimes," I said, "Concepts are in strange forms when I visit them. I never know what to expect. Some of them could be different every time. Some of them are consistent, but awful."

"Well, don't leave me hanging here," she said. "What's Trust like?"

I looked out the window, then back to her, eager to change the subject. "Hey, let's go get some pizza." I smiled.

"William," she called as I got out of the car and winked at her through the window. She climbed out of the passenger seat and shouted at me, "You can't leave me hanging like that, you jerk!" I crossed the street toward the small pizza shop across the road.

A few minutes later we were sitting at a small table inside a cozy pizza place, blanketed by scents of fresh-baked crust, melted mozzarella, and crisped pepperoni. The eatery was quiet and cozy. The smells were delicious.

It was heavenly.

Elise had a mouthful of pizza, but she was staring at me. I knew there was another question in her mind.

"Go on, ask," I said.

"I just don't understand how it works," she said. "How do you see something that nobody else can see? Why can't I see them?"

"From my experience, I'm the only Caretaker who's able to travel. Being favored by Death comes with some perks. Good thing too, because it's a high price."

She looked at me as if she knew there was a lot more to that statement than I was letting on.

I took a napkin from the dispenser on the checkered table where we were eating. Outside the large window beside us, the bustle of the day was going on. People were starting their shifts at various casinos along the Boardwalk, others were getting ready to have a day of fun, and others still were suffering through issues of gambling addiction, drugs, and drama. It served as a reminder of how insane I sounded when I talked about how this all worked.

I placed the napkin on the table beside my plate of unfinished lunch.

"That napkin is you," I said.

"I'm not that pale," she replied.

"Okay, smart-ass," I continued, placing my plate of half-eaten pizza on top of the napkin. "If you're the napkin, what can you see?"

"Well," she replied, her eyes thoughtful as she stared at my pizza and the obscured napkin under the plate. "The table and the plate."

"Right," I said, "layers. Concepts exist as the pizza. They're there, but to you, they aren't visible. You can sense their warmth though, through the plate and into your world. That's their influence."

"Concepts are pizza," she said.

"Metaphorically."

"So, like a different dimension?"

"Sure," I said, "you can think of it that way. And layers within layers at that. Sometimes I visit crust, sometimes I visit sauce, sometimes I visit cheese, and sometimes the pepperoni. Some Concepts are pepperoni and some are crust, separated by layers between them, influencing each other and perhaps never meeting. Some are side by side, like ham beside pineapple."

"Oh, fuck that," she said. "Not Hawaiian. Don't do that to me. Cooked fruit makes me sad."

"Again," I said, "metaphorically."

"You sound baked," she deadpanned.

"I see what you did there. Okay, let's go." I winked, picked up my pizza, and shoved the rest of it into my mouth, cleaning off the table and getting ready for the rest of the day.

It was a short walk to the Boardwalk from our lunch spot, so we quickstepped our way into the shadows of steel and glass. Massive casinos stretched high along the coast, buildings packed with the hoots and hollers of gambling victories while draining the life from everyone within the walls.

There were no clocks inside casinos. There were no windows. Every minute of the day as soon as you walked in the door was a crafted illusion to make you think you were winning. Casinos were entertainment, but more often than not the entertainment was veiled trickery intended to make you laugh and smile while you handed over your hard-earned time and cash.

We made it to the Boardwalk. The massive wooden path stretched out, winding along the wavy coastline and providing an expansive welcome mat to all the shiny glitz and glamor of billion-dollar buildings pressed up to it. The sights, sounds, and scents assaulted us. At any moment I could breathe in deep the delicious air of popcorn, pizza, and fried anything. A moment later I was smelling the sickening combination of stale cigarettes, spilled booze, and an empty bank account on a broken gambler who'd just pissed away his entire life savings on a roulette wheel.

We strolled down the wooden planks. To any outside observer, we looked like a couple—a pair of young people having a day out like any other. We were catching quick glances and stares from every direction, many of them just other visitors people-watching their way through the day, but I felt some eyes lingered too long.

We were being watched. There were Stewards here for certain. Stewards were everywhere, whether they knew they were observing you for a Concept or not. Some were conscious confidants, like Emmanuel, while some were just people going about their day. In those cases, their eyes were like a set of surveillance cameras for a Concept that just wanted to peek around the mortal world, wondering how to better influence existence to their own ends.

Elise raised her hand and pointed forward. "There it is."

I tilted my head up and took in a magnificent structure. Thin steel rails stretched up and out from the earth. Shimmering windows, changing colors as my viewing angle changed, reflected the Atlantic Ocean before it. The building's top floors were wider than the base, making it look like a massive glass-and-steel nail driven into the earth by some world-smashing hammer. This was one of those buildings that made little sense, a feat of engineering so skillful as to fool you into thinking it would topple over at any moment as it hung with precarious precision over the landscape.

And in bright and twinkling lettering lit from a massive screen stories high, "Dolos Casino and Resort" shimmered above us.

"There it is," I said. "Dolos."

Elise and I both stopped and stared at the impressive structure and mammoth screen. Under the words was a stylish caricature of an ancient Greek figure flanked by columns, smiling ever so slightly as he poured an endless animated flame from a pitcher of water.

"Greek?" Elise asked.

"Common as a casino gimmick," I said as I studied it. Dolos. Greek columns. Fire and water juxtaposed.

"You're staring," she said. "Any idea what's in there?"

"Elise?"

"Yeah?"

"You're staying out here."

"What?" she asked. There was a hint of incredulousness in her voice. My request upset her.

"I don't want you to come in," I said.

"Fuck that, I'm coming," she said, looking at the hotel then back at me.

I shook my head. "It's not safe. I just want you safe, that's all. That was a close call last night."

"No, William," she said, jamming her finger into my chest. It reminded me of the blade slipping into the same spot. Elise's finger wasn't as sharp, but I found her determination just as potent.

"It's not—"

"No. You were dead a few hours ago. I dragged your ass out of that tub and stuffed you under a bed, and even though I had no idea what was happening, I did my best to help you. Now you will help me."

I moved her hand away from my chest and pointed to the hotel. "Taking you in there would not be helping you. That is the opposite of help. How would that help you?"

"Because as fucking crazy as all this shit is, I need to be a part of it."

"Why?"

"Because you're entertaining, and I'm stupid."

"Would you just put the sarcasm away for one moment and answer the question?" I prodded.

She looked around as we stood there arguing in the middle of the Boardwalk. People stared as they walked past.

She was processing an answer, and something told me it was hard for her to verbalize what she was feeling.

I sighed and looked down at the ground, lowering my volume to help diffuse our situation. "Just tell me why. It's dangerous in there. I've put you through enough; I don't need to put you through more. People get hurt when they're near me."

"I don't care."

"I don't have that luxury anymore," I said.

"William?" she asked.

"Yes?"

"I have nowhere to go. I have nothing to do. As scary as it was helping you last night, I think that was my purpose."

"What do you mean?"

She looked into my eyes, her mouth turned down. "I can't explain it, but I think I'm here to help you. I don't know where it'll lead. To be honest, it's like I'm already dead. I'm not afraid. Let me help you."

I smiled at her and nodded. I understood her. She was finding some purpose in this insane existence. Maybe she could help me find my own.

"So, like the Robin to my Batman, huh?" I joked.

"Okay, you're not that cool, and you're not rich, so no."

"Damn." I smiled.

"Is that a yes?" she asked.

I looked at her as I placed my hands on her shoulders, staring straight into her eyes. "Yes, but listen. We'll go in there, and I'll say some things. Can you do me a favor?"

She looked confused. "Uh, yeah. Sure. What the heck is going on though? Tell me why you're so spooked."

"As soon as we walk through that door, don't believe a word anyone says."

"Huh?" she asked, her eyebrow raised high.

"Believe nothing."

She looked at the casino, then back to me. "Who the hell is in there? A Concept?"

I took a deep breath, looking at the massive screen high above, then back to her.

"Yes. In the flesh."

"Which one?"

"Deception," I replied.

CHAPTER 12

DECEIVING THE DECEIVER

Elise and I walked up to the entrance doors of the massive Dolos Hotel and Casino. The bright sun and perfect afternoon sky reflected against the shimmering, ever-changing glass of the building's facade.

I was fearful of what was in this building. My new friend had made her argument well. I was torn but trying to trust her. It felt as though we'd been friends for years because of what we'd gone through in the last day or so.

If Deception was in this building in the flesh, putting Elise in front of it would either prove to be a stroke of genius or stupidity. The last thing a Concept would expect was a Caretaker with a helper.

We were rare, and we always worked alone.

I held the door open for Elise, and she rerolled her sleeves as she walked in, tying her hair back in a ponytail as she stepped into the glitzy world of the Dolos. I followed close behind, straightening out my canvas jacket, dipping into a pocket and pulling out two butterscotch candies in crinkling plastic.

We stood beside each other and looked forward over the blinking, whirring machines and chaos of the casino floor. I held out a candy for her. Without diverting her gaze from the casino floor, she took it from my hand, unwrapped it, and popped it in her mouth.

"Elise," I said.

"I know. Don't believe a word, blah blah blah."

I looked down at her shoes, then to her face. "Not that."

"What then?"

"Your shoe is untied."

She looked down. "No it isn't."

I smiled at her.

She narrowed her eyes and scoffed. "Dick."

I held out my arms and offered an innocent shrug. "I'm just saying, Deception is everywhere."

In front of us, the casino floor had a fair amount of activity for noon on a Saturday. The inside had that typical low-level light of most every type of gambling establishment. There were Greek-style columns rising from the ground to the ceiling high above. A large balcony circled the entire casino floor. To our left was a plateau of poker and blackjack tables. There were gamblers walking around holding glasses of alcoholic drinks and partying as if they hadn't slept in days and couldn't tell.

It was all trickery.

The lack of clocks was to encourage people to ignore time. The constant flow of alcohol was there to remove self-control. Lights and the sounds of coins clinking and clattering in every corner of the casino were a subconscious signal that money was flowing out. The exact opposite was true. The oxygen being pumped into the room left the air clean and electric.

Our surroundings assaulted my senses in every way possible. That bombardment was intentional and effective.

Every table, every machine, and every game in this building tricked you into opening your wallet and handing everything over. No other place in the world could take someone's life savings with such ease, yet encourage them to leave drunk and laughing. In a short amount of time, they'd have to put the pieces of their life back together after the buzz wore off, and that was when the realization would set in that this place had deceived them.

What they'd never realize was that Deception itself had arranged their circumstances. They'd blame their life, their husband or wife, their job, or their kids. That was Deception's greatest gift: destroying everything through trickery and never taking the blame.

Elise and I walked forward onto the casino floor. We passed a security guard giving us a long, dedicated stare with his bright green eyes. As soon as we crossed onto the colored carpet marking the entrance to the gambling area, a machine to our left sounded a siren. There was an older woman there, her hands raised in the air. She screamed with joy.

"I won!" she shouted. "Holy shit, I won!"

Elise and I stopped and stared. She looked as though she'd been camped out at the slot machine for days. Filled ashtrays and empty cocktail glasses littered the small shelf beside the machine. Above it, the words "Pot of Gold" shone bright atop a giant screen filled with dancing leprechauns and rainbows.

On the bright screen was a graphic of a massive pot of gold being dumped out and into the old woman's total along the bottom of the screen.

She had just won two hundred thousand dollars at the press of a single button.

Elise leaned over to me. "That doesn't seem like a very good deception," she whispered.

I shook my head. "No, it doesn't. Everyone sees it though, and they'll keep throwing money at this place hoping it happens to them, too."

Elise shrugged. "I suppose."

"Come on. We need to find out where the hell to go in this place."

We walked through the casino and made our way to the hotel entrance at the back of the ground floor. Beneath our feet was a shining area of dark marble. Before us, a concierge desk stretched on and on. There was a labyrinth of purple velvet rope to direct people to one of the kiosks where a hotel assistant could check you in. Behind the endless desk were posters for the various events and entertainment available at the casino.

"Um, do you see that?" Elise asked.

I looked around. "What?"

She nodded toward one of the posters along the back wall. As soon as my eyes hit it, I knew what had caught her attention.

Along the tall wall behind the check-in desks was a floor-to-ceiling animated screen featuring a tall, ghostly pale man wearing a tailored three-piece suit. A tie with an oversized graphic of a king of diamonds playing card hung down from his prominent Adam's apple. There was a pocket watch chain dangling from his vest and a black, wide-brimmed fedora tilted back on his head. He was rolling a poker chip along the top of his knuckles.

There he was.

A shiver crawled up my spine. He was an image on a screen, but it brought back the memory of the early morning hours and the trauma I'd put Elise through. I studied the screen. The image looped every few seconds, always in the same sequence.

He raised his head and smiled a wicked smile. The poker chip flipped from his pinky to his index finger, then back. In animated letters flashing across the screen were the words "You Will Be Deceived." Then his head tilted down, and on a black screen the words "Duncan the Deceiver—Live at 8 p.m.," shimmered into view, then disappeared.

"Well, would you look at that," I whispered.

"Not exactly being subtle," Elise remarked.

"It makes sense."

"How?" asked Elise. "It looks to me like they're being a little obvious. Plus, a casino magician? Not in Vegas? Lame."

I nodded. "It's perfect. Think about it. The very best deception is the kind that's right in front of you. You know you're being tricked, and there's not a damn thing you can do about it. Deception is telling you that it's right here as you gamble your life away. Honestly, I'm impressed."

We both stared at the screen, watching it go through another loop.

He raised his head and smiled that wicked smile. The poker chip flipped from his pinky to his index finger, then back. Again, "Duncan the Deceiver" showed up on the screen.

"Okay, not gonna lie," said Elise, "that's a pretty freaky advertisement."

"That's intentional. Everything is a show, and everything is a lie."

The loop ended and started again. He raised his head and smiled a wicked smile, but this time, his hands were empty.

"You're seeing this, right?" I asked.

Elise's eyes were glued to the screen. "Yes."

He turned his head, slow and steady, and appeared to be looking straight at us. On the screen, Duncan the Deceiver reached into his pocket, pulled out a golden coin, held it between his fingers, and blew on it as it disappeared in an instant.

It entranced us.

He pointed to his pocket, his black eyes as cold and predatory as a great white shark with a pearly smile to match. He winked, and the screen faded to black. A moment later, the original loop began to play.

"What the fuck was that?" Elise asked. I could almost hear her heart pounding.

"Check your pockets."

I watched as she jammed her hands into her jean pockets. Her face went white as she pulled an identical gold coin from her pocket.

She stared at me with her mouth hanging open. "How?"

"Are you ready?" I asked her.

"No."

"Good. Hand me that coin. Let's go to the concierge."

We made our way through the labyrinth of velvet rope marking off the entry lanes of the check-in counters. To the side was a large desk with a tall, well-dressed woman waiting for our approach. As we stepped toward the counter, she reached up and adjusted her glasses. Her hair was tied in a perfect bun on top of her head, and she flashed a bright, welcoming smile.

"Welcome to Dolos. How may I assist you?" she asked.

I smiled and checked her name tag. "Mary Anne, is it?"

"Yes," she chirped.

"William St. Denis, here to see Deception."

The concierge nodded. "Absolutely! We have tickets available—"

I slammed my palm down on her desk, the sudden sound echoing off the walls. Casino patrons turned their heads toward us, drawn by the noise. The concierge's smile faded to a scowl. I picked up my hand and pushed the gold coin toward her. Elise was staring at me, trying to temper her surprise at my behavior.

"I'm not talking about Duncan's cut-rate act."

Mary Anne shook her head. "Sir, I don't know what you're talking about, I'm sorry."

Elise put her hand on my shoulder. Her eyes darted between Mary Anne and me. "William, chill, maybe she—"

I leaned forward and clenched my teeth as I stared at the woman.

"I am Caretaker William St. Denis. I am here to see Deception. Quit this fucking act and tell me where to go, or so help me I will erase from existence every Steward in sight, including you."

A pause hung in the air.

The concierge's scowl disappeared and a smile returned.

She took the coin from the counter and placed it in her pocket, then pointed down a long hallway flanked by elevator doors. "Penthouse elevator at the end of the hall. Enjoy your visit."

I turned and walked toward the mirrored elevator doors at the end of the hall, Elise following close behind. Before we could press the button, the doors slid open, revealing a spotless, mirrored elevator interior. We stepped in and turned around. There was one button on the wall labeled "Penthouse." Elise pressed it and the doors slid closed. The droning hum of the elevator started as we found ourselves being lifted to the unknown.

"What did you mean by erasing every Steward in the casino from existence?" Elise asked.

"I told you," I answered. "Believe nothing anyone says. Including me."

Elise nodded. I watched her for a moment as the elevator kept humming with our ascent. She looked nervous.

"We're in Deception's territory. This whole building. Everything that hits any of your senses could be a lie."

"Yeah, but were you lying, or is there something you could do?"

I wasn't sure how to answer the question. I stayed silent.

"Like could you touch someone and bring death or something?" she asked.

I shrugged.

"I'm serious. Do you have some kind of special thing you can do to just erase someone?"

"Maybe." I smiled.

"So you could've just reached out and touched the concierge to kill her on the spot?"

"Not exactly," I said.

"Then how?"

"I would've had to pick up the cash register and beat her to death with it."

"Oh," Elise said. "Well that's not nearly as exciting."

"The blade can do things, but I have to be careful."

"Why?"

"It makes a statement. An unmistakable statement."

The elevator bell let out a crystal ring and the doors slid open. Before us was a long hallway carpeted in gold and purple tones. Along the wall were golden sconces every few feet, casting the long hall in a warm amber light. There were no doors, save one double mahogany set at the very end of the hall.

We made our way forward through the hall and stopped in front of the double doors.

"I have no idea what's beyond this door, but I'm sure we'll find something unexpected."

"How are you so certain?" asked Elise.

"If you were Deception, you'd do anything for an advantage. If this Concept has my Blackwood Blade, I'll not get out of here with it unless I do some favors. But Deception won't be expecting me to have you, so I think we're walking in here with the high ground."

Elise nodded.

"Just follow my lead, okay? Don't react to anything and let me do the talking. I've got this handled, I promise."

She smiled and held out her fist. I gave her a fist bump and a wink.

I swung the double doors open and Elise and I stepped into a grand penthouse suite. We entered confidently and tried not to be too stunned at the beautiful interior.

As I looked around, I spotted small fountains along the walls, the trickling water echoing throughout the huge room, providing a soothing natural soundtrack. The lighting was bright and cheerful, and there were plush, thoughtfully arranged sofas and seats everywhere. This was a gorgeous environment, disarming in every way.

Along the back of the room was a floor-to-ceiling wall of one-way glass looking down upon the casino floor stories below. In front of the glass wall was a white desk with a pencil and notepad resting on it.

Behind the desk sat a man who appeared to be in his late thirties. He stood up, walked out from behind the desk, and made his way toward us.

His clothing confused me. He wore a pair of broken-in sneakers, whitewashed jeans, and a comfortable flannel shirt with the sleeves rolled up. That outfit was far too casual for the environment we were in. He was an inch or two shorter than me, with a head of thinning dirty-blond hair and a short, rugged beard.

Elise shrieked.

My head whirled around and I saw her with her hands outstretched, tears in her frantic eyes. She trembled as she looked at the man.

"What the fuck?" she shouted at him.

I looked toward the man, then back to her. "Elise, what the hell is going on?"

He looked at her with a soft smile and held his arms out. "Come on, Elise, give me a hug. Don't be like that."

It puzzled me beyond comprehension and I lost any shred of patience in an instant. "Would someone tell me what the fuck is going on?" I asked.

Elise kept her eyes locked on him and reached out for me, clutching my arm with her hand.

"William," she said, trembling and trying to keep herself from sobbing.

I stepped in front of her, blocking her view of our unassuming host. "What is it?" I whispered.

She swallowed and stared at my chest.

"Well?" asked the man behind me. "Can I get a hug? Elise, sweetheart, it's been so long. Please."

Elise looked into my eyes.

"That's my dad," she said.

CHAPTER 13

GUESTS

Elise and I locked eyes, ignoring the man behind us.

"Well," we heard him say, his footsteps echoing throughout the suite as he made his way to a soft white sofa, "I'll go sit down. When you two are ready to converse, join me."

"Close your eyes," I said to her.

Elise nodded and closed her eyes. I leaned close, pressing my cheek to hers to whisper into her ear. I cradled her head with one hand and kept a tight grip of her arm with the other. "Elise, it's impossible for that to be your father. This is Deception trying to gain an advantage. It surprised you, but I need you to stay with me."

She nodded and took a slow, deliberate breath. She was calming down.

"I've got you," I said, "I promise."

I leaned away, placing my hands on her arms. She opened her wide hazel eyes and looked into mine, then swallowed and nodded.

We turned to face him, but he was nowhere in sight.

Sitting on the sofa with legs crossed, a heel dangling off the end of her foot, and a relaxed arm outstretched across the plush seat was our concierge, Mary Anne.

Elise looked around, putting the pieces together of what this experience would be like.

I walked over to an opposing sofa, sat down, and sighed. Elise sat next to me, lowering herself to the sofa slowly and deliberately, fixated on Mary Anne.

Mary Anne looked toward Elise and let loose a wicked chuckle. "I'm so sorry, princess. I just had to see your face." She slipped a cigarette from a silver case, lighting it and blowing a cloud toward the ceiling. "I wasn't sure it would be you with the infamous William St. Denis. The dad thing was a guess. Duncan described you to absolute perfection after meeting you at the hotel last night."

"That's enough," I said.

Mary Anne turned her attention toward me and a slow smile crept across her lips. "Oh that's so, so rich," she purred as she leaned forward, resting an elbow on her crossed knee and taking another drag of the cigarette. "Since when did the famously cranky William St. Denis become chivalrous? This last century of bringing death to everything and everyone finally getting to your conscience?" She looked me up and down, as if having thoughts of devouring me. "Actually," she mused, "it suits you."

Elise shook her head. Mary Anne noticed and turned her attention toward her. "Would you rather me go back to Daddy?" she asked, condescension soaking the air between them.

"No."

For the briefest moment, the figure before us shimmered like the morning sun reflecting off gentle seas. Mary Anne disappeared in an instant, and before us was a girl with long black hair and sunken eyes. She looked to be in her twenties. The cigarette transformed into a hypodermic needle. She looked gaunt and sick.

"Cassie," Elise said, her voice sad.

"Is this better?" she said, itching her arm and holding the needle to her skin. "You saved me. Why did you leave, Elise? You'll kill me. I'll die without you. Come back!"

"Fucking stop it," I said.

She turned to look at me. Again, a shimmer hit the air and before it dissipated, I knew who was sitting across from me. Her sun-bronzed skin and soft summer dress were unmistakable.

Elise looked at me and I looked away.

"What's wrong?" Elise asked. "Who is that?"

"Nobody," I said. I didn't want to talk about Destiny, about history, or about what was happening. It was time to focus. I was here for one reason. The blade.

I spotted another shimmer out of the corner of my eye. Destiny dissipated and before us was a tall, broad-shouldered man in a tailored pin-striped suit. He had a clean-shaven square jaw, manicured fingernails, and looked as if he could be on the cover of a magazine as sexiest man of the year. He stood.

"Wait," he said, his voice deep and smooth. "You haven't told her?"

"There's nothing to tell," I replied.

He held out a hand toward Elise. "Hello, my dear. I'm Deception. Pleasure to meet you."

Elise looked at me, then back at him, throwing a confused sideways glance at our host.

"Oh, just shake the hand, sweetheart," he scoffed. "I'm done teasing you for now."

Elise stayed silent and sat on her hands. She looked at me with obvious questions on her mind. I felt uncomfortable sitting there. For whatever reason, I didn't want to bring up Destiny. Not to Elise, and not to Deception. Dee left me feeling too vulnerable.

"I'm here for the blade," I said. "Tell me what you need, hand it over, and we'll be on our way."

"Oh, no." He smiled. "No you won't." Deception took a few steps around me, walking to the back of the sofa and squatting down so his head was between us. He looked entertained by the sudden tension in the air.

Elise still looked confused. "William, what is he talking about?"

Deception laughed as he looked back and forth between Elise and me. "Oh, Caretaker," he said, letting every syllable of speech drift in the air. "Who's the deceiver now, hmm?"

As uncomfortable as I was in this situation, I was learning. Deception was showing his hand. He knew about my feelings for Destiny, so it was likely he had my entire history. He knew Elise, enough to mimic her father's likeness down to the smallest detail. Most importantly, he understood why we were here, and he'd been expecting us. My visit to Love, Elise's history, all of it was within his reach. To deceive someone, you must have knowledge of who they are and every facet of their emotions and tendencies. Deception didn't do this on his own. There was a lot of help.

Deafening silence filled the room as Deception walked back around the sofa and sat down across from us, lounging against the cushions and smiling wide. He was soaking in every moment of this interaction. It seemed like the more uncomfortable he made us and the more confused we were, the more satisfied he became.

Perhaps that was why those closest to us were also those easiest to deceive.

"So," he said, soaking in the environment he'd created over the last few minutes, "let us discuss what you'll be doing for me, Caretaker."

"Do you have the blade?" I asked.

"I do," replied Deception. "It is being held here, under guard."

Elise shook her head but stayed silent.

Deception leaned his head down to attempt eye contact with her. "You don't believe me?"

"You are Deception," she said with a shrug. "I don't."

He looked at me. "Your sexy little sidekick here has some brains, Caretaker."

"She's not my sidekick," I said.

Elise scoffed at Deception's remark. "Easy there, buddy. You aren't my type."

Deception bit his lip and shot her a playful look. "Oh honey, that's adorable, but you aren't my type either." He tilted his head toward me as he smiled at her. "He's more my speed."

"Enough already," I said.

He winked at Elise. "Your chivalrous Caretaker has a thing for Concepts. Don't you, Mr. St. Denis?"

"Get to the point," I said. Every moment he drew us into his banter created more opportunity for him to pull us into his world, learn more, and increase his influence over us.

"Oh fine, Caretaker. You'll have your precious little blade back in no time, but I need a favor."

"Go on," I said.

"First, did you hear about that poor librarian? Hit by a falling piano, of all things."

"Saw it in the news," I said, which was true. That was the story on the newspaper that had pointed me toward Trenton as my next stop. Emmanuel had told me to look at the paper. Now I was seeing why that was important.

"Shocking. Such a shame losing a librarian. Kids these days don't read as much as they should. You can gain so much knowledge by opening up a book," said Deception, looking at his fingernails as he settled into the sofa, crossing one ankle over his opposite knee. "She passed away this morning from her injuries. Your employer at work in the world, I suppose. There was an object of great importance to her. Perhaps a book. I need you to find it and retrieve it for me."

"A book?" I asked. "Why not just send one of yours out to fetch it?"

"Because I'm not sure if I'm right. You, Caretaker, can pull memories from the dead. It's one of your many special talents. I need you to do that. Find out what it was and bring it here."

I wasn't sure what this puzzle would reveal, but pieces were being put together. The librarian had been a target. It made sense that the blade had marked her. The news headline said she'd thwarted a robbery and found herself crushed by a falling piano being delivered to a studio through a building window a manner of stories up. If that wasn't the blade, it was one hell of an unlucky commute home after fighting off a robbery. If I knew anything after being Death's Caretaker over the last century, it was that sometimes it's your time.

"Dig into her memories, find this book or whatever it is, and return it here."

"Yes." Elise and I looked at one another, then I turned back to him. "And after that, you'll return the blade?"

"Correct," said Deception with a smile.

I was certain he'd just lied.

I stood and Elise stood beside me.

"She lived about an hour away. Nice neighborhood in a town called Cherry Hill. Mary Anne will give you the address," said Deception. He stood, walking toward the entrance to the suite and opening the double doors for us.

"Fine," I replied, turning to face him after exiting into the long hallway. "How much time do I have?"

"Be back in two days," he said, smiling at Elise. "Duncan will be less friendly if I send him out to retrieve you again."

We walked down the hall as the doors closed behind us. Neither of us seemed to want to talk about what had just happened. The elevator doors slid open and we entered. I looked to Elise and her eyes met mine.

The doors slid closed.

"I'm not sure what just happened," she said as we began our descent to the casino floor.

"I know," I replied. "Concepts are all very different. If I'd known about the shape-shifter thing, I would've warned you."

Elise looked down at her shoes. "I know."

The hum of the elevator slowed as we came to a stop. The doors slid open.

We walked toward the concierge desk. Mary Anne held a small piece of paper out for us. I snatched it from her without a word. Elise and I turned toward the casino floor. Out of the corner of my eye, I saw the digital poster of Duncan the Deceiver. It looked as though he was laughing and waving goodbye to us both. I was glad Elise didn't spot it.

"I can't wait to get out of here," she said as we made our way toward the exit doors.

The contrast between outside and inside felt huge. All the blinking and artificial lights of the casino floor subsided the moment we hit fresh air. Gone were the sounds of clinking coins, laughing customers, and the horrible sense that everything in the last hour had been nothing but a lie.

I breathed in the salt-scented ocean air and it was a welcome experience. Elise stood beside me, soaking in the sun and scent of fresh air with me.

"Can I ask you something?"

"Go ahead."

"What was all that stuff about your destiny?" she asked.

"We all have a destiny. It's set in stone."

"He said you have a thing for Concepts. Was he talking about actual Destiny? Are you and her, like, a thing?"

"It's complicated."

I walked over to the railing separating the elevated Boardwalk from the beach. Ahead was the magnificent ocean, bright and blue. Elise followed close behind and we leaned over the railing, resting our elbows against the cool metal barrier. In front of us were kids playing in the beach sand, behind us there were couples taking selfies and laughing, posting their pictures to social media. Elise looked contemplative, processing everything that had just happened.

"These people all around us don't know what's going on," she said. "I'm not sure if I'm fortunate that I know, or sorry they don't."

I shrugged. "Perhaps a bit of both. I've been feeling like that for the better part of a century."

"Are you lonely?" she asked.

I thought about the question. "Yes," I admitted. "Very."

"Destiny was beautiful," she said.

I nodded.

"Is it okay for you to feel the way you do about her?"

"I don't think so. It's hard to describe what I'm going through. You love who you love, you know?"

Elise nodded. We understood one another.

"Do you still want me around?" she asked.

"I do. Very much so."

"I'm glad," she replied. "I want to help you."

"This may sound weird," I said, "but it seems like I've known you forever. Complicated things are going on, but I just can't shake this feeling that we should be on this path together."

"Maybe it's our destiny to be best buds."

"I'm sure I sound crazy," I said.

"Um, you sounded crazy from the first moment I met you, but it's cool. I kind of dig the insanity. It's not every day some guy describes the inner workings of alternate psychological dimensions with half-eaten pepperoni pizza, then takes you to visit Deception, who ended up being a flirtatious shape-shifter."

"Welcome to my world," I laughed.

Proximity to the ocean gave me a sense of perspective. Even though I was small compared to the near incomprehensible size of the horizon and all the mysterious depths underneath, I was Caretaker for Death. Something so fundamental as to be part of the fabric of reality. Earth would one day die. Planets would die. Stars would fade and disappear. We would be in a universe that had long since lost entire galaxies to space and time. Was I part of that process, integral to that story?

It was a question I'd never slowed down enough to think about.

There was something about our meeting with Deception that had changed me. This was the first time I'd seen a concept in human form, as flesh, in this world. Sure, I'd seen a pug, but my brain had a hard time registering Romeo the pug as Romeo, Love incarnate. Deception, for as much as there were words and feelings and emotions stirred up, was in this world. My world. And he didn't seem human at all.

It made me think about Destiny in a way I was unaccustomed to, and I wasn't sure I wanted to ask those questions, much less answer them.

I turned and leaned my back against the railing, letting the sun hit my face and ground me in this world. There were bigger questions, existential ones, but I had a blade to recover, and to do that, I needed to visit the house of a dead librarian.

I looked to Elise. "So, how about a trip to find a book?"

"Sure," she replied. "Do you think anything he said was true?"

"Perhaps," I said as we started walking back toward the car. "Something about that librarian is making me wonder."

"You think he killed her?"

"I think he's involved," I said, "and I have a hunch she was a Caretaker."

CHAPTER 14

STORY TIME

It was Saturday afternoon and Elise and I sat in the car, looking out over a winding suburban street. We were surrounded by manicured lawns, shady oak trees, and homes that were well cared for. This could've been a neighborhood from a Norman Rockwell painting. Houses were close together, and nice, newer cars were in every driveway. There were a few kids running around and playing on one of the front lawns, their giggles and shouts echoing down the road. Fall colors from the surrounding trees and gardens painted the neighborhood in hues of vibrant yellow, vivid red, and deep orange.

Across the street from where we were parked was 88 West Oak Lane. It was a modest home, at least compared to those surrounding it. It had white siding, a nice yard with a small flower garden in front of the front windows, and a mailbox painted like a ladybug.

"That looks like a librarian's house," said Elise.

"Yeah, she must've been a damn good librarian to afford this place."

Elise turned from the window to look at me. "You think something's off?"

I shrugged. "Don't know. I guess we'll find out when we break in."

"Break in?"

I smiled at her. "Well, if she's dead, we can't knock and wait for someone to come to the door. There's nobody here right now. We need to get in."

"Dude," said Elise, "we're in a stolen car. In New Jersey. With a gun that isn't ours. We can't just break in. What happens if we're caught? You can't rot away in prison, but I sure as shit can."

"Relax," I said. "We'll go around the back, head in through the door or window or something, poke around, and I'll see if I can snag her last memories."

Elise narrowed her eyes at me.

"I'll be quick. Promise."

Elise looked back out the window to the house, silent. I knew she didn't approve of the plan. This was an inevitable point of contention between the two of us. I couldn't die. She could. Time mattered less to me in the grand scheme, but it mattered to her. I may be on this earth for another century or more. Over time, I'd forgotten what it was like looking at kids playing and wondering deep down if I would outlive them or they would outlive me. Now when I saw a young mother holding a baby, I felt an apathetic resignation to their fate and my own.

Every baby I saw would grow old and die long before I ever would.

If I got attached, all I would ever feel was loss. It was part of why Dee was so important. I'd known her for over a century. Those cherry blossom trees in front of her farmhouse were always there. She was always there, always beautiful, always in that dress, always offering affection. In a world that sometimes passed me by in the cruelest of ways, being able to breathe and dream beside someone who was always there was a comfort I couldn't deny. It was why I didn't accept help. Why would I invest time and emotional energy into something that didn't have the same permanence that I did?

I craved that feeling of being home.

Elise turned and looked at me. Doubt filled her eyes.

"I know," I said.

"Okay, look. We'll go in, but we gotta make it real quick."

I nodded. "Exactly."

She looked back to the house. "At the first sign of someone pulling into the driveway or walking by and staring, we book out of there."

I looked across the street. It was quiet enough that we should be fine. "That's smart. Also, nice pun."

"Then we need to steal a different car."

I stared at Elise and smiled. I hadn't expected that.

"Oh, don't give me that," she said, punching me in the arm.

I laughed. "I didn't say a word."

"Hey, I'm going to wipe that sarcastic smirk off your face with a brick before long, Mister Caretaker."

I held up my hands, unable to erase my smile. "I'm just saying, you've taken to this kind of life instantly."

Elise scoffed, but I saw her smile just a little.

We got out of the car and walked across the street to the sidewalk in front of the house. I looked around the neighborhood. It seemed quiet, and except for the occasional car winding its way past us, we didn't find ourselves within view of anyone. We quickly walked to the back of the house. There was a small stone patio with a lawn chair and a side table. I imagined our librarian would come out here with a delightful book and a warm cup of coffee to enjoy the sounds of birds and feeling of the calm air. I could picture her there, her fingers flipping through the pages of her favorite story, absorbed in the tale.

It would never happen again. In times like this, death felt surreal. In a blink, someone was gone, and all the little details they'd left behind seemed so intense right after. After a few days, a few weeks, or a few years, those imprints on mortal life faded and disappeared. Before long, memories did too. Impactful life moments drifted into hazy recollections, and hazy recollections drifted and faded like the dust to which we all returned.

Unless you were Death's Caretaker.

Elise was trying to open the back door by wiggling it back and forth, but it wasn't opening.

I reached into my coat pocket and pulled out a small black pouch. A quick unzip and I had the exact lockpick I'd need to get the door open.

"You're quite the criminal," said Elise as she stepped aside, watching me work.

"Well," I said, trying to manipulate the tumblers in the lock, "when you've lived as long as I have, you pick up skills. I know it all seems criminal, but after a while I forgave myself for all the theft and unsavory activities. I have a responsibility."

Elise watched as I worked the lock. "Do you kill people?"

I stopped and stared at the doorknob. I was uncomfortable making eye contact with her, at least for this question.

"I do."

"That must be hard," she added.

"It used to be," I said. "If I'm keeping score though, I've killed myself a lot more than I have anyone else."

She laughed.

The lock clicked, and the door swung open. I held out my hand. "Ladies first."

Elise rolled her eyes and walked in. "Deception was wrong, you know."

"About what?"

"Chivalry doesn't suit you."

We stood in the kitchen of the empty house. There were two dishes on the drying rack beside an empty sink. The refrigerator was humming, and in the living room just out of sight I heard a ticking clock. Everything was tidy. Dish towels were folded, resting on the counter, and in the dining area just beside the kitchen, a small table had a quilted fall-colored table runner and a small decorative pumpkin in the center.

"This is the most boring house I've ever seen," Elise whispered.

"Librarians aren't known for their wild parties. Come on, let's go upstairs."

We walked up a set of carpeted stairs to a small hallway on the second floor. There was a sparsely decorated spare room to our right, a bathroom to our left, and straight ahead, what looked like the master bedroom. We walked in and began looking around.

"Do you even know her name?" asked Elise, opening a nightstand drawer and shuffling through its contents.

"No."

Elise held up a small bracelet with a charm that looked like an open book dangling from it.

"Hand me that?" I asked. She tossed it to me. It wasn't anything special, but minor items like this, worn on many days, would help me feel connected to her. I was hoping to build the steam for memories this way. Elise moved to her closet, riffling through sets of clothes and dresses. I kept opening dresser drawers and looking around for anything that might give me a better feel for who this person was.

Pulling memories was always inexact. Unless it was a very intense moment, I wasn't sure if I was seeing what I wanted to believe or what was real. Memories always wound their way through our existence unseen, unheard, and unfelt to those not in tune with Concepts.

"Hey, what do you think?" asked Elise.

I turned around to face her. She had a dress on a hanger pressed against her, straightening her arm and looking down at it.

"Can you go put that on?" I asked.

She lowered the dress. "What? No. No, that's just a little too weird."

"Listen," I said, "I'm trying to get a feel for this person. You look to be about the same size. I'm hoping it'll help me. I promise. I'm not being creepy here."

Elise narrowed her eyes at me.

"The bathroom's right over there," I continued. "Please?"

"Fine," she said, heading down the hallway to change.

I turned my attention back to the dresser. Hanging on the mirror above the dresser was a lanyard with a badge on it. I turned it over.

"Juliane Santos," I said to myself. "Research Assistant at Rutgers University."

"What's that?" Elise called out from down the hall.

I craned my neck toward the door, studying the lanyard. "Her name was Juliane Santos," I said. "She was a smart one. She looked kind."

There wasn't much to go on in the bedroom. I got frustrated at how simple this woman's life seemed to be. There had to be some connection between her and Deception, I just had no way of knowing what it could be. The more time I spent in this room, the less I thought she was a Caretaker. By the picture on the badge, she seemed to be in her thirties. She had shoulder-length brown hair and an amiable smile. She looked the librarian part, for certain.

Elise walked in. "So, what do you think? Looks like we were the same size."

I turned my head to her, but I didn't know what to say.

Long gone was the transient youthful woman I'd met just a short time ago in a parking garage in Philadelphia.

Elise's blond hair cascaded down past her shoulders, framing her face. She held the dress skirt out with her hands, moving her bare foot around and looking down at herself.

"You look beautiful," I said.

Her bright, wide hazel eyes looked up and met mine and her smile faded. In a moment the sweet young woman before me disappeared. She looked sad.

"Keep that dress," I said.

"William!"

"No, I'm serious. Listen, I know it seems weird. Believe me, I get it. But we have to understand opportunity. Juliane Santos is gone. If there's something we can use, we should take it. I steal my clothes from laundromats."

Her mouth dropped open in mock shock. "Oh my god, you're the worst kind of human."

I shrugged. "There's a bag over there. Take a few things. Just what you can use, never too much. Juliane won't miss it. The rest will end up donated anyway."

"Damn, man. That's just cold."

I looked down at Juliane's bed, neatly made in the center of the room. It'd been only a blink since she was in that bed, waking to the dawn light, the sun stretching out, gentle and warm, to greet her from behind her curtains. The world would wake up, as would she, and her days would begin.

I summoned a memory. Then I saw her.

She was lying on her bed in oversized flannel pajamas. She was on her stomach. Beside her was a children's book, and she was staring at a cell phone screen. She whispered something I couldn't make out.

I tried hard to focus. The book had an illustrated owl on the cover. I couldn't make out anything on the screen of the phone. In an instant, the memory dissipated.

"Hey!" Elise shouted, snapping her fingers toward my face. "You okay?"

I shook my head. "I saw her. We're looking for a book."

Elise looked around. "Yeah, well, there's like nothing in this house."

I leaned down and checked underneath the tidy bed. I reached under it, grabbed a book, and pulled it out as I stood up.

"This is the one I saw," I said.

Elise finished stuffing a few clothes into the bag and looked up. "Oh, hey! Oliver the Owl! I loved that book! My dad used to read it to me when I was a kid."

I stared at the cover. "A kid's book under the bed in a librarian's house? What's it about?" I asked, opening the cover to look inside.

Elise smiled, slinging her fresh bag of clothes over her shoulder. "Well, it's about a wise old owl named Oliver, and he has the answer to everything. So some rotten kids ask him questions about what they can get away with."

When I flipped open the cover of the book, I froze. This book wasn't what it seemed.

Elise turned away, grabbing a pair of pants and a shirt from the dresser to go change into something more casual. She continued, "Oliver warns them about what they're asking about, but they don't listen, and there are consequences for the kids."

I reached into the hollowed-out pages of the book and pulled out a small, slim cell phone.

She must have sensed my silence and turned around. "What is it? Since when do you have a cell phone?"

"I think we have what we need. Get changed. Let's get out of here."

CHAPTER 15

LOL

I pulled into a hotel parking lot right off a highway exit. Elise and I had spent the last twenty minutes on the drive trying to figure out the connection between Juliane, a cell phone, the hollowed-out children's book that hid it, and Deception.

Nothing was making any sense.

If this was her cell phone, why was it in a hollowed-out book under her bed? The more likely scenario would have been a phone in her possession, taken and kept with her things when she was rushed to the emergency room. Why not have it on her?

Had Juliane known the accident would happen?

The only thing Elise and I could come up with was that it was a burner phone, a secondary phone used for some secret purpose. Had Juliane been up to something illegal? It made sense to us, if there was a connection to Deception. He was a Concept who's only purpose was to sow deceit and peddle his influence, measuring his success by the amount of physical money he raked in. He would need many acting on his behalf.

Elise ran into the lobby of the hotel to snag a room. We'd decided, since we had plenty of time before meeting with Deception again, to stay a night and rest. I couldn't die, but I could feel like it if I didn't sleep. The only significant rest I'd had was a few hours dead in a bathtub. It wasn't ideal.

I grabbed a few belongings from the trunk of the car and walked into the hotel. Elise was just finishing up at the front desk, and we made our way up the stairwell to the third floor. Our room was neat and clean, a far better option than the Four-Leaf Clover Motel I'd died in the night before.

I put my belongings down and set aside a change of clothes in the bathroom. I put the hollowed-out Oliver the Owl book and Juliane's cell phone on the desk.

"You look like shit, man. You need to get some rest," said Elise, unpacking a few things out of her backpack onto the nightstand.

"I feel even worse. I'm going to jump in the shower, then get some sleep. Don't let that book or that phone out of your sight."

"I got you, Caretaker."

I smiled. Minutes later I was standing in the shower letting scorching water trace across my body. I hadn't realized how sore my muscles were from the events of the past few days. I was used to sleepless nights, crazy hours, and abuse of my body, but it'd been a difficult few days, both physically and emotionally. I felt the scars over my heart. There was a large patch of discolored skin with scars on top of scars, each representing a visit to a Concept out of space and time.

I missed Dee.

I stood there with my hands against the shower wall, letting the spray of scalding water soak my head and trace down my spine.

Then I cried.

Inside my head and heart was a hurricane of emotion, suffering, and fear. For more than a century I'd cruised through my day-to-day life. I'd stolen, lied, and been responsible for the deaths of countless people, Harvey being the latest. Maybe bringing Elise into this world had been the wrong idea. As Death's Caretaker, there was no objective way to look at the course of my existence and think it hadn't been wreaking absolute destruction on everything.

And now Dee was involved, but I still didn't know how. I didn't want my atmosphere of entropy and death to encircle her, but I supposed that may have been inevitable. Death's influence reached through me. I'd allowed myself to get close to her, find comfort in her, fall for her.

Love her.

By being burdened with an existence I hadn't asked for, I'd jeopardized countless numbers of people, not to mention Concepts themselves.

I dried myself off and took a few extra moments to dry my eyes before slipping into a comfortable pair of sweatpants and a loose T-shirt. I stared at myself in the mirror. I'd been a twenty-six-year-old for over one hundred years. It occurred to me this was the type of thing friends joked about when they were in their thirties, saying they were twenty-six for every birthday past twenty-six.

If I turned twenty-seven next year, I'd be thrilled to be a year older.

I walked out of the bathroom, content to fight with the complex emotions of meaning and existence another time. Elise was sitting back in the office chair, her bare feet on the desk, Juliane's cell phone in hand.

"Something's not right," she said.

"What do you mean?"

"When was the last time you had a cell phone?" she asked.

"Never."

She held it up to me. "Well," she said, "it doesn't turn on, there's no charging port, there's no headphone port, and there are no buttons. It has a label from some company I've never heard of."

"What's the company?"

"It's 'iKnow.' Some cheap-ass knockoff of an Apple phone."

I took it from her hand. She was right. There was no case on the phone, it was just a sleek device with a perfect screen and a shiny silver back with the label "iKnow."

"Do they make phones with no ports?" I asked.

Elise shook her head. "Nope. Not yet, at least."

I flipped it over, pressing my thumb to various points to see if there was some way to turn the device on. There wasn't any kind of seam, button, or hole anywhere. There was no tiny microphone to speak into, and no place to hear anything. This was a strange device, to be sure.

"Are you sure that's what you saw in that memory?" she asked.

"I mean, there's no way to be sure," I said, turning the phone over and pressing on the screen. I sat down on the bed, studying it.

"Maybe it just needs a charge?"

I shrugged. "Maybe. But how would you charge it? If it was so important she kept it in a hollowed-out book, you'd think it would be ready to go at any moment."

I handed the phone back to Elise. "I sure as hell wouldn't know how to activate it. Telephones weren't a thing when I was born."

"Old man," she laughed. She held the phone in her hand as she stared at the blank screen. "This is so weird. What on earth are you?" she said.

The screen lit up. There was a ding noise and a text message notification. Elise and I looked at each other. She touched the screen and opened the message.

KNOWLEDGE, LOL. HI ELISE.

I watched as Elise turned white. She looked at me, then back to the phone. I should have known. Juliane Santos was a part-time librarian, a part-time research assistant, and a full-time Caretaker for Knowledge.

I sighed and stared at the phone. "This is terrible."

Elise shook her head. "I don't believe it. Is this a Concept? Knowledge? A fucking cell phone? Did fucking Knowledge just 'LOL' at me?"

"Concepts can be weird like this. But it makes perfect sense. I should've known it would be something like this," I said. "Go ahead. Ask it something."

Elise turned her attention back to the screen. "Uh, what is the square root of 763?"

Ding.

YOU HAVE THE ENTIRETY OF ALL KNOWLEDGE IN THE KNOWN UNIVERSE AT YOUR FINGERTIPS AND YOU ARE ASKING ME A MATH QUESTION?

We both sat there with our mouths hanging open. Elise shook her head.

Ding.

FINE. 27.6224546339. WHAT'S NEXT? CAT VIDEOS? THE WEATHER IN SRI LANKA? HOW LATE IS TACO BELL OPEN? DO YOU WANT TO ORDER SOME TOILET PAPER? DO YOU NEED TO TWEET IDEAS ABOUT YOUR NEXT HALLOWEEN COSTUME? LIKE OMG DID YOU SEE WHAT CELEBS WORE TO THE OSCARS?

"Well," I said, patting Elise on the shoulder, "Knowledge has your sense of humor."

I attempted to be light about this situation, but this was a grave circumstance. Two Caretakers no longer caring for their Concepts. Death and Knowledge drifting around Earth as objects.

"What do we do?" asked Elise.

"I don't know," I answered. "Knowledge is powerful. Do we want to hand Knowledge to Deception? I can't imagine how magnified his influence would become with another Concept in his possession."

"You think we need to trade?"

I nodded. "I need Death back in my hands. She's my responsibility. I realize Juliane was a Caretaker too, but I can't take care of two Concepts."

"Dude. We can't just hand Knowledge over to Deception."

Ding.

Elise and I looked at the screen.

HAND ME OVER TO DECEPTION.

"What on earth does he want with you?" she asked into the phone.

Ding.

HE'S DECEPTION, SILLY. LOL. I HAVE NO IDEA. I CANNOT PREDICT THE FUTURE AND I HAVE NO KNOWLEDGE OF THE MOTIVATIONS OF FELLOW CONCEPTS BEYOND MY UNDERSTANDING OF WHO THEY ARE. ESPECIALLY DECEPTION. BUT THE DUDE DOES KNOW HOW TO THROW A GREAT PARTY. CREDIT WHERE DUE AND ALL. YOLO. BUT NOT REALLY.

"Well that's not helpful," said Elise, "and it LOL'd at me again."

"Listen," I said, "I know it seems counter-intuitive to hand Knowledge over to Deception, but at some point I have to put things back together here. Deception used Death to get me to locate Knowledge. That was his goal. We need to make that trade."

Elise put the phone down on the desk and stared at me. It was clear she was unhappy with this situation. I was too.

"What choice do we have?" I asked.

"We could, I don't know, keep Knowledge instead?"

"To what end?"

Elise began gathering up a change of clothes from her bag, shaking her head. "It just seems to me like Deception could do a lot more damage with the knowledge of everything in the universe than he could with your Blackwood Blade."

I shrugged. "Maybe, but we don't even know what he wants other than that phone. That blade is my responsibility. I have to get it back."

She was holding clothes under her arm as she turned to look at me. "So you can go visit Destiny, right?"

"Elise, that's not fair."

"But it is," she added. "I know nothing about your motivations. What am I getting myself into here? I think I can trust you, but then you make me wonder. Do you have a job? Do you even do your job? Or do you just want the knife because you have some crazy love thing going on with Destiny?"

I threw up my hands. "Then ask me something!"

Elise looked around the room, and she was incredulous. "Seriously, William. Who are you? I get what you do, but who are you?"

"I don't know. I'm just a Caretaker. That's my identity."

"Thing is," she said, "Deception had a point. Who's the real deceiver here? Are you deceiving me? Or yourself?"

I shook my head. "I don't want to argue with you right now."

Elise walked toward the bathroom. "I don't want to argue either. I just know these things about you and this life you're living, but for whatever reason you're not telling me about who you are."

I turned to her. "You know I die and come back, and I've seen your dad's memories. You know what I do, and this whole messed up existence of Concepts. You know I've taken life and I steal cars and clothes and cash. You know Knowledge itself is texting with you right now. You know I'm twenty-six and I've been around for more than a hundred years. You know my real name."

She paused at the entrance to the bathroom, looking at the floor as she shook her head. I wasn't sure what more I could say to her. We weren't communicating well.

"I mean, what more do you want to know?"

"I know Deception wants more influence," she said. "I know he wants that phone. I know he wanted you to get it for him. But I don't understand who William St. Denis is, or what William St. Denis wants."

I sighed and looked at the phone. "Sorry. I'm not sure I know those answers either."

Elise walked into the bathroom, closed the door, and in a moment all I could hear was water running and my own thoughts spinning out of control.

I stood and walked over to the window overlooking the parking lot of the hotel and the highway not far past. Dusk turned to evening in front of my eyes. Everything felt heavy. I'd argued with Elise, but she was right. I'd hidden my feelings and my emotions even as I put her in danger. Harvey had died because I'd needed to spend a few blissful moments with Destiny. While I held her, while we kissed, he was being cut and doomed to death.

Was I a monster?

On the highway were countless cars with countless people shuffling off to all manner of activities. Couples were going to late dinners or out dancing. People were going to bars or friends' houses to watch sports together. These people lived in the present moment with friends and loved ones. It was a perspective that hurt me every time I thought about it.

I turned around and picked up the phone, staring at it for a long while.

"I have a question," I said, keeping my voice just above a whisper as Elise continued her shower.

The cell phone screen lit up.

Ding.

HELLO, WILLIAM. NICE TO FINALLY MEET YOU. ASK.

"How did I die the first time? Destiny said I jumped off a bridge, but I don't remember."

Ding.

ON MAY 14, 1915 AT PRECISELY 10:53 P.M. YOU COMMITTED SUICIDE BY JUMPING OFF THE CROOKED RIVER RAILROAD BRIDGE IN TERREBONNE, OREGON.

I nodded. All I'd ever been told about my history had come through conversations with Dee. Now with Knowledge, I could probe some things I'd wondered about for the last century. There were some questions I was afraid to ask, and some I was unsure I had the right answer to. At least I could get some validation.

"Okay. Why can't I remember?"

Ding.

SELF WON'T ALLOW IT. ALSO, IT'S COMPLICATED.

I hadn't even realized Self was another Concept exerting influence and hiding information. Putting aside my anger at being denied my own memories of life before 1915, this answer was telling. This meant that every time I summoned a memory, it was a collaboration. There was a negotiation between my Concept, Death, and the Concept of Self. Maybe even others. I was being denied these memories. Dee always rejected the probes into my history, choosing to focus on the short time we had together. It took years before I came to grips with the fact that these memories were locked away and I had a new existence to sort through.

I turned on the nightstand light. The room had turned dark as night approached. The shower stopped and I heard Elise brushing her teeth and finishing up in the bathroom.

"Okay," I said, "how do I visit Self?"

Ding.

JUST DO YOU, BOO.

I'd been afraid of that answer. Concepts always tended toward vagueness. It felt like the stronger I desired a straight answer, the less chance I'd get one.

"Is Destiny in danger?" I asked.

Ding.

EVERYBODY CLOSE TO YOU IS ALWAYS IN DANGER.

I felt the blood drain from my face. My heart began pounding. I had to know more.

"What happens if she's, I don't know, destroyed?"

Ding.

HUMANITY LOSES ITS WAY. OTHER CONCEPTS WILL SEEK TO FILL THE VACUUM. THERE WILL BE NO PATH. A NEW HUMAN SOUL WILL BE PLUCKED FROM EARTH TO TAKE HER PLACE. WEAK. INFLUENCED BY OTHERS. DOOMED TO BE A PROXY FOR AN AGE. EARTH RAVAGED. MATURE CONCEPTS ARE THE STRONGEST. SO YEAH. THAT WOULD BE PRETTY BAD.

Elise stepped out of the bathroom. She was in her pajamas, a pair of sweats, and an oversized sleep shirt. Her damp hair had been tied back in a ponytail. She looked at me and sighed. I placed the phone down on the desk.

"Learn anything?" she asked.

"A little," I replied.

I made my way to the queen-sized bed in the center of the room, sitting down on one side. Elise sat down on the opposite side. We sat there, back-to-back, for more than a few minutes. The lack of words in the air became heavier with each passing second. I had no idea what she was thinking. I didn't understand what I was thinking either. After a few minutes we lay down beside one another, facing opposite directions. I felt sleep pulling at me.

"Can I ask you something?" whispered Elise.

"Anything."

"Do you care about me?" she asked.

"You helped me when you could've just run," I said. "I do."

There was a lengthy pause as we both drifted toward sleep.

"Good night, William."

"Good night, Elise."

CHAPTER 16

ANSWERS

Soft sheets warmed my face as I took a deep breath. The quiet hotel room was just beginning to brighten from the sunrise outside. As the fresh day dawned, I stretched.

I peeked at the alarm clock beside the bed. It was just after seven. As I woke, I could tell I'd had a decent night of sleep. I felt ready to go. Gone was the depression of last night's conversation. There was a renewed sense of wanting to regain control over my friendship with Elise, my place in this world, and my responsibilities. It was the cry. I always felt better after a release of emotion. Intensity of emotions clouded my objective view of the world and my circumstances. Purging that intensity drained it from my mind. I was focused now.

Gentle dawn light streaked in through the parted curtains, as if a hand touching my face and urging me to wake. I turned away from the clock to face Elise.

She wasn't there.

I sat up, looking around the room. I slipped my hand to her side of the bed. It was cold. The room was quiet, her things gone. I stood up and looked around the corner to the bathroom. It was empty.

Panic hit me hard. I looked to the desk. Oliver the Owl and the iKnow were both missing.

Elise had disappeared. Knowledge had disappeared. I must've been the only Caretaker in existence to ever lose two Concepts in mere days. I'd hurl myself out the window, but it would just waste time and hurt when I landed. Like a whirlwind, I gathered up my things and threw on a fresh pair of jeans and my canvas jacket. After a quick stop in the bathroom, I ran out of the room and down the hall to find Elise.

I sprinted down to the front desk of the hotel. There was a young man working behind the counter who seemed startled at my abrupt approach.

"Excuse me, Elise Campbell, Room 29. Did she check out?"

He leaned over to look at a bin of papers beside his computers and trailed his finger along the top one. "Yes, sir. About an hour ago."

"Fuck."

"Uh, I'm sorry?" he asked, startled.

I took off through the sliding doors to the front of the hotel. Dawn was in full swing and the soft light of the day was brightening the world around me. I looked across the quiet parking lot.

There was no car.

I couldn't believe it. After all of those moments the last few days, this was how it would be. A transient Elise going back to finding her way on her own, but this time with a stolen Concept. In twenty-four hours I'd have to face Deception. He would hunt her down regardless of my wishes, and this time it wouldn't end with a poker chip and a "call me," it would end with Elise dead. Duncan, the Guardian who'd introduced himself the night before, was capable of hunting her down easily.

I sat down on the curb outside the front door of the hotel. If this was a normal circumstance, I'd have some kind of plan or idea for direction. I had nothing. No Death, and no Knowledge.

And I'd lost a friend.

My mind ran away with overwhelming thoughts of every single word I'd said to Elise in the last twenty-four hours. We'd become fast friends, but was I hurtful? Was it a comment that seemed innocuous at the time but cut deep and I hadn't picked up on it?

Was it just me?

I was overwhelming. This life, my circumstances, my reluctance and near inability to state what I was feeling because I was never sure of what I was feeling. I supposed what she'd found was a better alternative to my identity. I wasn't the best company, and I came with a lot of risk. She'd noticed as much when we were sitting in the car outside of Juliane Santos's house.

"Well this just sucks," I said to myself as I looked over the cold parking lot. Frost had descended last night, casting a shimmering white coat on the world before me. As the sun rose and kissed the tops of the trees, frost gave way to brilliant hues of deep orange and bright gold.

It was a simple, glorious pleasure for my eyes in the midst of the disaster blanketing every facet of my life.

I reached into the pocket of my canvas jacket and pulled out a butterscotch candy wrapped in crinkling plastic. With the rising sun bathing my face in warm light, I popped the candy in my mouth and let out a deep sigh. The cool fall air was still and peaceful. If I was going to lose, I might as well lose on a beautiful day with a piece of candy. There were worse situations. I had no idea what to do. Without a clear plan, taking a step in any direction seemed like a waste. I'd just as soon waste my time wallowing in indecisiveness instead.

All of this was my fault, and my mind was spinning going over last night's conversation. Elise was right. I didn't show who I was. I'd spent so much time being private, I just didn't know how to open up, and when I wanted to, my words didn't come out right. I supposed I feared being judged by others, so I didn't open up and ended up being judged anyway. The result was always a measure of self-loathing that was difficult to get past.

A black SUV with tinted windows pulled up to the front door of the hotel and stopped, the engine idling. It looked brand-new. I heard the driver's side door open and footsteps coming around toward me.

I looked up, and Elise looked down at me. We stared at each other for a moment.

"Well, I'm not your fucking Uber. Get in the car."

I stood, grabbed my bag, and got into the car. It was a pristine, luxurious SUV. Elise climbed into the driver's seat and shut the door, smiling. She looked at me, and we sat there in silence.

"You thought I left," she said.

"I did."

"Bet that didn't feel good," she said, looking out the front windshield.

"No. It didn't."

She nodded.

"Face it, Caretaker," she said. "We're our only friends. Like it or not, you're stuck with me. We don't have to always agree, you know."

She was right.

"Where did you get the car?" I asked.

Elise smiled wide. "Knowledge is awesome. Don't worry. It's clear."

"You asked Knowledge where you could get a car?"

"I did." She smiled, rubbing the steering wheel. "Isn't it gorgeous? I don't think I've ever been in a brand-new car. It has nine miles on it."

I looked around the interior and nodded. "So, all the knowledge in human history at your fingertips and you use it to lift a car?"

She smiled, put the car into gear, and pulled out of the parking lot. "Yup! It was a ten-minute walk away. And now we'll take this swanky ride somewhere we can have breakfast and figure out what we're doing today."

I looked out the window and watched the neighborhoods go by. I felt foolish. I'd panicked this morning, and I hadn't trusted my friend. I didn't trust myself. If I was being honest with myself, I didn't know how to act in this situation. With so much time spent alone, it was weird being this close to someone else. I didn't have to worry about finding another car, and I had a resourceful friend by my side who was making my existence easier.

It was weird, but nice for a change.

A few minutes later we pulled into a parking spot in front of a bustling diner. I reached into my pockets, realizing I had zero cash. Elise was a step in front of me.

"Don't worry," she said. "I got it."

Knowledge was handy, it seemed. I wouldn't question where Elise had scored the car or the cash. I trusted her to make decisions that weren't too damaging to our well-being or need for discretion. She understood. I had concerns about this kind of power in the hands of a person who wasn't used to this world and had little experience. Information was power. And with it at her fingertips, Elise had scored a perfect car and a pile of cash in under an hour.

A few minutes later we were sitting in a quiet booth in a busy diner, each of us sipping on coffee while waiting for food to arrive.

"Listen," I said, "I know I've upset you, and I know I need to trust you. It's just hard."

"Because you literally don't know who you are?"

"Something like that," I said.

"Knowledge isn't just good for cash and cars. I asked about you."

I stared at my coffee.

"Oregon, huh?" she asked.

"Apparently."

"You remember nothing?"

I shook my head.

Elise reached across the table and put her hand on mine. I looked up from my coffee into her bright hazel eyes. Her hair was pulled back, and she looked strong and sweet. There was compassion in those eyes.

"I don't know why I jumped. I tried finding out. For decades, I tried. Researched, followed dead-end leads, asked Concepts, always came up empty."

"I want to help you," she said.

I nodded. "I believe you."

Elise let go of my hand as our waitress came to the table, placing plates of eggs, bacon, and toast in front of both of us.

"So," said Elise, "what's the plan?"

"Well," I said between bites of breakfast, "we have to figure out what to do with iKnow. If we're trading, then we trade. But I'm not going to just hand the thing over, not until that Blackwood Blade is in my hand."

Elise sipped her coffee and stared at the table in thought.

"After that," I said, "I need to get a handle on what is actually happening. I, um . . ."

She put her coffee down and looked into my eyes.

For some reason the words weren't coming out. I was here again, stuck wanting to verbalize a thought that wasn't coming out.

"You need to visit Dee," she said.

I looked away.

"Why are you so afraid to talk about her?" she asked. "Is love making you an idiot?"

I popped a piece of bacon into my mouth and let out a sigh. "The thing is," I said, trying to form the words just right, "she's not, you know, real."

Elise narrowed her eyes. "What do you mean?"

"Concepts aren't people. They can look like people. They can be in this world and touch you, or influence you from afar, but they aren't real. I've fallen in love with an idea. Is it actually love if it's not another human?"

"You don't seem all that human yourself," she said, "so does that matter?"

"It does. Look around. Look at all the couples having breakfast, sharing laughs, having families, growing old and living through the end of their lives fulfilled and happy."

Elise looked around the diner.

"And here I am," I continued, "stuck. I've pulled the veil back on this world and how it works. There's no mystery anymore. If someone in this place is going through a hard time but finding the will to move on, I know it's Perseverance influencing them. I've met Perseverance. Have you ever seen *The Matrix*?"

"Yeah," said Elise. "Keanu's the best."

"Well imagine Neo taking the red pill, seeing everything he saw, but being stuck in the Matrix anyway with no way to escape. No phone calls. Stuck forever. Not even death is an escape. That's kind of what it feels like."

"Why does that matter then?" said Elise. "So what? You know they influence things, you know what they are, but it doesn't change what you feel, right?"

"But it does," I said, "because if I'm feeling angry, I can go visit Anger and tell him to knock it the hell off. But if I'm unhappy about what my life is, I can't change it. Destiny can't just change one person's fortune."

Elise looked thoughtful. She took a bite of her last bit of breakfast and leaned back in the booth seat. "If she's

Destiny, can't she just, you know, set you on a distinct path?"

I shook my head. "No. She's a representation of it, but she can't change or alter it. Her existence sets everyone on a balanced path. Destiny doesn't exist without her, but she can't just play with it. Changing one path is impossible without changing the others. Imagine what life would be like if a million people won the lottery at the same time."

"That would be awesome," said Elise.

"Until you think of an unfortunate circumstance," I replied. "Imagine a million millionaires destined to become mass murderers. Or a million millionaires hooked on drugs. Destiny's existence ensures that won't happen. We are free, or are we? Maybe our freedom to act however we like is our precise, well-balanced, predetermined fate?"

Our waitress came to the table and dropped off our bill. Elise placed some cash under the bill with a generous tip. We stood and made our way out of the diner and back to the car.

Elise started the car, and we sat in the parking lot for a few minutes.

"I have an idea," said Elise.

"Shoot."

"Use me," she said, turning to look at me.

I narrowed my eyes at her. "What do you mean?"

"Tomorrow we visit Deception. We'll hide the phone. Tell him we found it, and we know what it is. He won't give you the blade and walk away, but he will if you leave me there as collateral."

I shook my head. "No way. I'm not using a human as collateral. You aren't property."

"It'll work. You get the blade, I'll spend time there and see if there's something I can figure out or learn. Bring back the phone, you've got the blade, we leave."

"That's a terrible plan," I said. "What makes you think Deception will take you as collateral?"

"He knew how to look like my dad. Think about it. He knew me, and he knows you. I'm involved here too. And I think he knows what you're thinking," she said before cutting herself off.

I turned in my seat to face her. "What do you mean, what I'm thinking?"

"How you feel," Elise said with a shrug, looking out the window.

"You mean that you're important to me," I offered.

She looked down at her lap and swallowed, then focused back on my eyes. "Am I?"

"Yes," I said. "I think more than either of us realize."

Awkward silence hung in the air for what seemed like a day.

"Okay," said Elise, "where do we stash the phone?"

"I know someone I can trust for a favor," I said. "Start driving."

"Where to?"

"Philly. Right by where we met. We'll go visit my friend Emmanuel."

"Easy enough."

"Just a heads-up though. If he offers you something to drink, don't accept it."

CHAPTER 17

INTERNSHIP

I checked my watch. It was just before noon on a quiet Monday morning. Last night Elise and I had crashed in the car for a few hours after meeting with Emmanuel in Philadelphia. We were moving forward with her plan to be collateral in a Concept exchange.

For today to be a success, I needed the Blackwood Blade in my hand. I'd leave to retrieve Knowledge from Emmanuel, bring it back, and we would exchange. It sounded simple enough, but in Deception's home, anything could go sideways. Fast.

We stood outside the ornate double door entrance to Deception's suite. Moving through the casino floor just moments ago had been uneventful. There were no strange living advertisements on the wall, and everything felt quiet and unsettling.

Elise looked at me. "Any bets on what to expect behind these doors?"

"A big shiny room and a Concept wanting to knock us off guard?"

Elise put her hand on the door handle. "Let's find out."

With one smooth motion, she swung the door open. Before we stepped inside the room, we both had to stop and stare for a moment. Gone were the small fountains, cheerful lighting, and comfortable seating. The room was no longer bright white and minimalist.

Hues of deep burgundy tinted the walls. The tile floor was gone, replaced with plush carpet that matched the ominous color of the room. Sconces on pillars lit the ceiling and cast a thick coat of shadow along every object in view.

The room felt angry.

In front of the floor-to-ceiling glass overlooking the casino floor, Deception stood up behind his desk. His eyes were deep red, matching the walls. He was handsome, broad shoulders accentuating his silhouette in his jet-black suit.

"You had one fucking job, Caretaker," he said through gritted teeth.

Elise and I stepped into the center of the room to approach him. I could feel her nerves radiating like heat. It scared her. Fear left me alone, though I wasn't not sure if it was because I didn't care, or because Fear and Death had an unspoken understanding in order to help my duties.

"I have what you want. Give me the blade, and I'll bring it here."

"That's not the fucking deal!" he roared, gripping the edge of his desk and tossing it across the room. He took quick, determined steps toward us. I stood my ground. Elise flinched and took a small step back. I knew at this moment she was hoping there was another way out of this situation. I couldn't imagine she'd want to stay within the Dolos Hotel and Casino while I retrieved Knowledge.

It was too late to deviate.

Deception stopped a few feet in front of us, staring at Elise then back to me. He looked toward the ceiling and closed his eyes, drawing a deep breath in. The room shimmered, waving like haze produced by a scorching blacktop in the summer heat. Within moments the suite was back to its prior white, clean appearance. Gone were the deep red walls, gone were the shadows. Deception's minimalist desk was back to normal with a blank notepad and pencil resting atop it.

Deception lowered his head and looked between the two of us. "I'm sorry," he said toward Elise, flashing a brilliant smile. "I didn't mean to scare you, pet."

"I'm not your fucking pet," she said.

Deception turned and laughed as he made his way back to his desk. "No," he said over his shoulder before sitting down behind his desk. "You're his pet," he said, tilting his head toward me.

"That's enough," I said to him. "Stop wasting time. I want the blade in my hand, then I'll bring you what you asked."

"No," he replied. "You'll take off with your toy, and I won't have mine."

I looked at Elise. She looked to my eyes, and though I could tell there was fear, she gave me a determined nod.

We would make the offer.

"Elise will stay here with you," I said. "When I come back, we're both free to go. Until then she'll stay within the walls of the Dolos."

Deception's face was expressionless. He leaned back in his chair, placing his hands together on his lap. That he was even considering this felt like a victory. While we were in his domain, we had him thinking. Even the slight pause and leaning back was telling. He knew Elise was important to me. He knew I valued her. If he thought different, he would've dismissed the idea outright.

"Harm her, or play any trickery, and you'll never see it."

He leaned forward. "What is it? A book?"

"No," I replied.

"Does she know?" he asked, raising a brow and pointing toward Elise.

"Pry and the deal's off. Harm her and the deal's off."

Deception stood and sighed. "Caretaker," he said, "you have to know I'd want to have at least a little fun with sweet Elise here." He looked at her and smiled. "What do you say, my darling? Do you want to spend some hours with Daddy?"

He shimmered and waved, and before us once more was the spitting image of Elise's father.

Elise sighed. "I'm good. Thanks."

Deception shimmered and turned back to his typical form. The only difference was an exaggerated frown on his face. Elise's fortitude impressed me.

"Hey, look," Elise said to me, "he turned into a jackass!"

"Elise. Stop," I said. It was funny, but when you're inside the hornet's nest, you don't kick the walls. Her posturing would only make her time here more miserable.

"Okay, Caretaker," said Deception, smiling wide. "I'll tell you what. Deal accepted, but you will take something with you when you run off to retrieve Knowledge."

I narrowed my eyes at him. He knew Knowledge had been revealed. He was also smart enough to realize that I would've found out. I tried to think through this scenario. If he knew we were aware of what we had, and he was okay with an exchange, one of two things had to be true. Either Knowledge was more valuable than Death, or he needed the Blackwood Blade to remain in my hand.

There was no other reason for a Concept to strike a deal.

Deception looked down at his fingers with a thoughtful look on his face. "Yes, Knowledge. We all know what's going on here. Might as well acknowledge the elephant in the room, right?"

"Why do you want it?" I asked.

"It's Knowledge itself, Caretaker," said Deception, standing and turning around to look out the glass behind him, observing the massive casino floor below. "If I'm going to deceive these sheep, having more know-how is the way to do it. That's more influence for me, more currency in my coffers, and more of a grip."

Elise was paying close attention to what he was saying. I felt like she understood the high stakes of allowing one Concept to have another in his possession. I don't believe either of us trusted his reasoning, and I was almost certain he understood that, too.

"Are you going to destroy it?" I asked. Deception whirled around and looked at me with a mix of impatience and sarcasm. "It's a legitimate question," I continued, "and I'd appreciate an actual honest answer."

"Are you mad?" he replied. "Without Knowledge I have nothing. Do you think I want a world full of morons? No. That's too easy. I'm just going to borrow him for a while, then I'll have him back in the hands of his Caretaker."

"Since you killed the last one," said Elise.

I cringed.

His expression turned stern as he took a step toward her. "I did nothing of the sort, and consider staying in your lane, little girl. We need not make today uncomfortable."

Deception turned to me and stepped beside me, placing his hand on the back of my neck, skin on skin.

The feeling sent a chill through me.

Every time I traveled and visited a Concept, my feelings magnified. It was part of the reason visiting Destiny was something I craved again and again. The purity of feeling that your existence was in hands outside of your own was something I found soothing. There'd also been an undeniable connection between the two of us from the first moment we met. She felt right.

I tried to speak. I tried to get him to let go, but I didn't feel like I could move, or I didn't want to.

Deception's touch was impossible to comprehend. The intensity of pure deceit pulsing through my mind changed the entirety of my cognitive landscape. I not only wanted to lie and deceive, but I wanted to destroy lives by pitting motives against one another. I wanted content families to lie, cheerful couples to deceive each other, and relationships torn apart. I wanted to trick people into destroying themselves. If a used car salesman's deceptive tendencies were the size of a watch battery, it felt as if though I'd just grabbed a live wire carrying the world's electricity straight into my body.

He released his touch and smiled. Elise looked at me with concern.

"Fun, right?" he said, winking at me.

I shook my head, trying to orient my feelings back into the actual world. "What do you want me to bring?" I asked.

The door to the suite unlatched and opened. Elise and I swung our heads around at the sound. Standing in the doorway was a tall man with a tailored three-piece suit with a tie sporting an oversized graphic of a king of diamonds playing card. He strode into the room with a graceful gait and his lips curled into a smile as his eyes locked on Elise.

"No," I said. "Your Guardian can stay here. I'm not bringing him."

Deception ignored me. "Duncan, I believe you and Elise have met. This is William. He's Death's Caretaker. You'll be accompanying him to retrieve Knowledge, then you two will come back here, and he and Elise will be leaving."

"I'm not taking him," I said. "Out of the question."

Duncan walked past me, reaching into his pocket and pulling out the sheathed Blackwood Blade, placing it on Deception's desk.

It was the first time I'd seen the blade since I drove it into my heart with Harvey watching over me. I was overcome with that memory. That blade had cut Harvey and had likely cut Juliane Santos. It had been pulled from me by foreign hands while I was last with Destiny.

I was certain they'd placed the blade before my eyes because they knew I'd not be able to resist taking it. I couldn't leave without it. Not when it was this close.

It crossed my mind for a split second to grab it and fight my way out, but Duncan was beside me, a Guardian for Deception in his home. The reality of the situation was that Elise would perish, and I may not escape.

I couldn't chance it.

"Well, Caretaker?" asked Deception. "Is this a deal now, or are we done?"

I stared at the Blackwood Blade. I could feel it calling to me. It felt as though Death was happy to see me, or perhaps I was just projecting my hopes. I needed it in my hands.

Duncan reached down and picked the blade up, holding it out to me. "Take it, William," he said, his voice deep and smooth. "Let's get this over with."

I took the blade from him, and Death was in my hands once more. I took a deep breath and placed the blade into an inside pocket of my canvas jacket. I made a promise to myself that I would not allow the blade to leave me again.

Destiny was right. Love was right. This was my responsibility, and I was finding my way once more.

"I'd like Elise to walk me out," I said. "Duncan, I'll meet you outside."

Deception smiled. "Well, this is all so charming, isn't it? I truly feel like we can all be friends. Elise, darling, when you've walked William out, please come back up this way.

I'll make sure you're fed and we'll have a chat. I would love to get to know you better."

Elise stayed silent.

I couldn't imagine what was going through her mind. I walked toward her, shared a glance, and placed my hand on her arm. We turned and walked out of the suite.

We didn't say a word until we were in the elevator ready to descend to the casino floor.

"Is this a mistake?"

I shook my head. "Honestly, I don't know."

Her gaze fell to my coat. "So, um, that's Death?"

I took the sheathed blade from my jacket pocket and held it in my hands in front of her. "Where are my manners?" I said with a smile. "Elise, Death. Death, Elise. She's not very talkative."

Elise looked unimpressed. "It's not as grand as I imagined. And the name is still cheesy."

I shrugged, slipping it back into my coat pocket.

The elevator bell chimed and the doors slid open. The sounds of the casino floor assaulted our ears. We began our walk toward the exit doors where Elise would see me off and I would leave her to Deception's whims. I was trying to have faith that she would be okay.

"So what can you do with that thing?" she asked.

I looked around the casino. There were a few dozen people at various slot machines and tables. Even midday on a Monday gambling and drinking were going on. There were a few security guards walking around as well.

"There are close to a hundred people in this room with us right now," I said.

"And?" Elise asked.

I stopped walking and turned to her. "If I take out this blade and wield it the way I'm capable of, I can destroy every body and soul in this room within moments."

Elise swallowed and nodded.

I put my hands on her shoulders. "Elise, Concepts aren't to be messed with. When Deception touched me upstairs, I wanted to deceive the world. I wanted to ruin everyone. I wanted to lie to you and influence the world through deceit. Be strong."

"Okay."

"I have to go, but I'll be back for you in a matter of hours. Promise."

"Do you trust Duncan?" she asked.

"No, I don't. But I don't have a choice, and I have the blade. Don't worry about me."

Elise took a deep breath and looked around. "Okay. Go. Don't leave me here for too long."

"I won't. I promise you. If I have to destroy everything in my way, I'll do it to come back to you."

We walked the rest of the way to the door. I spotted Duncan outside, black fedora pulled down over his face, awaiting my exit. Between Duncan's unknown motives, Deception's blatant manipulation, and Elise's apprehensiveness, I was feeling overwhelmed. Not to mention my own feelings, which were near impossible to square away amongst all of this.

Elise and I stopped at the door.

"William, can you do something for me?" she asked.

"Anything."

"Can you hug me?"

I pulled her close and held her for a moment. Her arms slipped around my body and held me tight. After a moment we released, gave each other an awkward but genuine smile, and I slipped out the Dolos doors. Elise was behind me, and a trip with Duncan to retrieve Knowledge was in my immediate future.

I approached Duncan. He was looking out over the Boardwalk, his eyes darting back and forth with each person passing by. Up close, he reminded me even more of a crow, calculating and intelligent to support only his own ends. I remembered his face from the Four-Leaf Clover Motel the night I'd visited Love. He looked just as hollow now.

"Caretaker," he said, not diverting his eyes from the people passing by.

"Duncan," I said in return. His head turned to me and his unblinking blackened eyes fixed to mine.

"You are making a mistake. You're going to lose everything, and Elise will probably pay for your stupid mistakes with her life."

I shook my head. "Wait. What?"

CHAPTER 18

DUNCAN THE DECEIVER

For a moment I wondered if Duncan was being serious about Elise being dead, or if he was trying to manipulate me. I knew it would be insane to trust him.

"Well," I said, "forgive me if I don't believe a single word you say. Let's just get this done." I walked away. Duncan's hand grabbed my arm tight and turned me around. He tilted his hat up.

"William, I knew you were under the bed."

I looked down at his skeletal hand gripping my arm and thought about taking out the Blackwood Blade and cutting it off. I raised my head to meet his eyes and stepped closer to him. I felt like I had an ocean of fury deep in my being held back by the thinnest wall of impatience.

"Stop posturing," he said, his grip not changing. "Stop denying who you are."

"Oh?" I said. "You know who I am, then?"

Duncan looked down at my coat, as if peering through it to have a glance at Death herself, then back up to my eyes. "You are Death's Caretaker, and the longer you take to embrace that, the more pathetic you are. How long can one sad episode of denial last? More than a century?"

I ripped myself from his grip and pushed his arm away. "I can cut you down in a second," I growled. I felt the Blackwood Blade's icy presence in the jacket pocket beside my heart. My blood was pulsing. I was losing control. I was craving the sensation of harvesting bodies and cutting down souls.

Duncan's mouth curled into a wicked smile. "That's the William I need."

"Need?"

"Yes. The William who knows his purpose. Walk with me," he said, his relaxed voice tempering as he strolled away from the Dolos Casino.

"What do you mean?" I asked. The calm interaction messed with my body. My nerves felt intense and raw, and the urge I had to cut him down felt trapped inside of me with no way to expel itself. I felt like an erupting volcano with a lid.

"You are making a mistake," he said, "because he will kill Elise. He'll have Knowledge, he'll have your blade, and you'll be dead too."

"I've heard that before."

"Oh yes," Duncan said, a layer of sarcasm coating the words. "The mighty and invincible William St. Denis."

"Something like that," I said.

"He'll destroy her first, shortly after you bring Knowledge to him."

I listened, thinking over that possibility. I felt like Elise could handle herself. She was clever. But also, we had a trade to make. Duncan had to be wrong. Why would he tell me any of this?

"Keep walking," he said, "eyes are on us. We'll continue this conversation in the car."

I looked around, but it was clear Duncan was seeing something I couldn't. I hurried to keep pace with him.

Duncan pulled his fedora down over his face, focusing his eyes on the steps in front of him. The Dolos Casino was far behind us by now, and we made our way off the walkway and toward the parked SUV Elise had scored just hours ago. The afternoon sun was high in the sky, and the blast of cool air streaming between shaded stone buildings chilled my temper. I held my canvas jacket tight to my body.

We wound our way to the lower level of the parking garage. I unlocked the SUV with the key fob as we approached.

"Hand it over," Duncan said. "I'll drive."

"No," I replied.

He stopped and stared at me.

"No. Absolutely not," I added.

"Caretaker," he said, taking a step toward me, "I don't trust your head or your heart. If on a whim you steer into oncoming traffic, I die and you walk away. We both know that."

He had a point. Considering the situation from his point of view, I had an advantage being favored by Death. I nodded. "Fair enough," I said, dropping the key fob into his outstretched hand. "Consider this a first effort toward trust."

Duncan walked to the driver's side and climbed in while I settled into the passenger seat. He let out an emotionless chuckle as he buckled his seat belt and began pulling out of the parking spot.

"What is it?" I asked.

"You're a mushy, gullible fool," he replied. "It's funny. It's sad."

I shook my head. Deep down I was feeling unsettled. Perhaps he was right.

"I could beg you and you'd bend and break. 'Oh please, Mister Caretaker! Give me the blade! I'd feel safer if you didn't have it,' and you would hand it over like a browbeaten, disobedient child."

I turned toward him, my internal ocean of anger once again pounding its furious surf against a paper-thin wall of impatience. There was very little holding me back from doing terrible things. I'd seen Guardians at work. Endowed with skills and abilities far beyond that of normal human capacity, they weren't to be trifled with. Caretakers developed skills too, but they were less physical prowess and more geared toward the connectedness of all things.

We pulled onto a road leading out of Atlantic City. The car was quiet, the radio off, and my thoughts loud. I didn't understand if this was a trick or a trap, or what anyone's motivations were. What I needed were answers to put my brain at ease.

I broke the silence. "We're going to Philly."

Duncan's eyebrow rose. "You left Knowledge with Love?"

I shrugged.

"That's the smartest thing you've done in a long time."

"Why's that?" I asked.

"Love and Deception aren't friends. Congratulations on stumbling upon some good luck by accident. I imagine that's not something you're accustomed to. You found a Concept you could trust."

"Says the guy working for Deception," I countered.

"Chirp all you want, Caretaker. You don't understand what you're getting into."

I looked out the window. The sights and sounds of Atlantic City were far in the background. Right now we were on a deserted highway surrounded by trees and marshland. It wasn't pretty, but it was soothing seeing emptiness and expanse. Were it not for the company I was keeping, it would've been a pleasant moment.

"Now," I said, "I don't think anyone's listening, so why don't you spill some details on why you're so confident this won't go my way?"

Duncan's indifferent gaze focused on the road ahead. I couldn't imagine what it was like for someone aligned with Deception to straighten out all the thoughts, lies, and manipulation. I was hoping I could trip him up.

He let out a breath. "First, someone is listening."

I looked around the cabin of the expansive SUV. "We're alone."

"No," he said, "Death is right there, and she hears everything."

I shook my head. "I've been talking with her for years. I'm sure I'm just chatting with an inanimate object. Knives don't have ears."

Duncan slowed the SUV and pulled over to the side of the road. The car crunched the gravel and came to a stop. The engine idled as he turned in his seat to face me, leaning one arm on the steering wheel. He removed his fedora, placing it on the dash. Blackened, unblinking eyes stared at me. His chin-length midnight hair fell down to frame his gaunt face. There was a bright blond patch of hair on his left side, spoiling his otherwise symmetrical features.

"More than a century spent running around with her, and you still treat her like a possession? I'm surprised she hasn't given up on you and let your miserable self die."

"Don't tell me how to do my job."

He leaned forward. "Oh, I'm going to tell you, because even though I'm aligned with Deception and think you're a fool, the way you treat your responsibility offends me on the deepest of levels."

I felt anger welling up. "Offends?"

Duncan looked out the window, stretching a hand out as if to show me the world. "This whole place before you, and it has given you this gift, yet you spend your time whining and pining over things you cannot have. The literal end of life is something you hold in the palm of your hands and you just cry over Destiny and play this poor William routine. Yes. Offends. Other Concepts just feel sorry for you. It's embarrassing. Honestly, I think most just tolerate you."

"Keep fucking driving," I said. "I'll live my life. Now if you have nothing substantive to say, you can just shut it."

Duncan scoffed and let out a chuckle, speeding back onto the road.

"Elise will be dead in less than twenty-four hours," he said.

"I don't believe you," I said.

"Do you know why he agreed to keep her as collateral?"

"It was his only move."

Duncan threw his head back and laughed in a way that reminded me of a shot of electricity, as if lightning was crackling in his lungs.

I stared at him.

He shook his head. "Who was the first person to talk with Knowledge after you found the phone?"

"Elise," I said. "Why is that important?"

"Because she's a Caretaker now too, you idiot."

I felt blood drain from my face and a lump the size of a grapefruit forming in my throat. That couldn't be true. She hadn't agreed to it, and Knowledge hadn't indicated as much. Elise had spent time with him that morning out of my presence. She'd found the car and the cash. She'd asked him about me.

"See," continued Duncan, smirking as he spoke, "when a Caretaker is killed, the next person to interact with that Concept is the new Caretaker. It takes virtually nothing for that quick bond to form. I'm not surprised you didn't know. It's never a problem for you. That's your unique gift, I suppose. Maybe if you spent less time self-absorbed chasing something you can't have you'd actually learn about how this all works."

"No, you're being manipulative. I don't believe you," I said.

"I wonder why Destiny never told you," Duncan mused, sarcasm thick in his throat.

"I have zero trust for anything you say."

Duncan shrugged. "Disbelieve all you want. It's the truth. You left a brand-new baby Caretaker in Deception's house," he said. "She's done for. You'll hand over a Concept, Elise will give up any piece of knowledge that Deception wants because she stands no chance against his power, and guess what will be top on his list for a juicy little piece of Knowledge?"

I knew the answer before he said it.

"How to rid the world of the distraught William St. Denis," he said with a smile. He turned his head from the road, looking at my canvas jacket where the Blackwood Blade was nestled against my body, then to my face. "Don't worry, I'll take excellent care of her. I've always wanted to be a Caretaker."

I slid my hand into my jacket, grasping the hilt of the blade. I could feel the chill radiating through my hand and up my arm. My thumb came to rest against the sheath. In a moment I could draw her and turn the cabin of the vehicle into a frozen casket, ready to drain the life from Duncan sitting beside me.

"Before you do that," said Duncan, calmly staring at the road, "I have a proposition for you."

I stayed my hand.

"You don't believe me, fine," he said. "When we get to Love's territory and get the phone, you ask. Ask who Caretaker for Knowledge is. Ask if he knows how you can be killed."

I let my hand slip away from the blade resting against my heart and refocused on the road. "And?"

"And," Duncan continued, "if I'm right, you owe me a beer."

"A beer?" I asked.

"Can you manage that?"

"A beer?" I asked again, confused.

"That's all."

"Deal."

The car accelerated, and we stayed in silence for the rest of the drive. My goals were simple: retrieve Knowledge, find out who its Caretaker was, then find out if I could be killed. Then, when all the questions had answers, have a drink.

I'd had worse days.

CHAPTER 19

NO ANSWER

Duncan and I walked side by side toward LOVE Park in the heart of Philadelphia. The area was bustling. People were getting out of work, passing through on their way home or to a quick dinner. Sunset had arrived, and the air was getting a distinct chill. The city was windy, and dark clouds gathered on the horizon. A wicked vibe permeated the air, puncturing my lungs with each breath I took.

My intuition gave me that familiar feeling.

There was going to be death this evening. I felt it on the Blackwood Blade pressed to my warm chest. There was no explanation for my feeling; I just knew.

We made our way toward the iconic Love sculpture. Leaning against the statue, framed by dusk-kissed buildings of bustling Philadelphia streets, was Emmanuel. I spotted his glistening heart-shaped earrings. His spotless leather dress shoes reflected the shining red brake lights of the traffic exiting the city.

When Elise and I were here just hours prior, Emmanuel had been warm and engaging. He loved Elise, and he'd hugged me with a long and genuine embrace. Emmanuel had been thrilled to help us. Love was right that he was a friend who could be trusted.

That Emmanuel seemed to be long gone the closer I walked to him. Gone was the warm face and brilliant smile. His face was stoic. His eyes were critical.

"I think he likes me," said Duncan as we walked toward him.

"Shut up," I said. "Don't ruin this."

A frozen gust of wind cut through me and chilled my skin. Everything felt more difficult when the air froze. It was a loss of dexterity on gloveless hands attempting delicate work. It was hard to keep my wits sharp and active.

Duncan and I approached Emmanuel and stopped before him. He stared at Duncan, and Duncan stared back with his darkened eyes just underneath the brim of his fedora.

"Hello, Emmanuel," I said.

His eyes did not divert from my companion. "Caretaker," he said, his voice as chilled and sharp as the air around us.

"I've struck the deal, and I need—"

"You brought a Guardian here, William."

Emmanuel was not pleased. Duncan remained motionless, staring at him.

"I did. I had no choice. It was a condition."

He glanced at me, his eyes quickly diverting to lock onto Duncan once more. "You are making a mistake, my friend."

"I've been hearing that a lot lately," I said.

"Haitian?" asked Duncan.

"Yes," replied Emmanuel.

Duncan nodded. "I lost a friend in the Port-au-Prince earthquake a few years ago."

Emmanuel leaned toward me, keeping his eyes fixed to Duncan. "All he spits are lies."

"Oh please," said Duncan, relaxing his posture for the first time. "It's much easier to deceive with the truth, my Haitian friend."

"You are not my friend," Emmanuel snapped. "Caretaker, this is a mistake."

"Listen," I said, "I know this isn't ideal, but I have her." I patted the outside of my coat where the Blackwood Blade was nestled underneath.

"Two Concepts?" asked Emmanuel. He was incredulous. "You are going to trust yourself with two around this?" He gestured toward Duncan.

"I can handle this," I said. "I promise. I will handle this."

He let out a deep sigh, then reached a hand into his coat pocket and pulled out the slender, unassuming phone with the "iKnow" logo on the back.

Duncan smiled with wonder. "That's it? That's Knowledge? An Apple knockoff?"

I took the phone from Emmanuel and slipped it into my interior coat pocket. For a moment I let my mind muse about my circumstance. Here I was, standing in a darkening public park in the middle of a city. In one pocket I held Death herself in the form of the Blackwood Blade. In my other pocket I kept the entirety of all Knowledge in the form of a nondescript cellular telephone. I was over a century old, standing beside a Guardian for Deception and a Steward of Love.

Life was indeed strange.

"Thank you," I said to Emmanuel.

His eyes locked on Duncan once more, then back to me. "Be careful, my friend. There are things at work well beyond the surface of what you see."

Duncan tipped his hat toward Emmanuel and smiled wide. "Good evening, my Haitian friend."

We turned and silently walked away from the Love sculpture and toward the city lights. Our pace was slow, and neither of us seemed eager to say a word.

We wound our way past city hall and toward the tall glass-and-steel buildings closer to Rittenhouse Square. Moist heat from subway entrances blasted us as we walked past, PATCO trains rumbling beneath our feet as we made our way through the city.

"Stop over here," said Duncan. Dusk had given way to night and the cold air cut through us after every turn onto a new street. He was pointing out a small stone wall beside an old hotel along the city street.

We walked up to the building, shielding ourselves from frozen gusts of stinging wind, and leaned against the small stone wall.

"Go ahead," said Duncan. "Ask it."

I stared at him. At this point I wasn't sure what would be worse, Duncan being wrong, or Duncan being right. I took the phone out of my pocket and held it in my hand, staring at the blank screen.

Duncan watched me. His typical straight demeanor had given way to an almost childlike fascination of what I was about to do.

I held the phone close to my face and asked, "Who is your Caretaker?"

The screen brightened.

Ding.

ELISE CAMPBELL.

"I told you," said Duncan, "and if you weren't so shortsighted you would've understood that it was going to happen."

"Quiet," I told him. I was angry, both because Duncan was right and because I'd missed this possibility. Most of all, I was angry that I was indeed so self-absorbed that I hadn't considered this turn of events. I spent so much time evaluating the emotions of everyone around me that I forgot to stop and think. Elise as a Caretaker was far more valuable to Deception. He wouldn't have agreed to the trade otherwise. I'd been tricked.

I held the phone up to my face. "Can I be killed?"

Ding.

YOU HAVE DIED MANY TIMES. THAT'S KIND OF AN UNNECESSARY QUESTION, DON'T YOU THINK?

Duncan laughed. "Sense of humor. That was unexpected."

I sighed and held the phone close once more. "Permanently, I mean."

Ding.

YES.

I nodded, staring at the screen as it went dark. I brought it close again. "How?"

Ding.

MY CARETAKER KNOWS.

Duncan smiled and looked out over the traffic moving along the city street before us. "Oh, William," he said, as if gloating over victory. "You owe me a beer."

"Tell me how," I said to the phone. I needed answers.

Ding.

GOODBYE, WILLIAM. BRING ME TO MY CARETAKER. YOU HAVE YOUR DESTINY, THIS IS MINE.

The screen flickered off and I got the sense that any other question was going to remain unanswered. I placed the phone back into my pocket and looked down the sidewalk streets, hearing the soft hum of car engines pass me by and the soundtrack of Duncan's continued laugh beside me.

"I'm thirsty," he said. "Walk with me."

We walked between looming shadowed buildings, pressing against a dark and swirling sky. Brisk winds pushed menacing clouds past the city high overhead. There was a negative energy in the air and I was beginning to feel as if my emotions had been rubbed raw. Exposed nerves scraped against my thoughts and the reality of my situation. Tonight I'd received confirmation of something I'd wondered for more than a century.

I could die.

This little piece of knowledge ran rampant through my mind. How had I avoided it for so long? I'd been shot, stabbed, crushed, and drowned. I'd inflicted massive amounts of harm to myself and I'd always come back. I'd visited Destiny many times, and had always made my way back to this living reality. What ingredient was missing to avoid permanence in death?

It was clear that I wouldn't have the answer tonight. Tonight, all I was going to have was a beer alongside someone I didn't want to be around for another moment.

We walked a few hundred yards in silence before stopping at a set of stone steps leading to a tall set of well-worn oak doors. Beside the doors was a hand-carved wooden sign that had likely been posted on this building for a hundred years.

It read, "The Kerry Bog Pub."

Underneath it was a silhouette of a horse beside a pair of pint glasses. Affixed to the oak doors was a pair of upturned horseshoe door knockers that seemed to be as old as the pub itself. Taking in the facade, I found myself wondering if this building had been here longer than I'd been on Earth.

Duncan stepped up to the doors, his slender hand and gnarled knuckles grasping the door handle. With a smooth motion, he swung the massive door open, and we stepped inside.

CHAPTER 20

A PINT AND A SHOT

The interior of the Kerry Bog Pub was a warm wood-carved masterpiece bathed in the amber glow of wall sconces and candlelit tables. There was a bustling pair of bartenders and few open seats. Couples and friends filled the pub with cheerful conversation and bursts of laughter. The environment was soothing, and I found myself warm and comfortable being inside. It was a relief being shielded from the frozen night air carving through the city streets beyond those massive oak doors.

Duncan weaved a path toward a small table near the inside corner of the pub. He sat along the back wall.

"I'd like that seat," I said. "I prefer to see the exit."

He shook his head and slipped out of the chair. "Whatever you say, Caretaker. You're buying, so you and your anxiety can sit wherever you like."

Perhaps it was paranoia, but I always wanted to have everything in front of me. I'd distrusted everyone and everything in my life at various times, even my own wits.

Sitting toward the corner of a room allowed me to see everyone and everything. Even if I wasn't watching the people and actions going on around me, they were there, and I trusted my intuition to alert me if something ended up being off.

In the Kerry Bog Pub, however, I felt comfortable. It wasn't as charming as Love's bar I'd visited a couple nights prior, but for something within the realm of reality, it was charming enough.

There was a lengthy line of tables along the back wall, and many old wooden tables throughout the crowded establishment. The floors were crooked. This pub had seen fights, spilled drinks, and roomfuls of drunken patrons singing songs and hoisting glasses in devoted cheers.

Toward the front corner of the pub were three boyish men tossing darts at a well-worn dartboard on the opposite wall, high-top tables holding their half-drunk pints of stout beer.

A cheerful woman approached us with a spring in her step. She had long black hair, brilliant green eyes, and a bright smile between dimpled cheeks. She placed two drink coasters down on our table and gave us a slight bow. "*Fáilte*, gentlemen! What are you having tonight?" she asked.

"We'll each have a Guinness," Duncan replied. "And he's paying."

I nodded to her. "Please and thank you."

She winked at me and bounced away through the busy pub toward the bar, stopping to laugh with some patrons at another table and clear empty glasses on her way. The warm air of the bar was filled with an audible soundtrack of Irish song and Gaelic lyrics, the laughter and clinking of glasses drowning out the melodic music. I stared at the burning candle nestled in a small vase at the center of our table. Everything was on my mind. All at once. I was becoming overwhelmed.

"Cheer up, Caretaker."

I shrugged and looked at Duncan. "Excuse me. I occupy my mind with things other than a pint of Guinness."

"Look around," he replied. "Don't you see the complexity of all this?"

"Complexity?" I asked. "What do you mean?"

"What do you see when you look at this pub?"

I brought my head up and looked around. There was play, laughing, animated conversation about serious topics. People clinked glasses together and threw their arms around one another. There was a couple kissing over their own table.

"People going about their life," I said. "Some of them happy, some of them hiding their issues. All of them unaware of what's beneath the surface."

"And what's beneath the surface? You are referring to a world of Concepts? Our world?"

I gave him a smirk. "Our world? Yes. They're all just doing what they do. They don't realize that Death and Knowledge are sitting in a pub with them."

"Don't they though?"

"What do you mean?"

"William, you sadden me," said Duncan, removing his fedora and laying it on the table. His dark hair fell over his cheekbones, framing his pale, gaunt face. He stared at me with those black eyes, wide and unblinking. The shocking streak of blond hair drew my attention away from his eyes for a moment.

"Maybe I'm just having a hard time understanding your nature," I replied.

"Don't you see Concepts? Everywhere you look? Focus is here, wrapping herself around these people. Happiness is in here. Do you see that couple making out at that back table?"

I leaned away from the table, craning my neck to see a pair amid a very enthusiastic display of public affection.

"That's Desire," smiled Duncan. "Longing is here. Deception's influence is here too. There are hundreds of unknown Concepts exerting influence every moment, everywhere."

"What's your point?" I asked.

He folded his arms and leaned back in his chair. "My point is, you are Caretaker for a Concept that, at one point or another, will influence every soul in this place. All of them. Do you realize what that means?"

"I get it," I said. I was growing impatient with Duncan's lecture.

"No, you don't," he replied. "You spend your time worrying about William St. Denis and worrying about Destiny. These connections, this entire massive world, and all you know how to do is drive a knife into your heart and hang out with a pretend girlfriend."

I looked away.

"You need a shot of honesty," he said.

Our conversation came to an abrupt pause as our cheerful waitress brought over two tall glasses of Guinness, cascading foam slipping down the outside of the glasses. She winked at me again and bounced off once more to take care of the busy tables in the pub.

Duncan held up his glass. "*Slàinte.*"

I held up my glass and clinked it to his, though I wasn't feeling the mood.

"To newfound friends," said Duncan.

"Not feeling that one," I said, tipping the glass back and taking a long drink.

We placed our glasses down.

"William St. Denis, I want you to think about how you are being influenced and manipulated."

"I'm not."

"Oh, you are. I see it. Selfishness. Ignorance. Sadness. All of them have their teeth in you and you don't even realize it."

His comment grabbed my attention. "Fine. Who is influencing you, then? When was the last time you looked in a mirror?"

Rumbles of laughter, music, and conversation moved throughout the pub as Duncan's lips curled into a smile. He leaned close. "Deception. Greed. Ambition. Determination. Plenty more than that. Unlike you, I'm in tune. I know this world inside and out. I operate using logic and order."

"Happy for you," I said, lathering my words with a sarcastic tone. I held up my glass and tipped it toward him, taking another long drink before placing it back down. "And what does that get you? The privilege of being Deception's lapdog?" I asked.

"It gets me to this pub, sitting across from Death's Caretaker, which is exactly what I have wanted for years," he said, just above a whisper.

It was as if our moods shifted. Gone was the casual nature of our conversation. Something deeper was at work.

"What did you say?" I asked.

Duncan sighed and stood up. "I have to visit the restroom," he said. "Try not to have too much fun without me."

I stared at my half-empty glass of Guinness. My mind raced. What had just happened? He said he'd wanted to sit across from me for years. I looked up and around the pub. The commotion going on was just as it had been when we'd walked in together, but something felt off now.

There were still groups laughing and drinking. The bartenders were still pouring drinks. The couple at the table along the wall was still somehow making out. Songs continued playing, the waitress continued working the tables, but there was an undercurrent I couldn't place.

I looked to my left and four men at one table were staring at me, then diverting their gazes back to their drinks and erupting in laughter. My gut felt tight. Intuition was screaming at me, but I couldn't hear what it was saying. I looked at the bartenders and as they were working, they glanced at me, then back to their tasks at hand.

I didn't want to do anything sudden. I was being watched. If I stood up, it would draw attention. I let out a fake sigh and leaned back in my chair, raising the glass to my lips and having another sip of my Guinness. I looked over at the boyish men hurling darts at the dartboard. I noticed something.

Every dart they threw hit the bullseye.

I looked back at my glass and pretended to be lost in thought. I brought it to my face again for another slow sip, keeping my eyes just above the glass and staring at the dartboard once more.

Two of them playing. Four bullseyes in a row.

Duncan was out of sight. Our waitress approached the table, cheerful and smiling just as before. "Can I get you another?" she asked.

I looked at my almost-empty glass and sighed. "No, not for right now. I'll wait for my friend to come back. May I ask you a question?"

"Of course!" She smiled at me. Her beautiful green eyes focused on me and the dimples in her cheeks were pronounced beneath the low amber light of the busy pub.

I tilted my head toward the front of the pub. "Those fellows playing darts over there, are they a professional team or something?"

She held her gigantic smile. "No, why?"

I had the last sip of my beer and placed the glass down in front of her. "They aren't able to hit anything except for a bullseye."

Her smile faded in an instant.

The music stopped.

The chatter stopped.

Everyone in the pub froze.

"Oh, Caretaker," she said, her voice venomous. "You should not have come here."

Every person in the bar turned their head to face me. All of their eyes, brilliant green. Blood and adrenaline raged through my body. My heart was pounding. The icy

Blackwood Blade was aching for my touch. Death craved my embrace, and I craved to hold her.

I smiled and looked down at the table, nodded, then raised my eyes to the dozens of people with green eyes affixed to me. I was almost ready.

A chill embraced the warm pub as I stood.

Everyone stood in unison to match, all of them facing me, all of them ready.

Shadows crept up the walls as if poison was coursing through the room's corrupted veins. The warm amber light had receded to a faint glow. Death was here. Her heartbeat pulsed throughout the room. The blackened walls breathed with her, and my senses sharpened to a razor's edge.

Gazes shifted to the darkness tightening its grip on this place. The waitress, her faded dimples and wicked scowl focusing on me, moved her hand slow and steady toward the back of her belt. Nothing mattered to me right now except the impossible aching I experienced wanting to reach into my coat and grasp the Blackwood Blade.

"Listen to me, all of you," I announced to the silent group before me.

The room pulsed in darkness, synchronized with the beating of my heart, grew darker with each beat.

"My name is William St. Denis, and you are all dead."

Someone shouted, "He has the blade!"

A split second later, I had the Blackwood Blade in my hand as I swung my arm forward and plunged the blade through the neck of my once-cheerful waitress. Blood sprayed from the exit wound at the base of her skull and her lifeless head slipped off the blade as her body dropped to the floor.

In an instant, there was complete chaos. Rushing toward me were waves of attackers. I kicked my table over and began carving into the surrounding people. Sprays of blood from Death's edge painted the now midnight-black walls of the pub as I danced and slid around thrown punches and hurled objects.

I ducked down and sliced through legs, raised up and cut through exposed throats. When I felt two hands grab my shoulders from behind, I held and flipped my attacker to the floor in front of me, driving the Blackwood Blade straight through their brilliant green eye. I jumped up, carving flesh and bone, swirled my body as I swung the blade through chests, arms, and the faces of those attempting to surround me.

All I felt from Death at this moment was love, unconditional love for who I was and what I was doing. I wielded the blade with the precision of a legendary conductor, urging on the pounding speed and fury of Death's frantic orchestra. We were the perfect match. Together we produced a morbid cacophony of beautiful, dissonant carnage.

The room was frozen in an icy grip as bodies dropped to the floor, lifeless and soulless, until that last moment when I was alone. All I could hear was the faint echo of blood tapping against the floor from slumped bodies bent over broken chairs and tables.

The pulsing slowed. My heart calmed.

Shadow gave way to low amber light, casting a glow upon the sickening scene spread across the floor. There were bodies soaked in blood, severed pieces of flesh and exposed bone wherever I looked. Not a single wall or object was clean of coagulating human essence, except for Duncan's hat.

My breathing slowed, and then I heard it.

The bathroom door opened.

Duncan stepped out into the pub, wiping his hands with a towel. He had a cheerful ear-to-ear smile plastered on his face. "So," he said, "what did I miss?"

I walked toward him, the Blackwood Blade still in my hand and an urge to harvest one more bag of blood on my mind.

He held up a hand. "William, I was right here the whole time. I knew this would happen, and I was ready to help. But you didn't need it."

I stopped a few feet from him, pointing the blade at his heart. "You set me up."

Duncan's eyes fixated on the blade. "Oh my, isn't she magnificent?" he said in reverence. I watched him marvel at the interior of the pub. "The darkness everywhere. The chill in the air. This is breathtaking."

I felt rage. "You have five seconds before I cut you clean in half. Lengthwise."

He held up both hands. "Relax, William. This is incredible work. Truly. I am in awe."

"Get to the point," I said, stepping closer, holding the blade inches from his throat.

Duncan nodded. "You just saved Elise. I brought you here because I think I know who is against you. I know you don't trust me, and frankly I don't trust you, but we have a common enemy right now because both of our lives are on the line."

I shook my head. "Start making sense."

"These people," he said, gesturing around the room, "they stole the blade from you. They cut that kid when you were in that Nebraska warehouse. The blade was delivered to Deception by their hand after they cut Knowledge's old Caretaker, marking her and ensuring her death."

I let my arm drop, then opened my coat pocket and slipped the Blackwood Blade back into its sheath. The amber glow in the room returned and saturated the pub with color once more. He had to be right. There had been many opportunities along the way for him to manipulate me. But I still needed answers.

"Why not tell me? And who are these people?"

Duncan laughed. "Would you have agreed to come here if I had? Also, remember I am aligned with Deception, so where's the fun in being honest? I would've bailed you out if you'd needed it. But now I know you can handle yourself against Deception. You've reconnected with Death. It's beautiful to see. I'm not certain of who you murdered here, but I'm sure they earned it."

"You're the worst."

"You don't have to like me, but you should understand that you need me."

"Why's that?" I asked.

Duncan sighed. "Because I'm going to get you back to Elise. The only thing that can keep all three of us alive is you, and I want to make sure that happens."

"You're going to betray Deception?" I asked.

He shrugged. "He's gaining too much power and coveting too much more. Everything was easier before Ambition sunk her claws into him. Not all of us have the gift of immortality. I'd like to stick around without having my life threatened."

If Duncan and I had a common enemy in Deception, then I understood him. I had a feeling that I'd been wrong about him this entire time. As much as I hated the thought, he needed me at my best. Maybe his manner brought that out in me.

"Do you understand now?" he asked.

"I do."

"Are we good?"

I nodded. "For now."

"I'll take it. Grab my hat, and let's get out of here and get you cleaned up. We have precious little time before word gets out. We need to get back to the Dolos before anyone gets too suspicious."

I turned to look at the table and noticed a subtle movement out of the corner of my eye. Duncan's back was turned. From behind the bar, one bartender stood and raised a pistol.

"Get down!" I called out, and launched myself between the barrel of the bartender's gun and Duncan's back.

A shot rang out.

CHAPTER 21

REFLECTION

I opened my eyes.

I was falling from the sky. With what felt like the grace of an angel, I descended, slow and comfortable.

Through sky and stars and endless universe, I drifted toward solid ground, where my feet touched down. The clean air chilled my face. I felt like I was in a place not unlike the reality I was used to, but everything here appeared different. The light was soft as moonlight, but there was no moon above. There was only an endless, cloudless sky. I was in a world that felt lit by a haunting glow of bioluminescence. This place felt as strange as the deepest point in the oceans, but with perfect air to breathe.

It was light enough to see; it was dark enough for mystery.

I was barefoot and stood in damp, soft grass. This world was both dark and bright, a contradiction before my eyes, alit from the stuff stars are made of.

There was no fear here. It felt like home.

I breathed deep and the sweet scent of earth and pine filled my lungs. The pure taste of clean, fresh air pressed to my lips. A gentle breeze caressed my hair and I took a moment to close my eyes and breathe in the deep aroma of balsam on the delicate wind.

I heard no sound but the beating of my heart.

From horizon to horizon was lush green grass beneath my feet, painted with hues of midnight green. It was perfect land among the spectacle of the magnificent expanse of space above, itself dotted by an infinite number of stars and swirling galaxies.

I leaned down and planted a knee to the ground, running my hand through the cool grass in the chill of this strange, illuminated world. My hands were aglow. It reminded me of a photography darkroom brought to a human's visual spectrum by a single black light.

There were no distractions. I heard no sound from the grass or sky or forest in the distance. Even the steady breeze caressed me in what felt like a respectful quiet. I raised my head up from the expanse of emerald grass and noticed a figure approaching. It was a male silhouette with no discernible features from this distance. I stood and waited for him.

As he approached and came into focus, my heart was pounding.

It was me.

"I assume I need no introduction," he said.

I blinked and tried to focus.

"Welcome home, William."

I studied him. He looked like a younger version of my reflection. Gone were the scars and stress lines on my face.

The unkempt head of brown hair was still there, the look in his eyes bringing forth more innocence than my own.

We had the same well-worn canvas jacket. We had the same bare feet at the bottom of the same torn jeans. I peered forward, tilting my head to look at him from a slight angle. This didn't feel like a distinct entity or being.

There was no doubt I was staring at myself.

"You're me?" I asked, feeling dumb to ask such an obvious question.

"I am. Technically, I am Self. Not a Caretaker. Not exactly William St. Denis."

I looked around at the illuminated world and tried to soak in the feeling coursing through me.

"Aren't we both William?" I asked.

He approached me, draping an arm around my shoulder. I felt it on my shoulder and on my arm. I felt the cool grass on his feet and my own. I felt the clothes against my skin and against his. There were two of me. Separate, but connected in every cell, in every thought, in every way.

This was beyond strange.

"You are William," he said, strolling with me through the damp, midnight-green grass. "It's a label you take in reality. But is it you?"

"I don't know," I answered.

"Trust me, it isn't. Everyone calls you William, but what is William really? Everyone calls you Caretaker, but that's a responsibility, not an identity."

I soaked in his words as we walked, his arm draped over me as if we were best friends meandering under a starry sky.

"How did I end up here?" I asked.

"It happened so fast," he said, looking to the sky.

"I took a bullet," I said, "for Duncan."

He nodded. "You did. And in that moment of honesty and self-sacrifice, you reached a point where you were genuine, authentic through every weave of your complicated, stitched-together soul. It nailed you in the right temple. That's why it feels a little fuzzy right now. You died that instant."

"You brought me here?" I asked.

Self shook his head. "No. You brought you here. Over a century of life as a Caretaker for Death and you and I have never met. I think your subconscious realized that to move forward and to understand, we needed to converse."

That was true. Most of my other deaths had been deliberate, specific to a particular objective, or with a Concept in mind to visit. A sudden moment, an instinctual instant born from a split-second decision, had placed me in the only place I could be. Connected only to myself.

My instinctual action with no planning or thought ensured this was the only place I could end up. Self smiled at me as we walked, squeezing me a little with his arm as if to offer a comforting hug.

"You understand," he said through a warm smile. It wasn't a question. He knew and felt my realization because I knew and felt my realization.

We approached deep woods just ahead—shaded, mysterious, and enticing.

"What is this place?" I asked.

He closed his eyes and breathed in scents of balsam and earth. I could taste it on his tongue and in his lungs.

He stretched out his arm as if to present the environment to me. "This is your world, William. Think of it as your own planet. You, the alien on this small and ever changing ball. Your own tiny Earth where Self recedes and resides. When you are in distress, I am here, distressed under the storm-stricken sky. When you are at peace, I am here on a perfect, bright, beautiful day."

"And when I'm angry?"

Self looked down in reflection as we walked. "Crimson atmosphere scorched and swallowed by massive hurricanes of rage and flame."

"I'm sorry," I said.

"I know," he replied. "You know what you do to yourself. I am here to help you understand what you do to me."

We stopped walking and stood staring at one another. "Isn't that the same thing?" I asked.

"Yes," answered Self. "And no. William, I need not explain to you this near impossible time you have considering yourself. You consider others, die for others, and protect others. That's your nature."

I looked to him with a question on my tongue that I couldn't form.

"Now I am here," he continued, "with you. In front of you. We are the same, but we are separate. I need you to understand that when you are inconsiderate of yourself, you are inconsiderate of me. Yes, I'm a Concept, but I'm also you."

"What happens when I hate myself?" I asked.

I watched as Self reached into a pocket of his canvas jacket, pulling out a small butterscotch candy wrapped in crinkling plastic. He shook his head in resigned disapproval as he untwisted it, placing the empty wrapper back in his pocket. He popped the candy into his mouth. I could taste it.

"Beasts," he said, pointing into the forest just past where we stood.

"Beasts?"

"Pure loathing in beast form. Bleeding ichor and hatred from their own pores. They come for me, and they overwhelm me. The longer you are in that state, the longer they spend devouring me. Poisonous clawed appendages rending my flesh and muscle. Tearing me down to the bone. Hardened fangs consuming me."

I shook my head, confused at why I would treat myself this way.

"And you get over it," Self continued, "and I regrow. But your self-loathing consumes me in the same manner every time."

"I'm so sorry," I managed.

Self nodded. "I know. So am I. Come. Let's make our way through this forest. I've been looking forward to showing it to you."

We walked forward, broaching the boundary into the rich wood ahead. In this place there were trees, tall, young, and fallen. The light faded more, the universe above dimmed by the canopy of lush green leaves sprouting from what seemed like ancient growth. The air was thick with the lush aroma of earth and decomposing fallen trees, feeding the sturdy life around us.

"Why would there be a forest here?" I asked.

Self stepped over gnarled roots and branches, the slight sound of crackling twigs echoing into the distance as he led the way. He looked back at me and smiled.

"This forest is your mind. These massive oaks are your thoughts and ideas. The ones you have valued and held on to." He paused by a massive tree, gnarled old bark curling around its trunk. He placed his hands on it and gave it a gentle pat, looking up to its top high above us. "This must be an idea you've had for a long time."

"Wait. This is my mind?" I asked.

He kept walking, stepping over trunks and fallen branches, over tiny bubbling creeks and various eroded stones, their sharp edges long gone over ages of time and thought.

"Each of these trees on the ground, dead and decomposing, is an idea or thought you've had that you've forgotten or dismissed. Collapsed in the land of ideas, submitting to entropy. Just like your ideas in the actual world, they die and decompose, feeding the fresh growth around us."

I was standing in my mind, surrounded by the natural presence of my own thoughts and ideas. It was a humbling experience.

Some had grown into something incredible and towering. Others were just beginning as they struggled to find some light through the canopy. Some had failed and were collapsed, hollow, rotten, forgotten, and being absorbed.

We cleared the woods and moved on to a rocky shore.

Sea spray tickled our faces as we approached a large rock on the shoreline and sat upon it, pondering a never-ending sea before us. The water defied all physical rules—dark and raging in a hurricane, seconds later sweet and still and calm as glass.

Self draped his arm around me once more.

"Welcome to your heart," he said through a smile.

I sat and stared in marvelous wonder, watching the water and its massive ebb and flow. Lightning struck calm seas, waves as tall as mountains rose above brilliant blue water, smashing down under a clear night sky.

"My heart. This makes little sense. Water doesn't move that way."

Self held me close and patted my shoulder. "It's okay. It's hard to understand, I know. This deep ocean, filled with constant motion and movement. Forever calm. Forever raging. In constant contradiction of itself at all times. You have a very confused heart, William."

Sea spray droplets perched on my arm from small crashing waves at my feet and I felt close to my heart. This place was comforting but uncertain. I was tiny compared to the tumultuous sea before me, but I still felt in control.

I had a million questions for the sea, but I knew every answer. I wanted to dive in, but I felt terrified. I wanted my heart to swallow me whole, to feel that intensity, but I knew it would never let me go.

Self smiled and let out a soft laugh. "It only makes perfect sense because it doesn't, right?"

I looked to the sky, packed with the brightest stars from horizon to horizon. Self looked skyward with me. "Your dreams." He sighed a deep sigh. "Those are my favorite, you know. When you feel inspired it's magnificent. Dazzling, honestly."

The stars were shooting, shining, forming, and darkening. This was a sky filled with every hope from the sea of my heart and every idea from the ancient woods of my mind, blanketing this world. It appeared to be in constant flux. While there was no singular steady point in the universe above, it didn't matter.

I looked to Self and our eyes met. Our pupils had been replaced by swirling galaxies filled with billions of stars—each a hope, each a dream, too massive to comprehend, too far to reach, but all within our sight and all within.

My dreams were my dreams. They were me.

Self stood and reached out a hand to help me up. We kept walking side by side along the shoreline of the raging sea in the silence of our surroundings until reaching a point where we could walk no farther. We stood on the border of a void. There was no earth, trees, or sky. There was no color, scent, sound, or feeling.

"I know what this is," I said.

Self turned and looked to me, then to the absence before us. "An unfortunate place."

"That's my history, isn't it?" I asked.

"It is. Your life before your current life. There is no beginning or end, and you can't understand it."

"Why can't I remember?"

"Because I won't let you," said Self.

I turned to him, staring at this reflection of myself, feeling everything he felt, knowing everything he knew, yet in this space beside us, emptiness. "Why?" I asked.

"William, have trust and faith. In me. Revealing this place will consume everything here. Every idea. Every thought. You can't risk it. I know that not having the answer is driving you mad, but you must have faith that this void belongs here. Just as those trees are your thoughts, those stars are your dreams, and that beautiful raging sea is your heart. It belongs."

I sighed. "I need to know."

Self pulled me in and held me close in a warm hug. "You will someday, and everything here will disappear. Replaced. Including me. It will reshape us both for all time."

"It would change everything if I found out."

Self pulled away from the hug, leaving his arms on my shoulders. He nodded. "Yes. It will change everything. It is inevitable, but not today."

We continued walking past the emptiness beside us and back into the clearing where I first fell.

"Let's not make this an awkward goodbye, okay?" Self asked.

I smiled. "Fair enough. I don't know if I want to leave. I must be healing."

"You are. In moments you'll be out of this place. Back in reality. Neither of us know where you will end up when you arrive back."

"I guess not. I don't enjoy going in blind."

"True. This visit had to happen, though. Now I need to ask you for something, William."

"Anything."

"Take care of me," said Self, his eyes showing longing emotion for the first time. It was because I didn't want to leave. We both felt it.

"I'll try. I promise."

"Stay connected, please. Grounded. Know me. You will always place others first, but when you do it to the detriment of yourself, this place is a terrible nightmare."

"I understand," I said. "But how will I know I'm making the right decisions?"

Self shrugged with upturned palms. "You don't, but you will. Things will end up working out. Chance has nothing to do with it. You have the power to change Destiny."

"Nobody can change Destiny. Not even herself."

"Wrong," said Self. "You can. Know you can."

I didn't want to leave. I wanted to stay and take care of Self. Deep down, we both knew that was why this visit with the Concept of Self had to happen. This was the reconnection both of us had longed for.

I felt like I was home, with an ancient towering forest of ideas, an incredible sea of heart, and an entire universe of dreams, hopes, and possibilities shining down upon me.

This world was not letting me stay. I felt the familiar pull. Somewhere in actual reality, the dead body of William St. Denis was healing and ready to draw life and breath once more.

"Will I ever come back here?" I asked.

"You are always here," said Self. "And you'll always be here, as long as you are authentic and honest with me, and I with you. Goodbye, William. It is time for us to go. I love you."

I felt weightless. My feet lifted from the ground as I ascended.

"And I you," I said, drifting toward the billions of speckled stars in the sky high above. I wanted to fight and scratch and claw to stay, but Self was pushing me. It was too comfortable here, too lonely. We both knew it. I tumbled out of control into the sky, all the grace gone in place of violent twisting and turning as my world faded to a speck in the distance and I lost sight.

I closed my eyes.

Once again, I was the alien, drifting through space and time to an unknown destination back in the reality that would now feel so foreign to me. My entire being went numb. All things faded to nothing.

I tried to open my eyes, but they felt stuck together.

As I took the world in, my other senses painted a picture. I felt raindrops on the back of my head. Pungent scents punctured my body as I drew a first breath through the startling pain of slumbering lungs expanding once again. Life returned to me.

I brought a hand to my face and rubbed my eyes. Placing my palms on the ground, I felt cold, wet asphalt coated in steady rain and what felt like grease. I looked around. I was in an alley, beside a foul dumpster with trash scattered around me. Across the dark alley in the pouring rain stood a tall figure with a black fedora pulled low over his face.

"Finally," he said, acerbic and impatient.

I couldn't move. I tried pulling my legs up underneath my body. Propping my torso up with one arm, I reached with the other to my coat pocket. The Blackwood Blade was missing. My other pocket was soft and empty. Knowledge was not on my person either.

I heard Duncan's footsteps echo through the alley among the tapping of the falling rain. My clothes were drenched, my hair soaked and falling just past my eyes.

He leaned down and grasped my coat with his pale hands. With little effort, he lifted me up as he stood, pinning me to a building wall beside the dumpster. His eyes, pitch black as a crow's in a moonless night, looked up and down my body as they rested to meet my own.

"Caretaker," he said in a low, tempered voice.

I let out a strained gurgle from my throat.

"Hmm. Good. You're back," he said, still pressing me to the wall, my feet dangling inches above the ground as they had when I'd visited Self just moments ago.

I attempted to swallow. I couldn't speak. My head was pounding.

Duncan held me up with one hand as his other hand moved toward his belt. He raised to my face a gleaming straight razor, extending the blade with an effortless flick. My rain-soaked, blood-crusted reflection stared back as he held the blade up to my face and leaned in close.

"You and I, Caretaker. We need to have a chat."

CHAPTER 22

DEATH SENTENCE

Duncan's face was only an inch from my own, the brim of his fedora shielding us both from the rain as he held me against the concrete. He pressed the cool steel of his straight razor against my cheek. I felt it cutting through the top layer of my skin, but I didn't care.

"What was that stunt?" he whispered, his eyes searching mine.

I wheezed, still choking on my dry throat. I had no idea how long I'd been out for. It was night, I just wasn't sure which night. The alleyway was long and quiet save the out-of-sync slapping of collected rain streams pouring to the ground from the rooftops stories above. The only other sound I could hear was the occasional motion of what I figured was a large scurrying rat feasting in the dumpster beside me.

"Oh," he teased. "Oh, you can't speak."

Duncan slid the blade down my cheek to my throat. I felt it slicing a gash past my jaw as he left it to rest on my neck.

"Perhaps I should slice that throat of yours. Maybe that will let the words escape, hmm?"

With some effort, I opened my eyes wide in front of his. I'd just been home moments ago with Self, reconnecting with my thoughts, my heart, and my dreams. Now, at this moment, I felt fearless confidence.

I reached up and placed two fingers around his wrist, pulling the razor away from my throat. Duncan's face stayed close as he lowered me back to the ground, releasing his grip on my coat.

"Blade," I said. "Now."

"Answer my question," he countered.

Using my back against the concrete wall, I summoned all the strength I had, placed my palms on Duncan, and shoved him hard across the alley. I bent at the waist and used a hand to brace against my knee and stay standing. Strength was returning. This last death was a rough trip.

"I saved you," I said, choking on my own words. "Why is that a problem?"

Duncan walked back to me, leaning down as he spoke. "Because you saved me, Caretaker."

I stood taller, my sopping wet hair tickling my face as raindrops collected and slid down to my cheeks. "You have a strange sense of gratitude."

"That's the problem," he said. "Before that everything was easy. I deceived. I had a singular purpose. I've spent the last ten hours in this disgusting alley watching you like a hawk when I should have just taken the knife and taken the phone and left."

The low roar of pelting rain on every surface across the city filled our ears as we stared at one another.

"Okay," I said, still not understanding.

"That little act of yours was a crack in the wall. Now I'm sitting here keeping you safe. I'm feeling this weird sense of duty. I'm fighting off guilt."

I laughed at him.

With what seemed like preternatural speed, Duncan jetted forward, pinning me to the wall once more, his razor against my throat again. His eyes looked confused. The collision of my back against the wall helped clear my throat and my lungs and I began laughing harder.

"Why are you fucking laughing?"

I swallowed hard and settled my amusement down. "Because of all the ways I could hurt you, what hurt you the most was an act of kindness," I said. "How does it feel having Guilt, Duty, and Responsibility worm their way into your heart, huh?"

Duncan sighed and turned away. We stood in that alley getting rained on for a few minutes before either of us moved. He turned around to face me, reached into his pocket, and pulled out the Blackwood Blade and the iKnow phone.

I nodded in silence, took them from his hands, and replaced them in my own pockets.

"You've sentenced me to death, Caretaker."

"No," I answered, "I know Death. She won't touch you. I can promise you that."

Duncan looked down the long alleyway. His expression was half contemplation, half disgust. "Emotions are gross," he said. "You lived like this for a century? Riddled with all of this conflict?"

I nodded. "I still do. Every day."

He scoffed.

"Where are we?" I asked.

"A few streets away. It's almost six in the morning. I carried you out of the pub through some back streets. I was hoping the rain would wash away most of the blood you coated yourself in. It worked, but you smell much worse now."

"Thank you," I said.

He sneered at me. "Save your sentiment, it's vile. You make me feel gross."

"The bartender?" I asked.

"Oh, yes. The bartender. Before his finger twitched for a second shot I had cut him into a hundred pieces." Duncan looked down at his coat and shirt. "Not a drop of blood. Your work is very messy by comparison, but I must admit I am a fan."

I took a few steps to stand beside Duncan, both of us peering down the alley to the street up ahead.

He seemed to be deep in thought.

"I need a change of clothes. How far are we from the car?"

"Two blocks," he said, "but we need to be careful."

"Agreed."

Duncan looked down to the ground, then up to me. His expression was unfamiliar. "There's no room for a

Guardian who can't focus on the influence he exists for. Deception will sense it in an instant. I'm done for."

"What will he do?"

Duncan sighed. "Strip me of my gifts. Leave me human and defenseless. Arrange for my removal from this existence. That's just the start."

"Looks like we'll keep each other alive, then. Friends and all that."

He turned back to looking down the alley. "Stop being nice. I like you better when you hate me."

"Oh, I do," I said, the smile on my face betraying my own words. In a brief period, Duncan had grown on me. I appreciated his powerful sense of principle. While I still had some distrust, my mind was open to the possibility that he had his own gifts. I thought perhaps his steady focus was something I could adopt to improve myself.

We walked down the alley to the cross street in front of us. The city was just beginning to wake up. The reflection of bright lights were magnified in the rain pouring down. The sun illuminated the buildings in a gentle light. It was cold, and we were both soaked. I followed Duncan's lead as we wound our way around a few city streets. We both kept our eyes searching our surroundings, looking for anything or anyone that might approach us that would feel wrong.

After the events in the Kerry Bog Pub, we would be targets. Duncan had brought me to that pub to destroy a roomful of Guardians and Stewards. Deception himself would now be a target, as Duncan worked on his behalf. It'd been an age since I'd slaughtered so many in such a grand and public fashion. This was a re-announcement of my presence in the game. It upset me that Duncan had forced my hand, but I needed to unravel answers, and this would make that happen.

I only hoped Elise was safe. As Knowledge's Caretaker, she had a special connection with that Concept, but it was in my hands and not hers. It may be the only thing that was keeping her alive. We would need a plan to get her back. There was another loose end heavy on my mind after what had happened in the pub. Who were the green-eyed Guardians? They were here for a Concept walking around in this reality, but I couldn't tell which one.

Green-eyed agility experts hanging out in an Irish pub? Was Agility a concept? Subterfuge? Jealousy? Greed? Were they also agents of Deception? Had Duncan lied? My intuition freaked out trying to make sense of it. Before I took that bullet for him, he'd been pure deception. I had to be cautious.

Once we found ourselves out of danger, I'd get answers.

We wound our way through the streets toward where our SUV was parked, sticking to shadows and slipping under cover. I heard no sirens, and there was no emergency activity in the distance where the Kerry Bog Pub sat empty.

We arrived at our vehicle and I unlatched the trunk hatch and riffled through a bag of clothes in the back to pick out something to change into. A comfortable pair of jeans, a clean T-shirt, and a long-sleeved flannel to go over it would feel just right. I shut the back hatch and climbed into the back seat to change. Duncan stood outside the car, keeping a watchful eye. I left my soaking wet canvas jacket laid out in the back along with my soaked clothes, hooked the sheathed Blackwood Blade on the inside of my waistband, and slipped the iKnow phone into my front pocket.

I climbed into the passenger seat and gave the window a knock. Duncan opened the driver's side door and peered around one last time before sitting and starting the car. He pulled out of our parking spot and started down the city street, hanging a quick left.

"Where are you going?" I asked.

"I want to drive by the pub," he answered. "Curious if there's any commotion."

"Somebody could see us."

He looked at me, sarcasm across his smirk. "You destroyed everyone in there. I don't think they'll be outside pointing at you. Relax."

We looked out the window as we passed the front of the Kerry Bog Pub. The morning sun glinted off the bronze horseshoe-shaped door knockers. It looked quiet and untouched. I felt some relief that nobody was around and settled into my seat.

Duncan turned onto Market Street, beginning to wind his way out of the city. Traffic was picking up, so we weren't able to move as fast as I'd like, but it was still progress.

"How do you do it?" he asked.

"Do what?"

"You are Death's Caretaker, but you feel all this emotion. How can you feel that, but cut down dozens in a bloodbath like last night? Is Conscience not a Concept that influences you?"

It was a legitimate question. For more than a century I'd been carrying out Death's will. Sometimes it was marking someone deserving of a mark. Sometimes it was protecting someone who deserved protection. On rare occasions I'd be standing in a crowd, spot a single soul, and feel the blade calling to me, knowing that person was her target.

"Well?" he asked.

"I'm thinking."

"Maybe that's the reason you spend your life torturing yourself."

I shook my head. "No. Since day one it's been an inherent understanding. Death isn't evil. I'm not evil. I'm just an instrument."

Duncan had a thoughtful look on his face as he wound through traffic, making his way toward the highway out of the city. He didn't seem satisfied by my answer. "How do you know it's Death and not your own twisted will on a rampage?"

"Think of it this way," I said. "I'm not just out there murdering people; she's bigger than my motivations."

"Yes," answered Duncan, "but how do you know what you're doing is what she wants? What if you're just a guy murdering people with a pretty knife?"

"You've seen what it does."

He sighed. "That's not what I mean. Obviously, that's Death. I felt the chill in that pub. I saw the shadows. How do you know you're carrying out her will, and not your own?"

"I just do."

"Do you feel remorse?" he asked.

"I did at first. The first pull I had to end someone's life wrecked my emotions for a long time. Not anymore, though. I didn't choose this path. She chose me. It's complicated, but I was handpicked for it."

"Ever wonder why?"

I nodded, looking out over the bridge we were crossing to the Delaware River below. "Every day, but I can't ask anyone. What about you? Were you handpicked by Deception?"

Duncan laughed, and it sounded strange that he seemed so disarmed during our conversation. "Something like that. I cut my teeth as a performer. Fooled many people, made a lot of money. I was born with a gift. They recognized it, the rest is history."

"Someone chose you, too," I said.

"Some of us have natural talent that's in harmony with a Concept," he said. "If it's potent enough, it gets noticed. I guess Death noticed that you have a gift for nihilism. After seeing you in the pub, it's easy to see why she'd stick with you."

I shrugged. "Maybe."

The traffic slowed to a crawl and ahead we saw bright lights flashing. It was hard to make out what the exact scene was, but some kind of accident had occurred. Duncan and I were fixated on what was ahead.

Duncan shook his head and let out an exasperated sigh. "It's always something."

With a quick tug of the steering wheel, he jumped into the shoulder and flew past some traffic, taking the next exit. "Fortunate that we're right by an off-ramp, I guess. This conversation is delightful, but the prospect of being stuck in a car with you for two hours in traffic is a nightmare."

We slid off the exit and began cruising along at a good speed on a less congested two-lane highway as we made our way back toward Atlantic City and whatever awaited us at the Dolos Casino.

"So," I started, "you never told me who was in that pub."

Duncan sighed. "That's because I'm not entirely sure."

"You brought me there. You knew what was waiting. Don't play with me."

"What I mean is, I knew something was there. I knew it was a nest, of sorts, for a Concept, but I'm not sure which one. Deception is involved. Anything is possible."

"Then how did you know?" I asked.

"Three weeks ago someone was at the Dolos visiting Deception. I saw a business card."

"Another Concept?" I asked.

"No. That would've been too obvious. A representative of some kind. A courier. Bright green eyes just like they all had. I really don't know. What I do know is that they really didn't like you being in that pub. And they're all gone, so it doesn't really matter, does it? I'm guessing it'll be revealed soon enough. You kicked that hornet's nest quite hard."

"So what's the plan?" I asked.

"Well, we need to get back to the Dolos," he said. "I'm going to have to hope he can't sense any changes. You give him the phone, and you bust that knife out and cut your way out of the building, hopefully with Elise in tow."

"You can't be serious," I said. "Fight my way out?"

"Dead serious," he replied. "I think by that time you're going to know exactly what we're up against, and you're going to know what the threat to Destiny is."

"What about you?"

"I know that building intimately," he said. "I'll get out and go into hiding. If you can get out with Knowledge, do it. But don't you let that blade get into anyone else's hand."

"I know," I said.

"Even Elise."

I looked at Duncan. He was focused on the road, but the look on his face was serious. He wasn't being manipulative. "Why not Elise? I trust her."

"That'll be the mistake that kills her. Maybe all three of us."

"Why?"

"She's been in Deception's home for a day. You have no idea how strong his influence is. Or maybe you do. Did he touch you? Did you feel it?"

I remembered that moment. Just a hand on me and all I wanted to do was trick the world and deceive everyone and everything. I wanted people to find out about how others had deceived them, sowing chaos and lies. It had been an intense emotion. Elise would surely fall victim to that feeling. I felt like I had to trust her, though.

"Do you think he's harmed her?"

"No." Duncan shook his head, peering up toward the sky out the front windshield, then back to the road. "It's not his way. Besides, he needs you to approach him with some trust. Everything has to appear normal."

I nodded.

"William," he said, turning to me as he kept his hand steady on the wheel, "do not lose that blade again. We both know he wants the phone, but he wouldn't have dragged you into this if he didn't need that blade for something, too."

I heard a buzzing noise in the car. Duncan peered out the window and craned his neck to look upward once more.

"Do you hear that?" I asked.

He nodded, looking around outside. All I could see was surrounding woods and a long stretch of road in front of us. I searched around the inside of the car, but the buzzing noise was coming from outside and growing louder by the second.

I looked to Duncan and noticed his eyes widen and panic shoot across his face. He yanked the steering wheel, causing the car to screech across the pavement. I caught a glimpse outside the windshield and saw a small private plane just along the treetops heading straight toward us.

In an instant, there was a massive crash and tons of steel flew into the air, spinning and smashing with the sound of twisted metal being hurled in every direction. The SUV careened, flipping over and over before nailing the ground. I felt cuts and gashes from glass across my face, neck, and hands.

Bones were broken.

We were on our side. It wasn't a direct hit, but enough to send us off the road and to the edge of the woods. My door was against the ground. Duncan was slumped toward me, his seat belt hanging on as he dangled above me, his blood from numerous deep cuts and gashes dripping down on me.

I smelled gas. I unlatched my seat belt and crawled out the shattered front windshield. I was sure I had broken ribs, and my vision was blurry, but I could function. I unlatched Duncan's belt and dragged him out of the car, pulling him to the grass a few yards away from the SUV.

I collapsed beside him. He was alive, but unconscious. Around us was wreckage. The wing of the plane had broadsided the SUV. Painted red plane parts were scattered everywhere. Not far away, half the plane rested near the car, the propeller still spinning and the engine somehow still running.

I winced, grabbing my ribs. It was hard to breathe.

Then I saw them.

Stepping out of the broken plane were three men. They were unhurt and unscathed, smiles creeping across their faces as they walked toward us. I tried to stand, but whatever adrenaline had allowed me to crawl out of the car wreck just moments before had given way to outright pain. I was broken, lying beside Duncan, watching them approach.

Surviving that crash without a scratch was impossible. They approached, standing over us, smiles wide.

"Take 'em both?" one of them asked.

"No," another answered. "Grab the unconscious one. He's the one we want. The other is that Caretaker."

I watched as two of the men grabbed Duncan's slumped body and began dragging him toward the road. In the distance, a car pulled up and the trunk popped open.

The man in front of me was tall and muscular with brilliant green eyes. In the distance, the hum of the propeller drowned out the conversation the others were having as they dragged Duncan to the waiting trunk of a white sedan. He bent down and looked me over, considering me for a moment.

"Good thing you wore your seat belt," he said.

I was in severe pain, barely able to breathe, but strong enough to speak. I felt a chill against my body. The Blackwood Blade was still on me. She was calling.

"Who are you?" I asked. My speech was labored. My lungs pressed against crushed ribs.

The man turned his head to look at the sideways, smashed airplane just past the wrecked SUV. The attached wing of the plane was tilted in the air and the propeller kept humming and spinning as the fuel hadn't spilled out of the engine yet.

He turned back to me. "A skilled pilot, I guess. Somebody needs to have a word with your chauffeur over there. But you're here too. With a pair of Concepts on you, no less. Must be my lucky day. Now, I'm going to need that phone, and I'm going to need that knife."

In the distance, I saw Duncan's body being tossed into the trunk of the car, the two men carrying him slamming it closed and turning to look at who was standing over me.

"Come on!" one of them shouted.

The Blackwood Blade felt like burning ice against my body. With as much strength and speed as I could muster, I snatched it from my waistband and swiped a strike at the man in front of me, drawing a long slice straight across his chest.

He backed up a few steps as I collapsed down again, blade in hand.

"Oh, you little fucker," he spat, winding up and kicking me in the face. I felt my neck snap backward, and I lay down on my back in the grass, icy blade still clutched in my hand. I was not going to let go.

I heard someone shouting and tilted my head up. There was a rattle and a pop in the distance. The man standing over me was looking down at the gash across his chest and didn't see a dislodged propeller blade flying straight toward him.

I closed my eyes and turned my head, hearing a wet crunch and feeling a warm spray of misted blood hit my face. I slowly sat up and saw that he was cut in half. Mangled pieces of body were strewn across the ground. In the distance, the sedan doors closed and the car sped off with Duncan in the trunk.

The plane's engine came to a silent stop. There wasn't a single sound in the surrounding wreckage except for my own wheezed breathing. I sheathed the blade, felt the phone in my pocket, and took a few breaths as I began to feel myself slowly healing.

In a matter of moments, everything became more complicated.

There were so many emotions in my heart. I needed to get back to Elise, and I needed to visit Destiny. Even though Duncan was a Guardian for Deception, I was feeling angry that he'd been taken.

I felt like I'd lost a friend, and I couldn't stop it from happening. Sadness was short-lived and gave way to fury.

It was time to take control of this situation, embrace my responsibilities, and illustrate to any entity unwise enough to get in my way precisely why I was Death's Caretaker.

CHAPTER 23

PERSPECTIVE

"Sorry," I said, wiping a small streak of blood from the passenger seat. I was in a busted blue boat of a car littered with empty drink bottles and snack wrappers. It smelled like stale weed. The owner of this vehicle was a twentysomething kid with a tussled head of hair and a broken-in flannel shirt.

"It's all good, chief. That was a hell of an accident. You sure you don't need a hospital?"

"No," I replied. "Just need a drop-off at Atlantic City. I appreciate the ride. Sorry about the mess."

"Nah, it's fine. I'm just running this piece of crap into the ground anyway," he replied.

After the crash, many people had slowed down and stopped. I was fortunate to find someone willing to give me a ride away from that scene before police arrived and started asking questions. A plane wreck, overturned SUV, and someone cut in half at the edge of the woods would raise a lot of questions. A harmless stoner in a ubiquitous beater of a vehicle was the ride I'd been looking for.

"So what's your name?" he asked.

"You know," I said, "I think it's better that you don't know much about me."

He laughed. "I like it. You're in the middle of some drama or something. Possibly illegal. Good times, chief."

"Good times?"

"Think about it," he said. "I happened to be driving by a few minutes after a plane hit your car? Now we're here, no names, just two lives that crashed into each other then move on. It's awesome."

I shrugged. "I guess."

"Perspective, chief. You never know when a single event could change your life forever."

That comment got my attention. I turned to my nameless driver and studied him for a moment. He focused on the road, drumming on the steering wheel and humming some tune I didn't recognize. I did my best to not judge, but I had no idea what to make of him. In the past week I'd learned a repeated lesson that there were no coincidences in my line of work.

"My name's William."

"Nice to meet you, Will! I'm Eric. Philosopher of life, part-time weed smoker, full-time optimist. Or maybe full-time weed smoker. There're two blunts in the glove box if you need to chill."

I couldn't help but smile at the cheerful nature of my driver. We were zooming past marshy expanses on our way toward Atlantic City. The company was welcome after the intensity of the past few days. I felt like Eric and I had a lot in common. We were both drifting through life, only my timeline was much longer. Optimism wasn't something in significant supply in my own experiences, but I appreciated his attitude.

"So why Atlantic City?" he asked.

"I'm meeting someone," I answered.

"Girl?"

"Yeah."

"No offense, buddy, but you don't look like you're ready for a date."

I laughed. "It's not a date. Just a friend in an unpleasant situation. I'm trying to help her out."

"Oh," he mused. "So going for, like, an intimidating kind of thing. It's all good, chief. If that's the case, you kind of nail the look."

"Thanks, I think."

Atlantic City appeared on the horizon, the grand buildings reaching high with the ocean close behind. I could see the Dolos Casino in the distance. I didn't understand what awaited me within those walls, but I was feeling a sense of intensity building. It was anxiety over the unknown and a strange sense of mortality about it all.

I'd had time to think over the last few days, but the time I had to ponder anything now had the added twist of knowing I could be destroyed, and someone might be planning it.

Eric snapped his fingers in front of my face. "You okay, dude? Lost in thought and all that?"

I shook my head. "Yeah, sorry. I just spend a lot of time locked in my head I suppose."

He studied my eyes for a moment and turned back to the road as we approached the city. "You're worried about something."

"I am," I said.

"I get that, dude. Remember though, things always have a way of working out."

"Not always."

"Name something that hasn't," he said.

I thought about his question. "Well, I've spent the greater part of my life in love with someone I can't be with. I wouldn't exactly consider that working out."

He smiled. "What is it you love about this person?"

"That's an excellent question."

Eric was drumming on the steering wheel, but his smile never faded. "We can overcomplicate love, my dude. Ultimately you just love who you love, you know?"

I narrowed my eyes at him. I felt like I'd had this conversation many times of late. "Well, when she and I first met, I didn't know who I was."

"Do you now?"

"I'm getting there. She was always the only person who understood how lost I was, and it didn't matter. She just wanted me to have comfort."

"Comfort?" he asked.

"Yeah. Peace. She just understood. It always felt like we were linked somehow, I don't know."

"Is that the girl you're going to meet?"

"No. This is just a friend I met by chance. She's in some trouble."

"Did you meet by chance related to this person you've loved your entire life?"

I smiled. I saw what he was doing during this conversation. "Yes. You could say that some events led us to become friends."

"Perspective, chief, I'm telling you," he said. "It's everything. Maybe you've had some awful luck with love, but there are gifts all around you that wouldn't have been there otherwise."

I nodded and stared at him. "Do I know you?" I asked.

He smiled as he kept his eyes on the road. "No, my dude. Just two people on two paths crashed into one another for a moment. It's the meeting that might just alter our trajectories, you know. Cosmic perspective and all."

"Cosmic perspective?"

"Right, dude. Like, everything in this universe is connected. Quantum entanglement, brother. You and I are made of the stuff of stars and here we are in this precise moment, together. Trillions of years on a giant cosmological timeline and we spent the tiniest fraction of it together and stuff."

I blinked. "And stuff?"

"Listen up, Will. Perspective school is in session." He winked and kept drumming on the steering wheel while he spoke. "On the tiniest of quantum levels there are particles and magnetism and electrical synapses through every infinite space in your body."

"Like atoms?"

"Pff, nah man! If an atom was the size of this Earth, I'm talking particles the size of you and me. You gotta accept the fact that there is a piece of you, however small, that recognizes a piece of me, or of this girl of yours.

Maybe that spark you feel with somebody new is just the remnants of an ancient celestial body recognizing itself, resting silently in another person. And you're drawn to them because at one time you were both the same star."

I stared out the window. "I wasn't expecting this conversation."

Eric laughed and drummed on his steering wheel, letting out an enthusiastic shout, "Yes! My dude, that's what I'm talking about! If I can plant a thought in your head in this fraction of a second in the grand scheme, it just might change the entire universe someday." He turned to me and winked, making an exploding motion with his hand right by his head. Mind blown, indeed.

He was right.

Eric's blue boat of a car slowed down a few blocks away from the ocean and a quick walk from the Dolos Casino, rolling to a stop right beside a small laundromat.

"Who are you?"

He smiled. "Can I give you a little advice?" he said, turning toward me and resting his forearm on the grimy steering wheel.

"Of course."

"When all the things seem sideways, maybe all you'll need is a hug to set it right."

"Um, I've never tried just hugging, but I'll keep it in mind."

He winked at me. "Good luck with your friend. If she's someone worth space in your heart, I'm certain she's someone you can trust. You need your friends, chief. You'd probably be surprised at how many of them wish you success."

I stepped out of his car and onto a quiet sidewalk a block away from the casinos perched along the Atlantic Ocean. In all likelihood, that had been a chance meeting, but Eric the full-time weed smoker and part-time philosopher seemed to be something more than random coincidence.

Had I just caught a ride from Perspective?

He'd left an impact, but I couldn't think about it any longer. Now it was time to focus. I had Knowledge, and I had Death. I'd lost Duncan, and Elise was being held as collateral in Deception's home. From this moment forward, I knew I had to be at my best. Still, the lingering questions of what was happening to Destiny were heavy in my heart. I needed to see her.

I ran into the laundromat just around the corner. The clean scent of dryer sheets and detergent assaulted my senses when I walked in. I'd spent many hours raiding laundromats for clean clothes. I adored the quiet hum of spinning dryers and the rhythmic swishing of water along the rows of washing machines.

There was an old man folding some of his clothes along a smooth table across the room, but otherwise the place was quiet with a few dryers spinning unattended along a long back wall. I peeked into the various windows to find some fresh clothes that would fit. Bloody pants and a shredded shirt wasn't the dress code for walking among the people enjoying the day by the ocean.

I found some well-fitting clothes in one dryer. I opened the door, snagging a baggy pair of jeans and a long-sleeved T-shirt with the word "NEMESIS" screen printed down the sleeve. Sure, I looked like someone who'd just recorded a skateboard video for my social media fans, but it was the best I could do with few options. With a colorful snapback baseball cap, I could complete the look.

I snatched a small towel and a long scarf from another dryer and slipped through a slender door to a small back hallway behind the spinning machines. The heat being generated in this compact space warmed the back of the laundromat, and I located what I'd hoped to find: a quiet, unoccupied bathroom.

I placed the clothes in a pile on a small counter beside an old sink that had separate taps for hot and cold water, sat on the closed lid of the toilet, and took a long breath. I knew it wasn't the case, but I somehow felt that I hadn't had solitude for years. The events of the last week had been so intense that I'd become lost in that stimulation. The emotional cacophony of everyone that had stepped into my once quiet world was deafening to my head and my heart.

I thought about my heart.

I recalled how Destiny ran her fingers across my chest. She was right that she knew my scars better than anyone. Most of them were from visiting her. I wondered where she was at this moment. I was about to confront Deception. He wanted Knowledge and Death, and both Elise and I out of the way. For all of Duncan's failings and his brusque manner, I got a sense that he'd been honest.

If my destiny was to die, I couldn't do it without seeing her one more time.

I was in a quiet bathroom in the back room of a laundromat, and Death was by my side. I had to take a chance. But there was a problem I had to solve first.

If I plunged the knife into my heart and visited her, I would be stuck in a locked bathroom until discovered by someone coming upon what would appear to be a suicide. Nobody was here to remove the knife for me.

I missed Harvey. I felt terrible that he'd gotten caught in my world. I recalled how he'd stood by me with so many questions on his mind about what was happening and had tried to defend me, even. It had been unexpected, and I felt significant guilt over it.

I took another long breath and grabbed the scarf, tying one end in a solid knot around a hook toward the top of the bathroom door. I kept my soiled clothes on, as I'd need to change after I completed the trip I was about to embark on.

It was time to visit Destiny.

I took out the Blackwood Blade, resting snug and quiet in its sheath, and tied the opposite end of the scarf to it. Its emerald pommel glinted in the artificial light of the small bathroom.

I would remove it from the sheath, drive it into my heart, and come to rest sitting on the toilet. If my estimation of distance was correct, I would die, slump down, and fall to the ground, causing the scarf to suspend the knife in the air and pull it from me as I fell. It wasn't a perfect plan, but I knew this was a time to take a risk.

I would only be with her for moments, but these were moments I needed to have. I didn't know how long it would take for my body to slip from my seat and crash to the floor, but soon after I would be back in this bathroom and in this reality. This was the chance I had to take.

I smiled. Risking everything to see someone you love and using Death to do it seemed pure and romantic to me. I sat on the closed toilet lid and held the sheathed Blackwood Blade in my hands in front of me. I closed my eyes and took fast, deep breaths. I could feel my heart beating faster. I could sense the blood rushing through my arteries. Life was pumping through my body. Adrenaline coursed through my veins. I would die once more.

It was time.

I drew the blade.

Icy, frigid air gripped the room and caressed me as I put the point to my chest. The walls darkened, reality pulsed and breathed around me. Sounds of dryers in the laundromat faded, as if traveling through some kind of colloid to my ears.

That familiar feeling was in the small bathroom with me, grasping for me. My hand was freezing holding the blade. Entropy filled the air. Death was the first and the last, and she had arrived.

But she felt different to me now. I felt affection and love.

I paused, suspended prior to death for a moment. I'd spent many hours throughout more than a century casting this blade around like an object. I hadn't realized or appreciated our connection, yet she'd been patient with me. Sometimes I felt like Atlas, but holding the influence of Death on strained shoulders. My eyes were open, but I never saw her. She was not a burden. She was the ultimate gift.

My gaze drifted down to the knife, the slick black air nearly obscuring it.

"I'm so sorry. I'm sorry for not understanding. I know you can hear me. I am certain of you now. Thank you. I love you, and I appreciate you."

I kept Destiny in my thoughts to ensure I would visit her and not end up somewhere unwanted. With a single smooth motion I'd honed over time, I slipped the blade into my heart and drifted out of this world in the loving caress of Death.

I closed my eyes.

CHAPTER 24

PROPHECY

I opened my eyes.

The saturated hues of lush green grass and magnificent blue sky filled my eyes. I brushed my hands across cool earth and the sweet scent of evergreen pine filled my lungs as I breathed in deep and stood.

The Blackwood Blade was sheathed on my hip, sleeping in silence against me. With gentle care, I placed my hand upon her.

"Thank you," I whispered, "for bringing me here safe."

I turned and faced a well-worn gravel path stretching toward the familiar yellow farmhouse a short distance away. Blossoms fluttered to the ground, drifting in the warm open hands of the breeze as they lay to rest upon the ground before me. The whispering breeze carried the cheerful calls of black-capped chickadees to my ear.

I made my way up the path toward the house. I had little time to soak in my surroundings. Somewhere in a reality far from where I walked, the body of William St. Denis was dead and slumping. In a matter of moments the blade would slip out, tied to a scarf on the door. My body would be out of reach, and I would return.

As I approached the steps to the farmhouse, the door swung open and she appeared at the top of the porch.

She took my breath away.

Dee launched herself down the stairs and into my waiting arms. Among the gentle drifting of pink and white blossoms, we held each other tight. Her sweet, sun-kissed skin pressed to me. Her hands drifted across my body before pulling away for a moment.

"Why are you here, sweet William?"

"I have little time, but I needed to see you. I'm lost."

"Come," she said, holding my hand and guiding me to the porch swing. We sat together, her hands caressing mine.

"Dee, I thought I had answers, but every time there's an answer there's another question. What's happening?"

She placed a hand on my cheek, her deep brown eyes soaking in my face. "I miss you every day."

"You need to stop being so cryptic with me. Please. I'm begging you. Please tell me something that will help me."

"I will die," she said.

It felt like my heart stopped.

"Stop that," I said. "Stop it right now."

"I am Destiny," she said. "It is my path, and I am so sorry for how it intertwined with yours, sweet William."

I looked past the porch and down the well-worn gravel path, soaking in the vibrant intensity of the emerald grass, pink and white cherry blossoms, and brilliant blue sky. I found such solace here. She had to be wrong.

"Who?" I asked.

She looked away.

"Who?" I demanded again.

"You cannot destroy every Concept, my sweet."

I released her hands and stood, anger boiling up. "Fucking tell me, Dee. Who's behind this? Why can't you say anything? Why do you keep these secrets from me? Is it Deception? Is it Love? Jealousy? Tell me."

"Please don't feel this way," she said, looking down at the floor.

"What else have you kept from me?" I asked. "I've begged you to tell me who I was, but you refuse. I've asked you to tell me about my life, and you always say no and that it doesn't matter and it would only hurt me."

She stayed silent.

"And now here I am," I said, holding out my arms and motioning around, "more than a century later and I have no answers. I just drift, never knowing who I am."

"You are my sweet William," she said.

I turned and faced away from her, exasperated.

"That's all you've ever been."

"But it's not real, is it?" I said, calming my nerves. "I'm here and you comfort me, but still there's no answer. There's something missing. Something is always missing, locked away in my mind." I turned back to her, my gaze meeting her deep brown eyes once more. "Tell me why Death chose me," I said.

"She took pity on you."

"Pity?"

"Yes," she answered.

"Why?"

"Because you were wronged," she said, tears filling her eyes. "Deceived."

"So it is Deception," I said. I felt anger coursing through my body once more.

"William, I cannot tell you any more. Nobody can ever know their own destiny."

"You do," I replied.

"I do," she said, standing and walking toward me. She laid her hands on my chest. "I must walk my path without deviation."

"Tell me what to do."

"If I told you that, you would deviate from your path."

I reached up, grasping her hands and pulling them away from my chest. I didn't want to be touched right now.

She looked crushed. "You've changed."

"I am changing, yes. Because I've realized something."

I felt a familiar pull. Somewhere in a reality far from here, my body was slipping and slumping, and the Blackwood Blade was slipping out, straining to stay resting in my heart at the end of an outstretched scarf tied to the door hook. Death was holding on, but losing her grip. Still, it felt different. She was desperate to give me more time here.

"I can't go on like this anymore," I said. "My indecision and refusal to see what was right in front of me has prevented me from fulfilling who I need to be. I've been a pawn."

She nodded. "Yes, you have. Since before you died."

"I know that now. And I know there are forces at work, but I'm no longer a pawn. I'm a conduit."

"For what?" she asked.

"Death," I said, looking down at the Blackwood Blade and resting my hand on it. "I've neglected her for so long. Left her unappreciated. You were right when you said she could hear me and was with me. I can hear her. I know what she wants."

The pull was growing stronger. Dee turned away and sat on the porch swing, her smile turning into a frown. "What does she want?"

"Understanding. My entire life she's been trying so hard to guide me, to teach me why I'm here and who I was. I was too shortsighted to realize it."

Dee nodded. "William, she has cared about you since before you died."

"I just don't know why. Dee, I'm drifting. I'm leaving soon."

She stood and walked to me, rising on her toes to give me a kiss on the cheek, her warm lips lingering for a moment.

This was feeling like a goodbye, and I cried.

"What do you mean, before I died?" I asked.

Dee stared into my eyes, her hands caressing my cheeks as she held my face in the warm glow of the shining sky. "My sweet William," she said, shedding tears to match my own.

"Tell me. Tell me just this one thing, please."

"I will. The next time we see one another, you will have answers. I promise you."

She sobbed.

I looked around, frantic, noticing the ground in the distance falling away. I was leaving. The sky washed into a faded, pale gray. Gone was the scent of evergreen pine and the cheerful songs of black-capped chickadees, replaced by a neutral essence of whitewashed nothing. It was the transitional space between two realities. I was at the border of her world.

"I'm leaving. Dee, why are you so upset?"

She looked fuzzy in my eyes. I struggled to focus as her appearance glitched in and out of view.

"I can't tell you," she replied through haze and choked sobs.

"Tell me!" I demanded. "You said we will see each other again! Why are you so upset? For once, just tell me anything!"

"We will see each other soon, and that is when your friend Death will take me."

I reached for her, clutching at the phantom of where Destiny once stood before me, but she had disappeared.

I was suspended in emptiness between two worlds. My only companion was a single, horrifying realization. If I was ever to see her again, it would mean her death.

I'd begged her for a piece of knowledge that had sealed her fate.

Everything faded.

I closed my eyes.

CHAPTER 25

I SEE YOU

I opened my eyes.

Frozen to the bone, lying in a puddle of my own sticky blood in a dingy, dark bathroom, I choked out a first breath. The air stung my lungs, turning them to ice. The Blackwood Blade, dark and breathing, dangled at the end of a long scarf two inches above my heart.

For once, a plan had worked.

I gathered the strength to move my hands and sit up. The small bathroom felt coated in entropy, the ichor of death soaking the air. Blackened energy webbed out from the blade like ivy. Leaving the blade suspended and unsheathed for a time had allowed Death to permeate this space in the world, breaking down the wall between reality and her influence.

I sheathed the blade, bringing the bathroom back to its normal appearance.

"I feel like I have to apologize again," I said. "Maybe I shouldn't have left you here like that, but I didn't know what to do. It's hard to know what's right."

I knew she wouldn't answer, but I had to get my thoughts out. I stood, covered in dried blood, but with clean clothes and a sink at my disposal. It wouldn't be a great shower, but I would feel close to normal by washing up and leaving this small bathroom behind.

I peeled my clothes off, spying my scars in the mirror. The area around my heart was all scar tissue. So many times I'd driven the blade into my heart. I recalled the first one, the scar still visible and offset from the others.

"Do you remember this one?" I said, speaking to the silent blade as I touched my scar. "Missed my heart. What a disaster. It took so long. Such fear."

I began washing my hands, using a small towel to wipe the blood from my arms, torso, and neck. I watched the red water circle down the drain and cleaned off. I scrubbed my face as best I could and soaked my hair. It was tricky trying not to look like you'd just died.

No matter how hard I tried to distract myself, a sense of dread hung over me.

"She said you would come for her," I said, staring at the Blackwood Blade resting beside the sink. "I don't understand."

I changed into my clean clothes, a baggy pair of jeans and the T-shirt with the word "NEMESIS" on the sleeve. Whoever had owned this laundry was a similar size, which was a pleasant thing not to worry about.

I placed all the bloodied cloth into a small trash can. Whoever would clean this bathroom would be left wondering a lot of things, but that wasn't my problem. I strapped the Blackwood Blade to my hip and placed the iKnow phone into my pocket. I still had a wallet with some cash that somehow wasn't lost after the events of the last twenty-four hours.

I'd have to score a fresh pair of sneakers, but at this point they pretty much just looked red, and unless someone was paying close attention, they wouldn't notice.

I opened the bathroom door and ducked through the warm hallway behind the wall of spinning dryers. It was light outside. I figured I'd been dead for less than an hour. It'd been a quick trip, but had revealed something complicated.

I was Death's Caretaker. She worked through me, and she would take Destiny.

I knew Destiny was working in this world. Each of our paths were set through all of our actions and circumstances tied to everything else in the universe. We didn't know our paths, and so we couldn't change them. Destiny knew all paths, and she couldn't change hers, either.

Maybe I could feel her presence, but I had a hard time not feeling as if it had destroyed my heart. To keep her alive, I had to stay away forever. It was a paradox I wasn't ready to dive into.

I stepped into the shade of surrounding buildings and the dry embrace of chilled fall air. I made my way toward the Boardwalk. It was time to visit the Dolos Casino and resolve a loose end.

Deception.

Dee's words rang powerful in my ears. They'd wronged me. They'd deceived me. It'd set me on a path of heartbreak, and now it'd led me to be locked away from the one being I'd loved since my normal life.

I wasn't feeling rage or revenge. I was feeling determination. A determination to unravel my history and right a wrong that had existed for more than a century. A determination to free Elise and to find Duncan.

As I turned a corner, I could see the famous Atlantic City Boardwalk once again, lit by a bright afternoon sun perched in a clear sky. Sea-salted air filled me with the feeling that I was small in this world, playing an important part. I walked up a long ramp into the bright light on the rows of wooden planks stretching along the seaside, dotted by massive hotels and casinos, with the Dolos in my sight.

The glowing sun warmed my skin, but for a reason I couldn't identify, I felt cold. I stopped walking and looked around. There were a few people milling around the shops and sights, and nobody close to where I was. I didn't feel like I was being followed or watched.

I rested my hand on the Blackwood Blade tucked inside my waistband against my hip. It chilled my palm, but not in a way I was used to. This felt different, a connection, an understanding. It was as if Death was trying to speak to me. Perhaps the respect I'd gained for her role and my responsibility allowed us to feel better connected.

We felt together, and I felt different, powerful.

I approached the Dolos Casino and noticed a large graphic next to the revolving door entrance. There was a picture of Duncan, his steely eyes looking at a fanned hand of cards in his skeletal fingers, his fedora pulled down over his forehead.

Underneath it read, "Rest in Peace, Duncan the Deceiver. Forever missed. Never forgotten."

I stared at it and my heart sank.

The last time I'd seen Duncan he was being dragged off from the crash into the trunk of a car and hauled off to some ending by people with sinister motives who even now stayed hidden in shadow. I realized I was standing in front of Deception's home, but this didn't feel like a trick. It felt real. I'd resigned Duncan to his fate after the events of the Kerry Bog Pub. There'd been resignation in his eyes that he would be found out and that Deception would see him as impure.

My act of selflessness had set forth a chain of events that would mean his end.

Still, I appreciated him. Duncan's willingness to urge me to make sense of my responsibility had left me better connected to Death. I'd embraced who I was because of his actions.

Elise, too.

My body chilled to the bone. She was calling to me. Connecting to me.

Standing in front of Duncan's memorial poster, I summoned a memory and closed my eyes.

I was looking through this person's eyes. They were in a dim bathroom washing their hands. Their knuckles were bruised and cut. Each stream of water pouring over their hands left a watery trail of diluted blood to trickle down fingertips and circle into the drain.

Their head lifted and they stared at themselves in the mirror with brilliant green eyes.

I watched this moment and tried to focus through the rage I felt at spotting another green-eyed being. Why was I in this memory?

His face had a straight jaw jutting from the neckline of a button-up white dress shirt. There were some stains of what looked like blood or dirt on the rolled-up white sleeves. He was washing his hands and checking his face for blemishes.

I tried to memorize his features. Memories could be filled with clues that were easy to miss. I needed to know why Death wanted me to see this person. He turned away from the mirror to grab some hand towels and dry off.

He swung open the bathroom door and walked with a swift step down a long beige hallway. I couldn't tell where it was. I watched as his bruised hand open a door.

He stepped into the room. "Nothing."

He was staring at another green-eyed man, wide and thick across his shoulders. He appeared as if he was ready to burst out of the tight white dress shirt hugging the curves of his muscular torso. His hulking frame sat behind a table with a pair of casino dice stacked in the center. "Try harder," he said in a reverberating baritone voice.

My vessel looked to his right. Along the wall was a baseball bat leaning against a glossy white cabinet. He looked back to the massive man.

"Use it. Even you won't miss," grunted the man behind the desk.

I stared out from his eyes as he walked across the room and his scraped knuckles grabbed the baseball bat from beside the cabinet. He looked back to the man behind the desk. The immense man stared at him.

I watched as he looked back down at the bat, then up to him again. "If I hit him with this, I'll kill him."

The massive man stood, and I watched as my vessel backed up a step and looked up toward him. His green eyes were ablaze with the fury of a supervolcano, ready to pierce the surface of the earth and destroy all life in its wake. He picked up the two dice.

"Shall we roll for it? I roll a seven, I beat you to death right here, right now. I roll anything else, I will fulfill your every wish."

"No thank you, sir."

"No? What's wrong? Don't like the odds?"

"No, sir."

I watched as the subject of my memory backed up a step, bat in hand. The beast of a man behind the desk growled, "He's a fucking Guardian. You can't kill him with a bat."

He rolled the dice. It was a seven.

"Smart play. Now go find out what happened in my fucking pub."

He had to be talking about Duncan. Was I watching what had happened after they took him away from the crash site? My vessel turned and opened the door, walking down the long beige hallway and turning through a large archway into an expansive room with a wooden floor, flooded with artificial light.

In the center of the empty room was a metal chair and slumped in the chair was my friend Duncan. There was blood splattered in patterns on the wooden floor around him. His hands were bound behind him, his clothes torn. Long black hair shielded his face, and that streak of blond hair on one side was stained red.

He was being beaten and tortured.

My vessel walked forward, bat in hand, and I listened as he spoke.

"Oh, my, Guardian. You aren't looking so hot right now. You know it didn't need to come to this."

Duncan stayed silent and still. Drips of blood fell from his face to a small pool on the stained wooden floor. My green-eyed vessel took a moment to peer behind him. The loops of rope binding Duncan's hands had dug into the flesh of his wrists, rubbing raw the layers of skin. His hands bled. A thumbnail was missing, exposing the swollen epidermal layer underneath. He looked dead, but it was clear his body was shutting down from pain.

Duncan and I had shared contentious moments, but it hurt to see him this way.

I watched as a bloody-knuckled hand reached out and grabbed Duncan's hair by a fistful, then pulled his head up and exposed his face. The side of his face looked battered almost beyond recognition. One of his eyes was swollen shut. Bruises and cuts covered his cheeks. His pearl-white teeth were stained crimson in a mouth full of blood and saliva trickling over a gashed lip.

I wasn't sure what was happening, and I didn't know who this vessel was, but he was dead in reality. He had to be. I couldn't summon a memory from the living, and if I was looking at Duncan, it couldn't be his memory.

My vessel looked down at the bat gripped in his right hand. He brought it up, clutching it with both palms and lifting it above his shoulder.

"Wake up," he demanded.

Duncan was still.

"Wake the fuck up!" he shouted.

I heard my friend take a breath. He squeaked out some kind of response, though the word was unintelligible.

I felt my vessel pull the bat back and take a full-on swing aimed at Duncan's ribs. There was a sick crunch of bone as his body lurched forward and blood flew out of his mouth and onto my vessel's shoes. I saw him throw down the bat, then lean down and grab a fistful of Duncan's hair once more, peeling his head back.

I watched as my tortured friend gasped for breath. His bloodshot black eye shot open wide, staring back at me in a frantic search to focus.

"So many more swings," the vessel said. "I don't miss. All you have to do is tell us what you told the Caretaker and how you knew about the pub. Do that, and swift release. Don't, and there's a line of my friends waiting for their turn. Fresh. Strong. So eager to exact their own vengeance for what you did."

Duncan's eye focused and his face relaxed for a moment. It felt as if he wasn't looking at the green-eyed man before him.

It felt like he was looking at me.

Duncan's swollen mouth curled into a bloody smile. "Hello there, Caretaker," he choked out.

"What the fuck are you going on about? Answer the question. What did you tell the Caretaker, and how did you know about the pub?"

Duncan was ignoring him. "I see you," he whispered to me, staring at me through the dead memories of this man.

My vessel strengthened his grip on Duncan's hair and jerked his head violently. "Who told you about the Kerry Bog Pub?"

Duncan's gaze shifted away from mine and back to the green-eyed man. How had he seen me? How could he have known I'd be watching?

"Fuck this," said the green-eyed man as he leaned down and picked the bat up off the floor, raising it above his shoulder. He turned back toward Duncan, who was now standing right before him, freed from the chair, staring at him with his broken, bloodied face.

With a lightning quick movement, there was a glint of steel between the two of them.

My vessel dropped to the floor, hands clutching his throat. Jets of blood squirted out from between his fingers as he looked up toward Duncan, towering over him. He was wiping his straight razor clean on his sleeve.

Behind the chair was a pile of cut rope. Duncan must have hidden the straight razor somehow and cut himself free at that very moment. He was an expert at sleight of hand and misdirection.

Duncan leaned down with casual, calm grace. He stared with one open eye into the eyes of my vessel, who gagged on the blood spilling out from his throat.

"Caretaker," he said, "I know you see me. Listen. Come inside. I know this place. I will find you. There isn't much time. It is safer in here for you than it is outside."

I watched through heavy blinking eyes, as this memory's play was almost at an end. Duncan leaned in close, using a hand to prop my vessel's dying eyes open in his last moment.

"William, do not trust Elise."

I saw him get up and step over the body as my vessel's eyes closed in death.

I opened my eyes.

I couldn't trust Elise? If that was the truth, it meant she was under the influence of Deception. Duncan was inside, too. How could I trust him? Maybe this was all a setup. My head was spinning to figure out this puzzle.

Standing outside the Dolos, I found myself once again staring at Duncan's memorial poster beside the revolving door entrance of the casino. It was a lie. I'd witnessed it myself. Death had helped him send the message to me through a memory, but I didn't know if I could trust it.

Out of the corner of my eye, I noticed something. Standing in a semicircle around me were about thirty people. White shirts. Bright green eyes. They were stepping toward me, encircling.

I took a deep breath and ran to the Dolos entrance, spinning through the revolving doors and into the sounds of the ringing chimes and bells of the casino floor.

I saw Elise. She ran to me, arms wide, her long and wavy blond hair bouncing behind her in a high ponytail as she bounded toward me. She threw her arms around me, hugging me tight. It surprised me, but my heart melted. I threw my arms around her and squeezed her against me.

"I'm so glad you came back!"

She pulled away and looked around, then pulled me close once more, her lips beside my ear. "Listen," she whispered, "I don't know what's going on, but I know they're expecting you. Everyone here is watching. Be careful."

I held her in my arms and nodded, looking around at people on the casino floor. They weren't looking at me, but I knew they were watching somehow.

"Duncan is dead," she said. "Deception is furious. You can't let him have the blade."

I loosened my hug, monitoring the casino floor. I caught a security guard glancing at me, then looking away.

"Don't worry. They won't take the blade from me."

Elise held on to the hug, whispering, "Do you have Knowledge too?"

"Yes," I replied.

"You should give them to me."

CHAPTER 26

REUNITED

I pulled back from our hug and studied Elise's expression for a moment.

Who was deceiving me?

The thought wasn't outrageous. Duncan had said it himself: Deception would smell the other influences on him. He'd known he was in trouble. They'd come after him, even dragging him away from the plane wreckage. Was I being set up? Was Elise the one I should trust? She'd been there for me when I was poisoned. She'd helped me locate Knowledge. She'd been my friend, the first real one I'd had in a long time.

I felt this inescapable urge to take care of her.

But she'd been in Deception's home for days. It was impossible not to fall under the direct influence of a Concept—even a little— after being in their presence for so long. After all, she'd only just learned about this world and how it worked.

"You know I can't give you the blade," I said.

She took a step back and narrowed her eyes at me before looking to the ground. "You don't trust me."

"What did I tell you the first time we came here?"

She waved a hand at me. "Fair enough. Seriously. No, it's fine. I only stood by your side as you ran around dying, dragging me into your insanity. Why was I trying to help you even though I don't owe you a damn thing? Maybe I'm the fool here."

I took the iKnow from my pocket and stared at the screen, then back to Elise.

"We both know that belongs to me now. William, I need you to trust me."

I nodded. She was right.

"Okay, Caretaker. Here's your Concept. Knowledge is your responsibility."

I handed it to Elise.

Ding.

I saw the screen light up as Elise held it close. Her eyes darted back and forth across the screen. The soft light of the phone flickered against her cheeks as she studied it.

Out of the corner of my eye, I saw three security guards having a conversation and looking over at the two of us. I looked back to Elise.

"Something's about to happen. Put the phone away."

Ding.

The iKnow phone lit up with a different array of colors. The artificial light flickered across Elise's face once more. Her eyes went wide. She looked angry.

"What is it?"

She shook her head, staying silent. In the distance, three security guards were joined by four more. The noise of the machines in the casino began to fade. A few gamblers got up and walked away from their tables.

Elise slipped the phone into her pocket.

Seven security guards turned to face us and began to walk forward, slow and deliberate. Others began appearing seemingly out of nowhere down the alleys of blinking, chiming casino machines. Eyes on us. Walking slowly forward.

We were about to be overwhelmed by what I suspected were Guardians. I put my hands on Elise's shoulders and brought my face close to hers. "What did it say?"

"We're trapped."

"Fuck that." I grabbed her arm and turned to the door. Duncan had said the Dolos was safer than outside, but I'd have to take my chances.

The door was gone. The entrance was a solid stone wall. Security guards began running for us. I pulled Elise with me and began running in the opposite direction. I needed to buy time.

"This way," she said, pulling me toward an access door in the corner of the casino floor. My head was on a swivel. There were people swarming toward us from everywhere. This wasn't a small group of people in the confined Kerry Bog Pub. There was no fighting out of this, even for Death's Caretaker.

The metal door swung open. The handle smashed against the wall, broke off, and skittered down cement steps with a melodic chime. We ran down a flight of stairs, turned the corner, and headed down another floor.

"To the basement! We need to get to the parking garage!" Elise shouted, jumping down sets of steps to go faster. I could hear the metal door on the floor above flying open again and the shouts of people chasing us from the upper floor. We made it to the lowest level of the stairwell. Elise pulled the door open and we both ran through, finding ourselves in the middle of a hallway deep in the underbelly of the Dolos Casino.

Right behind Elise was a green-eyed security guard winding up to take a swing. I grabbed her collar and shoved her to the ground across the hallway, slipping the wild punch.

The moment he took the swing, I knew his body would lurch off-balance. That was my opening. I wound up for a brutal kick straight to his prone leg. My shin came down to the side of his kneecap and a wet crunch echoed down the hall as his leg buckled backward. He shrieked and collapsed to the floor, vomiting on himself as he reached for his leg, gnarled and bent like a branch on a dying oak.

Without a thought, I snatched the Blackwood Blade from its sheath. Tendrils of shadow and the icy grip of death instantly filled the hall. The ends of the corridor faded to pitch black.

Lights dimmed to near total darkness.

She was free. She craved his soul, and she was magnificent.

I drove the blade into the side of the guard's throat, twisting it deep into his esophagus and ripping it out of his exposed neck. Arterial spray glistened across the hall, coating my face as sinew and vein snapped at the release of tension and curled up under his skin. A quick gargling noise burst from his neck, then only the sound of his life pouring out of his exposed throat.

I sheathed the Blackwood Blade, though I felt her fighting hard to be free. We were exposed here. It wasn't the right place for a fight. I would have her in my hand again soon. Darkness subsided, and I picked Elise up off the floor. Her wide eyes stared at the destroyed guard, dead in a twisted heap, soaking in a growing pool of his own fresh blood.

We took off down the hallway as the stairwell access door swung open behind us, guards pouring out. The sight of the dead body at their feet caused them to stumble into the hall in shock, slipping on spilled blood and vomit.

Elise and I were at a full run, and I didn't understand where we were going.

"That way," she called out, pointing down a side hall. There was screaming close behind. I recognized these halls. This was the area Duncan was in when I'd seen him in memory. I took off down the hall with Elise's footsteps right by my side. I knew that if we could find Duncan, we'd have a massive advantage escaping this place, finding Deception, and ending him.

There was an open door at the end of the hall. It looked as though we were passing the area in the bowels of the basement among the vaults holding cash, chips, cards, and casino dice. This was where all the inventory keeping the illusion of glitz and glamor of high-stakes gambling was stored.

"Get to the end of the hall!" Elise shouted. "That goes to the parking garage!"

I looked into every windowed door in the hall, trying to spot any sign of Duncan. It didn't matter how many people were chasing us. Death's Caretaker and a skilled Guardian could take down any group. I'd handled the Kerry Bog Pub on my own; Duncan and I could slice our way out of this situation in a heartbeat.

But he was nowhere in sight, and it was hard to detect details with only the hall lights illuminating the darkened rooms.

Something collided into me. I lost my balance, my feet flew out from under me, and whiplash sent a shock through my neck and spine. My head slammed against the ground as my body twisted underneath me and I slid across the floor and into the open door at the end of the hall.

I felt blood trickling down my chin. My lip must have burst open from smacking against the tile as I landed. I heard a door slam shut behind me. There was an echo, then silence. I was disoriented in the unlit room. The only light streaming in was from the window in the door.

I looked up from the ground and back to the door.

Through the rectangular window, I saw Elise. Smiling. Guards quickly surrounded her, but they weren't restraining her.

A shimmer, bright as the sun's reflection on calm seas, illuminated my surroundings in a blinding amber glow for a moment. Elise disappeared. Deception was staring at me from outside the room, a wicked grin across his face. I watched him flick his hand against a switch on the outside wall, making the fluorescent lights in the room flicker on.

The quiet sound of a throat clearing echoed in the compact room. I spun my head around, my hand reaching for the Blackwood Blade sheathed at my hip. It relieved me to find it there.

Duncan was sitting on the floor in the corner. His bashed and bloodied face lifted into the artificial light. He was cut, battered, and bruised. One eye was swollen closed. Flecks of dried blood dotted his cheeks and neck. His one bloodshot black eye stared at me, unblinking.

He sighed. "Caretaker, you are a fucking moron."

Duncan's voice was raspy but audible. It was obvious he was in pain from crushed ribs. He sat still on the floor, his elbows resting on his bent knees. His wrists—skin raw and shredded from being bound as they'd tortured him— were leaking clear fluid through their abrasions. If it wasn't for his gifts as a Guardian, he would've died numerous times over through his ordeal.

I stood.

"You told me not to trust her. I should have listened to you. It's hard to know what to believe anymore."

Duncan hung his head low, shaking it from side to side.

There was a knock on the door. I turned around and saw Deception smiling, rapping his knuckle against the glass. "The infamously cranky and endlessly illogical William St. Denis, caught in a cage," he said, his voice soaked with the melody of victory.

I walked up to the glass pane of the door, slamming my hand against it. Deception was inches away, but he didn't flinch. I felt the fury and rage of a thousand volcanos deep in my mind. My hand gripped the handle of the Blackwood Blade, aching to yank it out of its sheath and cut down the entire world.

"Death will taste you," I growled.

"Back away from the door."

"Open this door and I will cut you into a thousand pieces, I promise you."

Deception leaned forward, his face almost touching the glass. "Back away."

"Open the door," I said, feeling an icy chill radiate up my arm. She was calling to me, desperate to be free from the soft leather confines of her sheath. "Come on, you coward. Open it. Let's settle this. I want to carve you into ribbons."

"It's not time for that, William," Duncan whispered. I didn't care. I needed the door open. Death needed to be free. This needed to end.

There was a commotion down the hall. Deception stepped out of the way. Appearing behind him was the massive beast of a green-eyed man that I'd seen in the memory. At the end of his extended left arm he held the same baseball bat from the memory.

In his extended right hand he gripped a fistful of Elise's hair. She was crying, struggling, and unable to do anything but be dragged down the hall by his thick arm. Her feet were hovering just above the floor as he dragged her forward like some kind of lumbering troll with a prized trinket.

He stopped a few feet from the door, holding Elise in the air by her hair. She was kicking her feet to find the floor and relieve pressure on her scalp. She was in enough pain that she couldn't make a sound. Tears streamed down her face as she trembled in midair before me, held like a rag doll.

Deception looked her up and down, then turned to face me through the window. He sighed, amused.

"William, I'd rather not go through the trouble of finding a new Caretaker for Knowledge. It's too time consuming, and I'm an important Concept with many things to do." He held up the phone, showing Knowledge to me.

I put my hand on the glass. "Put her down. Right now."

"But," he continued, "if you don't put your back against the far wall of that room, my associate here will crush her skull to pieces. You'll watch as he breaks every bone in her body, shreds her alive, and sends her into the room through the crack under the door piece by piece. He's very patient, you know. He'll take his time."

"William," said Duncan. "Just back up. It's not time."

I stepped away from the door, pressing my back to the far wall, and I slid down to sit. The door opened, and he threw Elise into the room and onto the ground. The door slammed closed behind her, and I stood and ran over to her, picking her up off the floor.

Elise sobbed, throwing her arms around me. I held her, staring out the glass at Deception, who'd placed two hands over his heart in a mock gesture of emotion at our reunion.

"I've got you," I whispered to her. "We'll be okay, I promise. I'm so sorry you had to go through this. Maybe I should've come sooner. This is all my fault. I'll fix it, I promise."

"No, you won't," said Deception from behind the door. "I'll be spending some time with my new phone here. You three make yourselves comfortable. Oh, Duncan?"

I turned toward him, bashed and battered in the room's corner. He raised his head toward Deception. I could see his one blackened eye trying to focus on Deception through the glass pane of the door.

"You can still be in my good favor," Deception said to him. "Forgive and forget your stupid mistakes. All it takes is one moment. When the time is right, cut down William St. Denis, and let's have a real Caretaker for Death in this world. Do that, and you'll be free."

I watched through the window as Deception leaned down, and I heard something hit the floor. He kicked, and from under the gap in the door I saw a familiar straight razor blade slide across the tiles, coming to a stop at Duncan's shoe.

Duncan's skeletal hand—bruised and scraped—reached down to grab it. He brought it to his face, peering at it for a long moment with his one good eye. He slipped it into his pocket and sighed.

Elise and I looked between Deception and his disgraced Guardian, Duncan the Deceiver, waiting for the response. Duncan raised his head to look at Deception through the glass.

"Consider it done."

CHAPTER 27

AN IMPERFECT PLAN

The three of us sat in awkward silence for what seemed like hours. Elise clutched my arm, resting her head on my shoulder. On the opposite side of the room, Duncan sat, knees bent and arms resting on them, his head lowered. Outside the room, two guards stood in the hall, backs to us.

The only sound was Duncan's labored breathing. I kept my eyes on him. His last exchange with Deception was unsettling. He couldn't take me out in his current state, but having to keep an eye on him while trying to manage our situation and how to get out of it would be difficult.

I didn't think he'd do it. I felt like we'd developed a cautious friendship, but he'd been one of Deception's Guardians for an age, his right hand. There was so much uncertainty.

I didn't know if I could trust him. I'd thought Deception was Elise. Nothing in this casino was what it seemed. Squaring my own feelings was impossible. How could I make reasonable decisions?

Duncan raised his head to look at us with his one good eye and we stared at each other.

He broke the silence. "You know he'll kill all of us."

"Not if you end me."

"Don't be so stupid." He sighed.

"You said it yourself. Consider it done?"

Elise picked her head up and looked back and forth between us as we spoke.

"William, do you believe you can trust anything anyone says in this place? Everything in here is Deception. He's not just that shimmering jackass walking around the building. This is all him. It's illusion. This building, this air you are breathing, and this floor you're sitting on."

"Yeah, well, I know what I heard."

Duncan's back stiffened. "All you hear are lies. It's just a fact. If I'd declined, he would've killed me on the spot. You know what? The only person who was remotely fucking honest with you is staring at you with one fucking eye."

Elise pointed a finger at Duncan. "Check yourself, asshole. We're all stuck here and I never lied to him. That wasn't me."

"Please," Duncan shot back. "Your overconfidence put us in here. Along with William's stupidity for bringing you into this place. You're a child and you made him your Caretaker too, and he can barely fulfill his own duties. You have no business being anywhere in here. You don't understand it. There's no way you can last in this world."

I shook my head.

"Look at you two, over there snuggling up like some nauseating after-school high school romance. Neither of you have any respect or reverence for the world you're in and how it works. That's why you're locked in here."

I stood up. "Enough already. Would you just shut up so I can think?"

Duncan motioned toward Elise. "What about you? What can you do that has any value? You're baggage right now. Are you going to stand up and yell at us and say something stupid like, 'Oh guys, please stop, this is just what Deception wants,' or some other inane piece of advice you'd see in some bullshit teen movie?"

"Get the fuck off her case," I growled.

"Why? Wake up! Just when I thought I was through to you, you're back to the old legendary William St. Denis. You're an emotional overthinker who can analyze people and situations in a blink, but when it comes to what you are, you have no clue. What has she done other than complicate you even more than you already were?"

Duncan looked at the blade, pointing toward it with an upturned palm. "Would you just embrace your fucking identity already? It's right there in a sheath! Quit playing down to her and to me and to everything else. You're Death's Caretaker. Act like it already so we don't all end up dead because you're meek and indecisive."

Elise jumped to her feet and walked toward Duncan. I grabbed her arm and held her back as she leaned toward him. "Fuck you. I should've blown your brains out at the motel."

Duncan laughed. "Please. You think I didn't hear the safety click off? That's adorable. If I seemed relaxed, it's because there's nothing you can ever do to me before I cut you into perfectly sized pieces of confetti. You're a baby bunny in a wolf's den, Elise. Sit down and shut up."

He was right. I hated the manner in which he'd described it, but it was spot-on. Elise was in over her head, but that was why I was determined to protect her.

Elise turned to me, circling her arm around to break my grip. "You should fucking cut him down first."

"Elise, stop that."

"No! What the hell has he ever done for you? What makes you even hesitate? He's been Deception's Guardian for how long? He's lying! You heard the two of them. He's going to cut you down the first chance he gets. Is he even human?"

Duncan grunted as he stood, holding his ribs. "I break and I bleed just like you do, you insufferable brat. I'm just a lot harder to kill. That's the Guardian's gift. And William's is even better, which is why his lack of appreciation sends me into a fucking rage."

"Duncan, shut up," I whispered.

Duncan wasn't letting up on Elise. "You're just a fucking baby Caretaker. For Knowledge. Anyone in this building could cut you in half in an instant, so you and your angsty daddy issues can sit the fuck down and let the adults figure this out."

Elise shoved me. "Just fucking kill him already so we don't have to listen to him!"

Duncan turned to me and pointed his finger at Elise. "Are you even listening to her fucking tantrum, Caretaker? Now do you understand why you weren't meant to take care of anyone or anything but that blade?"

I felt my temper raging. Without a second thought, I unsnapped the Blackwood Blade from its sheath and held it out in the room.

In an instant, darkness enveloped everything in our sight. Duncan scrambled back and fell to the floor. An ice-cold void crept down the walls. Elise jumped back, pressing herself against a wall before being swallowed up by the frozen grip of Death's presence.

I drew a lengthy breath through a wide smile. The presence of Death filled my lungs. The walls pulsed in an unnatural curve, defying the physics of our reality. Frozen oxygen made its way into my body. She embraced me.

I felt Death's affection, and nothing else mattered.

I turned my head toward Elise and studied her wrapped in the dark. She looked to be experiencing pure terror, unable to scream or move. Fear's presence was unmistakable.

When I looked to Duncan, he had a slight smile across his lips. He understood why I'd drawn the blade. He stared at me from his spot on the floor, consumed by the darkness just as Elise was.

I spoke, my voice taking on an unnatural tone. "I will say this once. Duncan, I trust you. Elise, I trust you. You two will get along, and you will help me. If you don't, I swear I will leave you in darkness for a century and see if you come out of it with no scars. Deception is making a power play and everything is off-balance. I'll fix it with your help." I looked back and forth between them. "I will cut down every obstacle to save Destiny and set things right. Do not become an obstacle."

I closed my eyes and breathed her in deep one more time before slipping the blade back into its sheath. A moment later, her grip on our world had dissipated.

Elise sat on one side of the room, Duncan on the other. I sat down in the middle. A long, uncomfortable silence hung in the air. The guards outside the door hadn't moved, ignoring our shouting and unaware of Death's presence just moments ago.

"Elise, did you learn anything about Deception while you were here with him?"

She shook her head. "No," she replied, her voice soft and still laden with lingering fear.

"Think," I said. "Anything at all that can help us?"

"He wanted the phone. It's what he spoke about. And that I'm important. He said it surprised him how I've kept myself alive through dumb luck."

I nodded. "Okay, so he knew you were Knowledge's Caretaker, and he needed you alive because he needed something from Knowledge."

"He needs you dead and replaced, Caretaker," Duncan interrupted.

"He does."

"So he wants to learn how to do it," said Elise.

"You know how," I replied.

Elise looked away from me and to the floor. "How did you know that?"

"Knowledge told me. When Duncan and I retrieved him, I asked if I could be killed. He said his Caretaker knows."

Elise nodded. She looked up at me. "William, I promise I didn't say a thing. I told him I didn't know. He said it didn't matter, that he'd have his answer soon enough anyway, and he could only get it if they kept me alive."

"There you have it," said Duncan. "He'll trick Knowledge into spilling the secret."

"How can he do it?" I asked.

Elise shook her head. "The fewer people that know, the better." I caught her glance at Duncan.

"Say it. Everyone in this room needs everyone else. Duncan can hear it."

Duncan scoffed and rolled his eyes at Elise. He brought his hands to his head and plugged his ears with his fingers.

"Better?"

Elise sighed. "Okay, look, I don't understand. I asked it because I was interested in how you could drink poison and live. It's just weird and wrong. Knowledge told me it was possible for Death to end you outside of reality, whatever that means."

Duncan unplugged his ears. "I can read lips, you know."

Elise stuck her tongue out at him.

I looked at Duncan and he stared back with one eye and the same understanding I came to realize.

"I understand."

It puzzled Elise. "I don't understand."

"Death is the blade. When I visit Destiny, I do so by driving the blade into my heart."

"Doesn't that hurt?"

"You know, I'm unhealthy. That pain to me feels like a sacrifice. It has helped me cope. I'd be lying if I didn't say it was a little addictive."

Elise turned away and nodded.

"Anyway, that's how I get to her. When I arrive in her realm, I have the Blackwood Blade with me. It makes the journey because it's buried in my heart when I leave this world. What I think this means is that if he kills me with that blade, in that reality, I'll be dead. It's the only way. I can't die here. I've tried."

Duncan shifted his weight. "The question is why?"

"Well, what do you know about him? You've been his Guardian for how long?"

"Maybe not as long as you've been around, but a very long time."

I placed my hand on the blade, wondering what it would feel like to die by the same Concept I appreciated and felt such love for. I knew she cared for me, and I couldn't imagine my life ending that way.

"Well then. What would he want?"

"Power, mostly. Some kind of leverage over everything. And not small-scale, either. He wouldn't go through this kind of trouble for a short-term benefit. Could he have struck a deal with Power?"

"No," I replied. "Power wouldn't."

"Influence?"

"I don't believe so. Influence is too broad to make a deal with a single Concept. It wouldn't be sustainable. Also, she can be cranky about personal requests."

Elise waved her hands in the air. "Wait, you mean Power and Influence are Concepts? Have you met them?"

I nodded.

She let out a big breath. "This is messed up, dude."

Duncan laughed. "You have no idea."

There was something on my mind, and I had to let them know. "Destiny will die if I visit her again."

Duncan looked puzzled. "That's impossible. Destiny can't die."

"She can and she will. She told me."

"Oh no. Caretaker, this is bad."

"I know."

"Nobody should know their fate. She's the only one who knows hers and everyone else's. You asked her?"

"I pressed her, yes. I demanded an answer. She didn't want to say anything. I was so frustrated."

He shook his head. Elise studied the both of us.

"I visited her before I came here. She said I'll see her again soon, and when I do, Death will take her."

"Well that's easy then. Don't visit her," said Elise.

Duncan puffed his cheeks and blew a long, exasperated breath into the room.

"Elise, I've been on this earth for more than a century. Destiny is the only thing that has kept me from giving up and giving in. She pulled me through my darkest moments. She gave me something to live for. I don't know what fate is worse: seeing her again for one last time and knowing it's her end, or never seeing her again. She was one of the first Concepts I met. She was so gentle. I've loved her since that first moment I saw her. I can't explain why. It always felt right. We always felt connected."

I stared at the ground. The more I thought about this situation, the more I was torn up inside. There were still answers I didn't have and I had a feeling that the full picture would reveal the answers. I needed the answers.

"Why would she tell you though?" asked Duncan.

"I don't know. It's somehow linked to my life before becoming a Caretaker. That's what my gut tells me. She said they tricked me. They deceived me. I've been a pawn since before I died."

"Did she say anything else?"

"She said that telling me she would die would make me deviate from my path. And I made her tell me anyway. I made a mistake."

Elise let out a lengthy sigh and lay down on the floor. "But you didn't know your path already? Dude, this is a serious mind job. How do you know you're on a different path if you didn't know the one you were on?"

Duncan laughed with a hint of resignation in his breath. "Elise, that's why you can't know. Destiny is a curse to itself. The only Concept that knows its own fate and must walk that path, regardless. Sharing anything about someone's fate alters everyone's fate."

"How do you know that?" I asked.

Duncan shrugged. "Deception knew. He talked about Destiny often. I just figured it had something to do with you. It's no mystery he's linked you two."

"Okay," I said, standing, "Deception wants me gone. We know he talked about Destiny. He'll use Knowledge to figure out how to do it. If I visit her, I'll have the blade. If he finds some way to be there, he'll be able to kill both of us with the blade. That must be it."

"Yeah, but why? That's what makes little sense. Why does he want you gone?" said Elise.

"I'm not sure about that yet," I said, "but it's obvious part of his end goal is getting Destiny and me out of the way. Maybe to change his own fate? Remove Death's Caretaker and use Death to destroy Destiny?"

"So what do we do?" asked Duncan.

"When he shows up, he'll want to split us up and take us somewhere. He may hurt you both, and I'm sorry for that."

Elise's face went white.

"He's going to demand I visit Destiny, with your lives on the line."

"Then?" Duncan asked.

"I'll do it."

Duncan shook his head. "No. You can't trade our lives for Death and Destiny. That's too far out of balance."

I looked at him. His eye was swollen shut, crusted blood was on his face, and he had too many bruises, gashes, and cracked bones to count. Duncan was my friend, and I realized that my anger earlier was because I cared for him and Elise, and I hated seeing him this way, and putting her in danger.

"Please don't," Elise pleaded.

"Don't worry. Only Death's Caretaker or a Concept can visit another Concept."

Duncan smiled. "You'll lure him there by doing what he wants. That's risky."

"It is, but where else will I have him isolated with Death in hand? It's the only chance I have. Either I take him out there or he'll end us all anyway."

I unsnapped her from my hip and held the sheathed Blackwood Blade in my hands, twirling it in my fingers as I studied it. We'd been through so much together. I had no idea if she had the power to end a Concept, or if she'd somehow refuse.

Elise reached out and put her hand on my knee. I looked up at her, those sweet hazel eyes staring into mine and nothing but concern in her face.

"Protect Destiny."

"I know."

"I hate it, but Duncan is right. If it comes down to it, and you've got to choose, it's okay."

"I'm not choosing anything."

Elise smiled at me, her bright face coaxing a smile from me in return. "I'm just saying, I'm okay. This has been a wild ride. Do the right thing."

Duncan groaned. "Really, you two? Again with the nauseating high school routine? Caretaker, I'm not saying any of that. Don't screw up."

We heard footsteps in the hall. The guards walked away and Deception appeared behind the glass, a wide smile on his face. He was in a tailored tuxedo.

"Well?" he asked, his melodic voice echoing through the door and into the room. "Are you ready?"

We stood.

"For what?" I asked.

He held his arms up and let out a laugh. "The show!"

CHAPTER 28

THE DEATH OF WILLIAM ST DENIS

My knees ached. I was kneeling on a stage in a large theater. Before me on a small table was the sheathed Blackwood Blade. Past the edge of the stage was a sea of eager onlookers, greed in their eyes and hunger in their hearts. Varied people from varied nations, but all with the greenest eyes, visible even from up on a stage with spotlights shining in my face.

To my right, a short distance away, Elise was kneeling, hands bound. Her tearstained cheeks and strained breath were her only communication. Her eyes were frantic, searching the ground, the stage, and me.

This felt like an execution.

To my left, a short distance away, was Duncan, still bruised and battered from the torture he'd received hours ago. He was on his knees, his hands bound once more, his head hung low.

Guardians surrounded us, green eyed and staring with anticipation at what was about to occur. Both Elise and

Duncan had multiple Guardians around them, one poised behind each of them with a raised bat. They filled every seat in the theater. Deception was center stage, microphone in hand with a mile-wide grin stretching across his face as he considered the three of us.

He turned to the crowd, bringing the microphone to his face. Applause and shouts filled my ears as I focused on the blade in front of me.

"Ladies and gentleman, are you ready for a show?" he announced. He had the charisma and dramatic flair of a circus ringmaster.

Cheers echoed throughout the theater. I looked to Elise, who was no longer sobbing, but it was clear she couldn't think. I was trying to stay focused on what I had to do. In a moment, the spotlight would shine down upon me. And in front of hundreds, I'd have to commit the intimate act of killing myself with the Blackwood Blade, visiting Destiny, and being able to think on my feet to a point of destroying Deception in a realm outside of this world.

I'd been in weirder situations.

I considered the blade before me. Destiny had been clear. Death would take her when we reunited. That was her path and one that she had to walk.

"Friends," he shouted to the crowd, "let us put tonight into perspective!"

I stared at him with rage boiling in my veins. I wanted to grab the Blackwood Blade and cut him into ribbons in front of everyone. That would never succeed in Deception's home, and that was why I had to stay still.

Deception held out his hands, calming the crowd. They settled and I watched him take a seat on the edge of the stage, facing them as if having a small private conversation. He motioned for the lights to dim, and in a moment there was a single soft spotlight illuminating him.

"Tonight is the culmination of decades upon decades of effort. You are witnessing a consolidation this evening. A consolidation of influence. You have all asked and been promised a piece of this, and you shall all earn it!"

The audience rose to their feet and gave an ovation. Cheers filled the theater walls. Deception stood and walked over to Elise as the spotlight followed. Cheers died down as a shared spotlight expanded to highlight Elise and a bat-wielding Guardian right behind her. I watched her as she began breathing heavily, frantic eyes searching for any escape. She was in the grip of fear, and that flight response was overwhelming her. I needed her to not do anything stupid. She had to stay still and trust the plan. Any deviation was her end, and Duncan's too.

"Allow me to introduce you to the cast of this tragedy," Deception announced with a flourish of his hand. "Here we have young Elise Campbell, a down-on-her-luck street-wandering girl who stumbled her way into becoming Caretaker for Knowledge. She found love once in the form of a beautiful woman."

Deception shimmered and appeared in an instant as a gaunt young woman in her early twenties, sick and unhealthy. He was determined to tease and torture Elise.

He looked down at himself and made a face of mock horror, whipping the audience into a fit of laughter. "I'm not going to judge," he said, "but if you're attracted to something like this, is it any wonder you end up a homeless wretch?"

I watched as Elise stared up at the form of her lost love and began crying. Tears streamed down her face, falling from her cheeks and tapping against the floor. She was shaking her head. I couldn't tell if she was heartbroken or angry. She looked to me. I mouthed the words, "Be strong," but she was past the point of accepting help or advice. This was too overwhelming.

"Well, I have a surprise for you, Elise!" Deception continued. "We made sure that the real Cassie could join us today!"

A spotlight shone on the opposite side of the stage and an exact duplicate of Deception's form of Cassie walked out from behind the curtain. Elise caught sight of her and began sobbing, her unkempt head of hair obscuring her face, but not the tears streaming down. She lifted her head to look at Deception, who shimmered back to his tuxedo-wearing form, then back to Cassie.

Deception clapped his hands and Cassie shimmered and turned into a laughing green-eyed Guardian with a bright white shirt. The crowd roared with laughter.

"Just kidding," he announced to the crowd, a frown stretching across his face. A moment later he was joining them all in laughter.

Elise screamed and Deception jumped back in mock shock, putting his hand on his chest as if he was having a heart attack. Elise couldn't take much more of this abuse before she'd do something stupid. I could feel her willpower slipping. He was breaking her and looking for an excuse to punish her for lashing out.

"Would you shut the fuck up already?" called a voice from my left. It was Duncan. I closed my eyes and winced. He was attempting to save Elise by drawing the attention to himself.

There was no way he wouldn't pay for it.

The spotlight shot over to Duncan, already battered and broken, looking up to Deception with his one open eye. His bound hands strained, and the Guardian behind him was ready to bring a baseball bat down upon his head in an instant if he was told.

Deception walked toward Duncan. "Ah," he announced to the crowd, creeping across the stage in dramatic fashion. "Introducing the traitor!"

Boos and hisses echoed throughout the theater. There was cursing and shouting, people in the crowd standing and pointing fingers, screaming all kinds of terrible things toward him.

Duncan looked up at his Concept with no fear in his posture. He seemed accepting of whatever his fate may be. I only hoped it wasn't this moment. Elise was calming down, so Duncan's trick had worked, but I was bracing myself for the payment he'd have to make.

The crowd subsided as Deception reached into his pocket and pulled out a baseball.

"Mezzanine. Fourth row. Third seat," he said.

In the crowd, a spotlight shone down on the mezzanine level, and the person far off in the third seat in the fourth row stood and held his hands up in the air.

Deception tossed the ball to the bat-wielding Guardian behind Duncan, who took a swing and launched it into the hands of the man in the crowd, causing cheers and hollers to erupt once more.

"See?" Deception called out to Duncan. "He can't miss. Let's try again!"

He reached into his pocket but pulled out an empty hand, disappointment on his face. "Okay then," he said. "Left side. Rib cage. Third from the bottom."

With a quick swing, the bat-wielding Guardian behind Duncan launched the bat into his ribs. The sound of air being blasted out of his lungs and the wet crunch of a rib echoed in the theater before being drowned out by further cheers.

Duncan collapsed onto his face, curled up on the stage floor, gasping for breath. Deception leaned down to him, holding the microphone away. I heard him say, "The next one opens the back of your skull so this crowd can see your traitorous brain."

He stood up and pointed toward Duncan. "This, the reprehensible Duncan the Deceiver. A traitor for all time. Responsible for the deaths of many of your kin! I trusted him. Loyal for so many years. Who would have known that being influenced by Deception would turn someone into a traitor?"

He was playing the crowd in masterful fashion, raising the energy and the thirst for violence throughout the theater.

I felt the blinding heat of a spotlight on my face.

It was my turn.

"And here," Deception continued as the crowd fell into a hushed whisper.

"Caretaker William St. Denis, the star of tonight's show. For more than a century he's been misplacing one of the most powerful Concepts in existence." He sauntered over to the small table before me, picked up the sheathed Blackwood Blade, and held it up to the crowd.

A jolt of oohs and ahs reverberated through the theater.

"Ladies and gentlemen," continued Deception, "I present to you, Death herself."

I watched the crowd. Many of them stood, peering onto the stage to get a better look at the blade in Deception's hand. He placed it back on the table and turned to the crowd once more.

"Tonight, my friends, you will witness something so unsettling that you may never be the same. Death will be in this room with you."

Another shot of shock and gasps filled my ears.

"Do not worry," continued Deception, holding up a reassuring hand, "for she only comes for her Caretaker this evening. William will grace us with his exceptional talent. He will end his own life before you and travel to another existence right in front of your eyes."

Enthralled murmurs flittered through the crowd. Deception walked to the side of the stage and pointed to a balcony high above. Everyone looked toward the spotlight shining down on the massive green-eyed hulk of a man who I'd first seen through my vessel before Duncan had sliced his throat. He was the largest person in the room, a behemoth of a man. Massive muscles strained his dress shirt and his eyes blazed a brilliant green. He'd been the one dragging Elise through the hall by her hair a few hours ago.

I didn't understand who or what he was.

"Ladies and gentlemen," announced Deception, "let us also take a moment to recognize my guest of honor and personal friend, Faust. Without his influence, tonight would not be possible."

The audience rose to their feet, turned toward the balcony, and gave a rousing and long-lasting applause to Faust. His emerald eyes, matching the pommel of the Blackwood Blade, stayed affixed to my own. He did not move at the applause. He only stared at me.

"Though," continued Deception with a gleaming smile, "you know him by a different name." He laughed.

The ovation continued until he settled them. My head was spinning. That massive beast of a man was the key to this entire thing. He was right before my eyes in that last memory and it hadn't occured to me he could be so important. I had moments to put these puzzle pieces together before having to kill myself and attempt to destroy Deception. He must be a Concept.

My thoughts spiraled in a hundred directions, a hundred times faster than I could keep track of. My intuition ran wild trying to make this fit.

Faust. His name was Faust. I remembered the story. A dissatisfied man selling his soul to the devil. It made no sense in terms of Concepts, though. They already had incredible power and influence over reality. It had to be something else.

Deception walked over to me, hushing the crowd. He leaned down, holding the microphone away from his mouth to have a private word. "You will kill yourself now, and I will meet you there when you arrive. You know that, don't you, William?"

"I do," I answered.

Deception gently stroked my cheek with the back of his hand, injecting my being with the desire to deceive everything and everyone for a moment. He leaned down to meet my eyes.

"And that will be your end. You know that, don't you?"

"I do," I answered.

The crowd was getting antsy.

His voice dropped to a whisper floating to my ear. "And if you don't do as I say, those bats will brutalize your friends for days. Weeks. Months. Years."

"I understand," I answered.

Deception stood and turned toward the crowd, motioning with his hand to the lights up above. A gentle flood of warm light bathed the theater in its amber glow. I closed my eyes as I kneeled center stage.

I was the showpiece.

It was time.

I reached out and grasped the Blackwood Blade, and the entire theater went silent. I could hear my heart beating in my ears, faster and faster. Adrenaline coursed through my body.

I opened my eyes and looked at Elise, who was begging me to put an end to all of this with that look in her eyes.

I tried to reassure her by mouthing the words, "I've got you, I promise."

With the Blackwood Blade high above my head, I grasped the leather sheath in one hand and the hilt in the other. I took a deep breath and looked toward Duncan. He was in a heap on the floor, gasping for breath as if a fish out of a fishbowl, clinging to life.

I felt afraid. My head was spiraling out of control. I didn't know what to do and I didn't want this to be the end of Destiny.

This was ripping me apart. Insecurity and uncertainty was in every cell in my body.

"Your delay has upset my guest of honor," said Deception.

His words drew my attention, pulling me out of my lost headspace. I looked up and beside him on stage was Faust. The crowd stayed silent. Faust looked toward Deception with a disapproving scowl. He was not a fan of the show.

I watched Faust walk over to Duncan. He stepped behind him, taking the bat from the Guardian and casting him away with a strong shove. The bat looked like a miniature child's toy in his massive hand.

I reached out and held a hand toward him. "Stop! I'm doing it!"

Faust stared at me.

"Leave him alone!"

"No," he snapped.

Duncan raised his head off the floor and toward me, one sympathetic eye peering into mine. He knew this was his end. Faust raised the bat high above his head and drew a big breath. His muscles flexed as he prepared to swing.

Duncan gave me a supportive smile. "Good luck, Careta—"

The wooden bat came down on the back of his head with enough force to snap the bat into splinters, sending pieces of wood into the crowd. His head slammed against the stage with a hollow thud. Blood pooled from under his skull. His eye stared at mine and I watched it fade out of focus and close.

Duncan was dead.

My insecurity had cost him his life. It proved that Faust was a Concept. Only an entity as powerful as a Concept could strike a blow that could take a Guardian's life. The crowd gasped then stayed silent from either horror or shock. Faust walked toward Elise, grabbing the bat from the Guardian behind her and shoving him to the ground. He raised it above his head and stared at me.

Elise screamed.

Deception smiled.

I grabbed the Blackwood Blade and unsheathed it. Frigid air filled the theater in an instant. The walls darkened to black, bending outward and pulsing with Death's breath. I heard the crowd's surprise at the instant change, murmurs through time and space, as the absence of all life gripped the theater.

"Marvelous," mused Deception. "She is stunning."

Faust was poised to strike Elise. I grasped the hilt with both my hands. Darkness seeped out from the blade as if spectral fog floating across an ancient grave. It wrapped around my wrists.

She was guiding me. I could see the shape of Death's long, delicate fingers, made of blackened shadow, caressing my hands. I had never seen her shape before. This was as close as she'd ever been, touching me with her own hands for the first time. The skin on my wrists was frozen and numb beneath her gentle grip as she urged me to join with her once more.

She erased my insecurities in an instant. I felt validation and determination. Death embraced me with love and support, and I knew what I had to do. I trusted her.

"Thank you," I whispered to her.

With a fluid motion I'd executed countless times before, I drove the blade into my heart. It pierced and ripped my chest open as it slid into me. There was the stunning shock of feeling it drive into my heart, confused frantic beating causing spurts of blood to jet out from the opening in my chest. I watched my crimson life drain out over my hands, pouring in a steady stream to the floor between my knees.

I could hear Elise screaming among the frantic noises of the crowd. I watched as Deception stayed Faust's hand. Chilled air enveloped everything as the bright lights high above the stage dimmed in Death's presence.

She drained my life, the light, and the warmth of the theater.

Sounds drowned and faded to silence.

I heard my heartbeat cease.

I closed my eyes.

Chapter 29

The Sorrow of William St Denis

I opened my eyes.

I felt cool earth beneath my fingers and on the side of my face as I woke in that familiar glade. Cherry blossoms flittered to the surrounding ground, gleaming in the sunlight with their vibrant hues of pink and red. Warm air laden with the aroma of evergreen filled my lungs as the sweet sun bathed me in comforting light.

I picked myself up from the ground on that familiar well-worn gravel path. I turned and looked to the small farmhouse in the distance and started walking. My hand rested on the blade sheathed against my hip. I had no idea how the next few minutes would play out, but I had to end Deception and prevent Destiny from leaving me.

Dee was sitting on her porch swing. Her sweet summer dress draped down her slender frame, sun-kissed legs stretched out and bathed in the warm summer light. She raised her head and spotted me, then covered her mouth with her hands and began crying.

I ran up to the porch as she stood up and embraced her. Dee laid her head on my chest, her hands shaking as I wrapped her up in my arms.

"Shh," I whispered.

"You're here."

"I know. I know you told me not to come, but this is the only way. I had to draw him here."

She shook her head. "It won't work." I felt Dee's hand drift down my chest and rest on the blade. "She has come for me."

I pulled away, holding on to Dee's shoulders and leaning down to look into her sweet brown eyes. "I have her. Trust me. She will not take you. I won't let it happen. I promise."

"Sweet William, you don't understand."

"I do understand. I get it now. Death is with me. It's all so clear now."

Dee shook her head, staring at my face through tears. She frowned as she brought her hands up to touch my face.

"I've loved you forever," she said.

"And I you. I don't know why or how this happened, but you and I have had a bond since the first time I saw you. I will not let it break today. I swear."

She buried her head in my chest once more. Her tears soaked my shirt. I held her, trying to memorize every touch, the way her body moved when she breathed and how her hands felt pressed to my back. I kissed the top of her head, breathing deep.

"He's here," she whispered.

I let go of Dee and turned, using my arm to guide her behind me and placing my hand on the hilt of the

Blackwood Blade sheathed against my hip. A short distance away, walking up the gravel path in his perfect tuxedo with an enormous smile across his face, was Deception.

He looked around. "Lovely place you have here, Destiny. I forgot how homey it is. The last time I saw it, this homestead was enveloped in flames."

I turned my head to look at her behind me. Her wide, tear-filled eyes met mine. "What is he talking about? Flames?"

Destiny only stared at me, then sat down on the porch swing, staring at the floor below her dangling feet.

I turned back to Deception, who was now leaning against the stair railing, his head upturned, soaking in the sun. He reached into his pocket, taking out a cigarette and lighting it. He took a deep drag and blew a stream of smoke into the air above.

"Well, William? Are you ready?"

"Duncan was my friend," I said.

"Oh, please. He would've cut you down in a heartbeat if given the opportunity. I did you a favor. That would've been an uncerimonious way to go. He would've had to slice you into pieces, then find you in some alternate realm and do it again. So much work."

"Is Elise alive?"

"She is."

"Will she stay that way?"

"If you drive that blade into your heart right here, yes."

Destiny let out a choked sob behind me as she stood. Her hand pressed to my back. She was trying to comfort me. It always worked. Her touch could soothe me for a thousand years.

"You two have met before?"

Deception smiled at me. "Stop stalling, William. Faust is eager to swing that bat and knock Elise's head into the audience. I'm not there to stop him."

"Who is he?"

Deception's smile disappeared as his back straightened. He took a few steps up the stairs, standing an arm's length away from me. His eyes glinted with a predatory hunger.

"Tell me," I pressed.

He took a deep breath, his chest swelling. "I'll tell you nothing, Caretaker. I am Deception. I am a Concept in a Concept's land. You are insignificant, a mere pawn. Now, take that blade, and drive it into your heart."

I slid the blade from the sheath.

There was no darkness. Of all the times I'd visited Destiny with the Blackwood Blade on my hip, I'd never drawn it in her presence. It surprised me that nothing happened. It appeared as an ordinary knife.

Deception laughed.

I looked back at Destiny. She was staring at the blade, fear in her eyes.

Without a second thought, I lunged forward with the knife, straight toward Deception's chest. Light shimmered, and he disappeared.

I turned. Deception was sitting on the porch swing with Destiny, his arm around her. He was stroking her arm with his hand, pretending to calm her down. He looked at me and winked.

I gripped the blade tighter and took a step toward him. Another shimmer and he faded again, this time appearing on the gravel path just past the end of the porch steps.

"Do you seriously think you have a chance here? Come down here and try it again." He flicked his cigarette to the ground.

I walked down the steps, standing before him. Instead of swinging with the blade, I launched my fist across his face with a left hook. It was a surprise he hadn't expected. I felt his jaw pop under my knuckles, then another shimmer.

I turned around and Deception was behind me. In a blink, he delivered a kick to my chest, sending me flying down the gravel path, blade in hand. There was no darkness. There was no shadow. I'd expected Death to be with me, but she was absent in this world. I didn't understand why.

"Stop fucking around, Caretaker," he bellowed, walking toward me with his fists tightened. I stood up as he launched a strike toward my face. I slipped the punch, knocked his arm away, and drove the blade toward his chest.

Again, he shimmered and appeared a few feet away.

"Do it," he demanded.

"Tell me why."

"Be more specific, Caretaker."

"Why are you doing this? Who is Faust? Why is Destiny involved?"

Deception threw his head back and let out a genuine fit of laughter. There was another shimmer and he disappeared from view. I searched around for him, then felt a fist on my head, grabbing a handful of my hair with enough power to snap my neck. Before I could counter, he brought me to my knees. I was unable to grasp at anything. I couldn't reach behind me with the blade.

"Press it against your chest."

I brought the blade to my chest, feeling the point against me once again, but Death's presence was absent. There would be no magic. She was not here to keep me alive. Driving the blade into my heart now would only mean death. My eyes went to Destiny on the porch. She wasn't watching, only holding her head in her hands.

"Now think, fool."

"Who is Faust?" I asked.

"A business partner," he growled. "One that I plan on sating with the ultimate prize."

"What prize?"

He laughed. "The object of his obsessive and frankly childish affection."

I looked at Destiny, balled up on the porch swing, shaking her head in disbelief.

"You're killing me because he wants Destiny?"

"Naturally," he said, yanking on my hair with furious strength. I felt my neck crack as he shook me. I couldn't compete with his strength outside of my reality, not with a plain old blade.

"Who is he?"

"That kid died because of you. What was his name? Harvey?"

"Yes."

"What happened to you? How did that stupid fucking blade get stolen when you met him? Think."

"I was late," I said, wincing from the pain of my hair being pulled from my scalp. "I had a flat tire."

"Where did Duncan find you?"

"A motel," I said.

"What motel?"

"Four Leaf, I think? Four-Leaf Clover Motel in New Jersey."

"Mmm," he said, trailing a finger along my neck. "What was on the front door of the Kerry Bog Pub?"

"A horseshoe," I said, with a final understanding. "Faust. That's Latin."

Deception kept laughing.

"It means 'Fortunate One,' " I said.

How had I not seen it? The flat tire making me late, leading to the blade being stolen. Duncan finding me at the Four-Leaf Clover. The ladybug outside the librarian's house. All signs of luck. The freak accidents. A piano falling on her a day earlier. The plane hitting our car as Duncan and I drove to Atlantic City. Green-eyed bar patrons throwing bullseye after bullseye at a dartboard. The horseshoe on the door. Love asking me if I wondered why I was so unlucky.

Duncan's cut-off last words, "Good luck, Caretaker."

Faust was Luck. This entire time he'd been manipulating the tiniest events with a roll of dice to put me here in this moment. I had to break from Deception's grip. I needed one more shot at surviving this.

I was responsible for Duncan's death, Harvey's death, and countless others throughout history. I needed to make this right. Destiny would die; she knew her ending. If I drove that blade into my heart, it was her death sentence. I couldn't let that happen.

"Very good, you figured it out. Now do it," he demanded.

"One more question. Why you and Luck?"

Deception sighed. "Do you know how easy it is to gain power and to deceive when Luck is on your side? For an age that monstrous hulk was the only thing denying me influence. Fleecing people in a casino is easy, but one lucky spin or one lucky card and the house loses. Little white lies uncovered by lucky chance, stopping perfect deception from worming its way into the hearts and minds of man. Faust has been around influencing the world for almost as long as that ridiculous knife of yours."

"What happens to Destiny?"

"I don't fucking care," he replied, his voice growing angry. "That massive asshole has wanted her since before you were Death's Caretaker. She'll be his toy to play with. Now you need to drive that blade in, and I need to deliver her to Faust so I can get on with crafting lies and betrayal with Luck's favor. Elise has only moments left, I'm sure."

I pressed the blade to my chest, feeling the tip poke through skin with a sting absent of Death's embrace. The pain was shocking, different, and real. I winced and closed my eyes.

Deception shook and shoved my head again, craning it sideways, straining my shoulder and neck. "Do it!"

I opened my eyes, head sideways, and looked to Destiny. In that moment, puzzle pieces fit. When I'd hitched a ride with who I suspected was Perspective, he'd said, "When all the things seem sideways, maybe all you'll need is a hug to set it right."

I needed to hug to Dee.

"You win," I said to Deception. "I won't fight you anymore. I'll do it. But grant me a goodbye. One more embrace with Dee. Please. I'm begging you."

Destiny perked up and stood on the porch. Tears streaming down her face, she nodded. "Let him," she called out. "Please. I-I'll go with you. I'll go to Faust, I promise."

He sighed and threw his head back. "You two are so annoying I might literally vomit right here on this gravel path. Fine. You have one minute, then we all leave this ridiculous scene." His grip loosened on my hair. I stood and ran to the porch, sweeping Destiny up in my arms.

I held her tight.

"I love you, William," she said through choked sobs and endless tears. "I've loved you forever."

My cheek pressed against the side of her face, soaking her temple with my tears. "I can't lose you. I don't want to do this," I whispered.

"Sweet William," she whispered back, her voice full of resolve. "You are the only one who can set these wrongs right. Your entire life you've been a pawn. Play a different game now," she whispered. "You know what you need to do."

"It's time," Deception snarled. He was far enough away that he couldn't hear the whispered conversation between us.

"How?" I asked her.

"Grant me my destiny. Let me go with grace," she whispered. Her words were gentle across my ear. She looked down at the blade, then back up to me.

"No. No, I can't do that. Dee, don't make me do that."

Her hands caressed my face once more. "Have faith in me. You have to. You've been my every joy and my every love, always. Now give me a goodbye kiss, sweet William. Trust that I always loved you, and I always will."

I leaned in, pressing my lips to her for the last time. I tried to memorize the feel of her hands on me, the smell of her sweet skin, and the soft touch of those loving lips against my own.

"Now, or Elise is dead!" Deception demanded once more.

Destiny pulled away from our embrace. She looked afraid.

I caressed her face with my hand as she closed her eyes and cried, peace washing over her expression at my touch.

Reaching toward my belt, I freed the Blackwood Blade from its sheath.

"What are you doing?" Deception shouted. "No!"

I yanked Destiny's body against my own. With speed and precision I'd honed over a century, and through a tidal wave of tears, I plunged the blade into Destiny's heart as I held her close.

Her eyes shot open wide and her jaw dropped as she tried to breathe in.

I supported her collapsing body in my arm as I held the blade into her chest, feeling her heartbeat fading fast. Her warm blood radiated out, staining her sweet, thin summer dress and coating my hand in her warm essence. I lowered her, my tears raining down on her chest.

"I'm sorry," I pleaded. "I'm sorry! Dee, I'm so sorry! Please forgive me! What have I done?"

"Forgiven," she mouthed back, her body slumping farther. "You've been blind, but now you'll see."

Blood trickled from the corner of her mouth as her head relaxed and tilted back.

She was dead.

Skies darkened. Clouds formed. I stood and turned, shaking.

There was blood on my hands. Countless times over the last hundred years I'd pierced my heart and become whole again. All of those scars, and it turned out piercing someone else's heart was what broke mine.

Deception screamed in the shimmering form of gaseous fury. He was growing larger, taller, stronger. A hurricane of anger shone in his eyes as his massive presence shadowed me.

"Traitor!" he shouted, his voice erupting in deafening deep-toned wrath. "Murderer! Ruiner! I will exile you here forever, William St. Denis, and I will torture Elise for ten thousand years! I will burn to the ground everything you've ever seen or touched and I will annihilate Death herself!"

With a flash of light, he vanished.

I turned back to Destiny, sat down beside her, and brought her to my lap. I held her and broke down.

"What have I done?"

I looked up. The sky was fading to white, as if watercolor being drained from canvas. Driving rain washed away everything that surrounded me. The black-capped chickadees fell silent. Cherry blossom trees disintegrated into a faded pink dust. The farmhouse crumbled to nothing.

I was in a white void, holding Destiny in my arms, the Blackwood Blade resting in her chest.

I closed my eyes.

"Oh, William," I heard a voice say.

It startled me. I opened my eyes and looked around, but I saw nothing. I looked down at Destiny. There was no blade. There was only a hole in her chest.

I turned and looked behind me.

A tall woman was approaching, each step of her black boots echoing in my ears. She was in stark contrast to the white surroundings. She wore ripped black jeans and a half jacket, exposing a pierced belly button. She pushed her black-painted fingernails through her full, curly hair.

"Are you—"

"What have you done?" she asked, emphasizing each syllable. She shook her head as she stepped closer.

I laid Destiny down and stood, turning to face my visitor. She was shorter than me, but her huge mane of curly jet-black hair towered past my height. She stood before me, grabbing my hands and holding them in her own.

Her grip was freezing cold. She lifted one hand to my face, wiping my tears with an ice-cold thumb. I blinked. Her pupils were dark and wide, drawing me in. It looked as if there was a universe of a billion swirling galaxies shining in her eyes.

"Hi," she said, with an amount of awkwardness to match my own.

"Uh, hi. Are you?"

"Yes, baby. I am."

"Death?" I asked.

"That's the question I was answering, William. So yeah."

"Oh," I managed.

Death leaned to the side and looked at Destiny on the ground behind me. She frowned and shook her head before leaning back toward me. She looked concerned.

"William, are you okay?"

"No."

"Fair enough. You and I need to talk."

This felt surreal.

Death and I were sitting beside one another, Destiny's body lying before us. I didn't have the strength to cry anymore. Everything was numb. I sat with my legs bent, elbows perched on my knees. Disbelief tingled in every cell in my body at the scene of Destiny dead before me.

Existence felt wrong. I should be dead. She should be alive.

Moments ago Destiny had been in my life, in some capacity. Duncan had been alive. Elise had been in danger but safe until my return. Death had been inanimate.

In mere minutes I'd lost a friend, lost a love, doomed a friend to torment, and no longer had a blade. True, Death was sitting beside me, but that felt beyond awkward.

"Do I just call you Death, or do you prefer something else?"

"Kay works."

"Kay?"

"Short for Khali. That's what I went by the last time I was in form."

"In form?"

"Yep. Not that pretty knife you've been swinging around and murdering everyone with."

The way she'd phrased that last statement had me feeling apprehensive about how I'd been executing my duties as Caretaker. We sat in silence for some moments, staring at Destiny. Kay seemed deep in thought.

I felt like it was up to me to break the silence. "I'm sorry about the pub."

Kay scoffed. "Why? It was brilliant."

"You saw all of that, huh?"

She turned and looked at me. Her wide, spiraling eyes felt like they were burrowing through the back of my skull.

"Yeah," she said. "Or do you not remember that I was there? Because I was there. You were swinging me around and murdering a bunch of drunken green-eyed Guardians. It's hard to sleep through that. That blade for me is similar to hibernation. I'll take its form for age upon age, then wake up. Even in that half-asleep state, I still hear and absorb everything going on around me."

I shook my head, trying to regain some focus. "Right. Right, you're the blade. Were the blade. I'm sorry, I'm just not used to this."

"Talking to girls? Yeah, you suck at it."

"What? No. That's not what I meant! I mean not used to you being, you know, you."

Kay leaned back and raised an eyebrow at me. "Are you saying you prefer it when I'm quiet and inanimate?

Buddy, that's some patriarchy shit right there. You want me to go make you a sandwich now?"

I blushed. "No! I'm sorry! No, no, I'm glad you're here. There were just a lot of things I said to you as a knife, not thinking you were going to actually be here and now that you are I'm, you know . . ."

"Embarrassed?"

"Yeah."

Kay smiled and put a hand on my back, patting me. "Relax. Yeah, I've seen it all. I've heard it all. Wish there were a few things I could unsee. Sure, I didn't talk back, but I've been with you for the last century. Nothing is different. I'm just out of the sheath."

"I got carried away in the pub, I know that."

Kay laughed a pure, genuine laugh. "Please don't worry your little head over that one. None of them were very much human anymore. Casualty of Faust's grip on them."

"Yeah. Also, I'm sorry I lost you."

Kay shrugged. "You lost me a lot, but I never strayed far. This is all part of how Concepts work. It's not neat and clean. It can get messy and complicated. Emotions are. Concepts are. We don't all get along. Influence gets pulled in so many directions. When Concepts get together, it raises the complexity level exponentially."

"I guess so."

"You know so. Remember too that we are here through existence. What seems like life or death for you in a sixty-year lifetime feels like seconds to me. I've been around forever."

"Can I ask you something?"

"Yes."

"Why do they call you the First and the Last?"

Kay rolled her eyes and groaned.

"What?"

"Come on, man, you don't think that's the cheesiest phrase ever? I can't even. It all goes back to a Caretaker with a flair for the dramatic a very, very long time ago."

"He called you that?"

"Yes. *Prima et Ultima*,' he used to say. He had this long, grand speech every time he took a life. Meanwhile I was just like 'Get *on* with it already,' you know? He was so dramatic. That relationship didn't last long. I prefer you by far."

"Wait, relationship?"

Kay chuckled. "I mean, that's kind of what it is, isn't it? Not going out on a date, but a friendship and working relationship of sorts. Fine, then. Call it a situation-ship. I've spent most of the last century down your pants, William. Ever think of that?"

"Uh, I am now." I blushed.

"Yeah, so situation-ship. Anyway, he phrased it that way because I was first, and I'll be last."

"I never understood how Death could be first."

Kay smiled to herself and looked at her boots, brushing one of them off with her hand. "Thought Life would be first, right?"

"Yes. Life. Creation. Something like that?"

She shook her head. "Wrong answer, my man. For a universe to begin, the universe before must die. Think of that chicken and egg thing, but different."

I scratched my head. "Okay, but are you the chicken or the egg?"

"Neither," she said, a thoughtful expression across her face.

"Huh?"

She smiled. "I'm more like the frying pan, baby."

As charming as I found her presence to be, the emotions of the moment began weighing me down. I'd just killed Destiny. I couldn't bear to think of what was happening to Elise.

"Can I get back? I have a friend in trouble."

"Elise. I know. Remember, I know everything you do. I saw all of this. Elise is a firecracker. She's good for you. Spunky. I like her."

"Me too."

"Don't worry. We have time. You need to trust me."

She reached to my opposite shoulder and pulled me in close for a hug as we both turned to look at Destiny again. "We need to discuss this."

"I don't know what to say."

Kay sighed and held me close. My body was freezing against her, but it was still comforting. She felt like my oldest friend, rubbing her hand on my arm with much affection and understanding. She used her hand to pull my head to her shoulder and let me lean on her. I had difficulty wrapping my brain around how gentle and sweet she was.

"William, I need to show you something, and you won't like it. It'll be hard for you to watch."

I felt an emotional swell in my chest and began crying again. Tears welled up and drifted down my cheeks. I didn't feel like I could take any more. It overwhelmed me. She reached her other hand to my chin and turned my head to her. Kay was stunning, and while she looked human, there was something about her that felt alien.

"Be strong for me, baby. Please."

I wiped my eyes and nodded, taking a big breath. Kay reached into her pocket and pulled out what looked like a tiny metal puzzle, no bigger than a finger or two.

"What is that?" I asked.

Kay was fiddling with it, concentrating. "A curio."

"A curio?"

"Yeah. That's what we call them."

"Who?"

"Concepts."

"What does it do?"

"Think of it as a trinket imbued with a small amount of pure influence of a Concept. I borrowed this one from Reality."

"Reality gave you a puzzle, or is that actual Reality?"

"No, a curio is more like a little object given some power by a Concept. Not the Concept itself in need of a Caretaker. It only works for a little while. You know how you hear about objects being cursed?"

"Sure."

"Cursed objects are curios. A Concept puts a bit of pure power or influence into a physical thing, then loans it to someone, or sets it loose on the world to change the course of things. The Hope Diamond? That was Greed's work."

"Well, did Reality tell you how to solve it?"

Kay looked flustered attempting to turn the linked pieces of metal of the curio. Her brow furrowed and her tongue stuck out from her lips. "No. Reality can be a bitch sometimes, honestly."

"What is it supposed to do?"

The question had just escaped my lips when the metallic sound of the puzzle clinking together rang in my ears. There was a flash of blinding light, and Kay and I were standing on a well-worn gravel path winding its way ahead to a small farmhouse with a swing on the porch. Cherry blossom trees were on either side of the path. I smelled evergreen and the songs of black-capped chickadees rang in my ears.

"This is Destiny's home," I whispered.

"No, baby," Kay replied. "This is your home."

CHAPTER 30

THE PAIN OF WILLIAM ST DENIS

Kay reached out and grabbed my hand. "Walk with me."

We made our way up the gravel path, through the glittering blossoms hued pink and red. I felt the gravel crunching beneath my feet. There were no sounds in the distance other than the calls of songbirds and the breeze whispering its gentle way through branches and leaves around us.

"What do you mean, my home?"

Kay stopped walking and turned to face me. Her infinite, spiraling eyes focused on mine.

"William, it's 1911 and we're in Oregon, four years before your death. This curio enabled us to shift reality enough to be here. Nobody can see us. Think of it as stepping into a movie, the difference is, this movie is you. Your life. Right now we don't exist in current time or reality. We are outside the fabric of the universe."

"That's a lot to process."

Kay nodded. "I know. I'm about to show you what your life was like. It's time you learned your history. I'm sorry, but it won't be very pleasant."

"I don't understand."

She frowned and grabbed my hand again, walking with me in silence toward the familiar-looking farmhouse. I felt anxious. It was hard enough wrapping my head around Concepts being humanoid. Stepping outside of reality to look at reality felt overwhelming. We made our way up a slight slope and I heard a faint sound of wood chopping toward the side of the home.

There I was.

I looked so different, but so much the same. A few years younger, my skin was fair and less scarred. I wore a white button-up shirt with the top few buttons undone, trousers, and brown leather shoes. It seemed like I was alone at the chopping block, collecting enough to bring a few pieces into the house. I watched myself gather them up and smile as I walked up those familiar steps and brought them inside.

Kay and I looked at each other.

"Are you ready?" she asked.

"For what?"

Kay's voice softened. "Your daughter, Grace."

I stared at her, stunned. Sound caught my attention. We walked closer to the house and I heard a baby crying. I watched as my younger self stepped out of the house, cradling an infant. My shirt sleeves were rolled up and I held her close while the crying continued. I bounced her up and down, her head cradled in the palm of my hand, tiny and vulnerable. I was smiling at her, trying to quiet her fuss.

I sang to her.

"Amazing Grace, how sweet the sound . . ."

I stood in disbelief, watching myself sing sweet words to a child I didn't remember.

"That saved a wretch like me . . ."

I turned to Kay, who was watching me. She put a hand on my shoulder, her touch ice-cold in the hot midday sun. "I don't understand. Kay, what is happening?"

"I once was lost, but now am found . . ."

I stared at my younger self, singing my infant daughter to sleep in my hands.

"T'was blind, but now I see."

I closed my eyes, leaned down, and gave little Grace a sweet kiss on her forehead. That version of me, standing on my porch holding my sweet daughter, turned toward the screen door and said something quiet and inaudible.

Dee appeared at the door. She opened it without making a sound, kissed young William on the cheek, took baby Grace with the gentlest touch, and stepped back into the house. She looked young and beautiful and sweet. We were together. With child. There was so much love between us even in that brief moment.

I fell to my knees, put my hands over my mouth, and watched my prior life unfolding through welled-up tears.

Kay squatted beside me, rubbing her hand on my back to comfort me. Her icy touch was welcome. It felt just as familiar as the icy grip of the drawn Blackwood Blade. She loved me, and I knew it hurt her to watch me suffer through this memory.

"We had a life together?"

"Yes, baby. You had a family."

"I had a family with Destiny?"

Kay looked to the farmhouse and nodded, then dipped her head down to draw my eyes to hers. "That's just Dee. She wasn't a Concept. Not at this point. You built a life together here. You worked on the railroad."

"The bridge?"

"Yes."

"The one I jumped from, that started this whole fucked up existence?"

Kay sighed and shook her head at me. She looked stern. "You're going through some things, so I'm going to let that one slide. I understand this is a shock. We have to move on. You'll be back on the bridge again soon."

I looked back to the farmhouse, noticing the phantom silhouettes of Dee and my younger self moving as I watched through the windows.

Kay was fiddling with the Reality curio. I heard the metal clink together and in an instant we were standing on railroad tracks a short distance away from what looked like a tiny town. It was night, and a faint drizzle was coming down, but I couldn't feel the rain. Kay was right, we were just watching, unaffected by the reality we were standing in.

Ahead, I saw a few buildings. There was a general store, a church, and a saloon. On the opposite side of the street was a large train station beside a town hall. The sky was dark but warm light poured from the windows of the buildings, illuminating the soaked dirt road cutting through the buildings and beyond.

"Where are we, Kay?"

"A short distance from your old home. A lot of small areas like this sprung up to support the workers on the railroad, and the bridge."

"When is this?"

"About two years after what you just saw. 1913."

"I died in 1915."

"Yes, baby, you did."

"Why are we here?"

Kay pointed toward the rain-soaked scene ahead. I saw Dee burst out of the general store, carrying two-year-old Grace bundled up in her arms. She looked panicked and flustered as she hurried down the wooden stairs. The store doors flung open right after her and the vast shadow of a man appeared in the doorway.

Faust.

I watched as he ran after Dee, who seemed to realize she was too slow. Dee set Grace down on her feet and stood in front of her, facing him, shaking her head and holding out a hand.

"No!" I heard her say. Again and again. "No. No. No."

Faust approached her, grabbing her arm in his massive hand and pulling her toward him. Grace stood alone to the side, wailing in the rain, her feet sinking into the muddy street.

Kay grabbed my arm just as Faust grabbed Dee. I looked down at her hand and back up to her. Stars swirled in her eyes as she stared into me. "There's nothing you can do, baby. I'm sorry."

I turned my attention back to the scene in the rain-soaked street. Words were being said between Faust and Dee. Grace kept screaming. I watched as Faust's massive hand struck the girl and she fell back into the mud. Silent now, unable to scream, she was too shocked to bring air into her lungs. Dee shrieked and Faust brought her to him, kissing her as she tried to fight him off.

I fought against Kay's grip, but she held on to me like a frozen vice. I was stunned at how powerful she was. It felt like I was trying to rip my arm out of a cement building. She stood calm. I couldn't free my arm unless I cut it off. I wanted to.

I watched Faust shove Dee to the muddy ground and point at her as he stood over her and Grace.

"Mine," I heard him say.

Dee scrambled to pick up Grace, running off down the street and into the night as Faust walked up the steps and his hulking frame disappeared into the building.

"What the fuck just happened? Why was he there? What was that about? What the hell is going on?"

"Easy, William."

"Easy? Are you joking? That fucking massive monster hit my daughter. Forced himself on my wife!"

Kay nodded. "I know this is hard, but you need to understand what's happening and that this is bigger than you, and bigger than Dee and Grace."

"Why is he here?"

"Because Deception is here too, and those two have been working on a deal for a long, long time. Here in 1913 you were working the railroad. You had a life and a family with Dee and Grace. Faust was here while Deception manipulated his way through the West. The railroad was perfect for him."

"Why?"

"Cheap labor. Profit. Power. All he ever wanted was more power. Faust saw Dee and wanted her. He was obsessed with her. But he couldn't have her, not with her being mortal."

I watched as Kay fiddled with the Reality curio once more. The metal clinked together, but we hadn't moved. There was no rain, and the moon was higher in the sky. It looked like we'd advanced only a few hours.

"What's going on?"

She pointed to the general store. Behind the store, I saw a light. It looked like a flickering flame approaching the store. I walked forward and spotted a figure.

It was me, carrying a flaming bottle. I watched as I hurled it into the window of the building.

A blast of fire spread to match the sound of shattered glass and within moments the entire building was aflame, the dry wood inside igniting in an instant. As the building became engulfed in a raging fire, I saw Faust walk out the front door and into the street, turning and staring as the place burst into a raging inferno. I watched as on the opposite side of the building, I stared at the flaming building, revenge in my eyes.

"Revenge," I said.

"Started a chain of events. Yes." Kay took the Reality curio out from her pocket, and a moment later there was another metallic clink.

I saw the farmhouse smoldering, nearly burned to the ground. Small flames burned inside, and sagging posts and beams, charred and blackened, twisted and fell onto the foundation. Close to the house, in a heap together, I saw Dee and my young self. We were a pair of darkened silhouettes in the foreground of the destroyed life burning to the ground before us.

"What happened?" I asked.

"Embers from your stove cracked, popped, and made their way onto the wood floor."

"Where's Grace?"

Kay stepped in front of me, ice-cold hands on my shoulders, her gaze focused on mine as she shook her head, swirling eyes laden with sadness.

"She didn't make it?" I asked.

"I'm so sorry, baby. It was terrible luck in an accident. This is the night Grace died. But I need you to focus on that. It was rotten luck. Faust is Luck. This was his doing."

"Why?"

"Well, as Concepts we live through ages. He couldn't have Dee as a mortal—she would've grown old and died in what was a fraction of a moment of his lifetime. So, wielding his considerable influence, he arranged the death of the prior Destiny."

I thought for a moment. "He killed a Concept? I didn't think that was possible without you?"

Kay nodded and shrugged.

"He used you."

"Yes, William, he did. He had the Blackwood Blade this entire time."

"And others?"

"Yes. He manipulated many of us, and he hid it all with the help of Deception. Those two have been responsible for Concepts being tricked, manipulated, used, and destroyed. That's what I mean when I say it's much bigger than you. It has affected life and the trajectory of human civilization. You were the pawn he used to turn Dee into Destiny, and he used Deception to destroy you, to break her down."

I understood. Faust had gone to work with the help of Deception many, many years ago, and somehow I'd ended up at the epicenter of it all. He couldn't have Destiny without me gone. He couldn't have her without destroying a fellow Concept. There was nothing he couldn't accomplish without the help of others and the subterfuge of Deception.

I felt the incredible pull of revenge once more.

"What now?"

"Look at Dee," Kay replied.

I stared at her, beautiful and sweet even in a state of complete distress. Then I noticed what Kay was alluding to. I hadn't seen it when I first looked at us. Dee was pregnant.

"She lost the baby after tonight," Kay said, resting a hand on my back. "Would have been your son."

"Because of all this?"

"Yes."

"How did she become Destiny?"

Kay sighed, staring at the smoldering house and shaking her head at the destroyed couple—my younger self and Dee. "Leverage. Faust and Deception secured her installation as the new Destiny. That's a story for another time, though. There are two more things I need to show you."

With a quick twist of her hands, the Reality curio made another clink noise, and I was beside Kay in a compact room. It looked like a hostel. Cold, unforgiving, and cheap. I was alone on a bed, sleeping. Moonlight struck my face through a small, grimy window. There was a shadowy corner to our right. Kay and I directed our attention there.

Deception sat in the corner in an old wooden chair. He looked different, wearing period clothes like a waistcoat and flat cap, but his cut jaw and confident look was unmistakable. It was him. There was a shimmer in the room, and he took the form of what looked like a four-year-old girl.

It was Grace.

He stood in the form of my deceased daughter, walked across the room, and tapped me to wake me up. In my half-awake state, I rubbed my eyes and scrambled back in the bed, shocked at her sight.

"Daddy, why did you let me die?" I heard her say. Kay clenched my hand.

I watched my younger self stammer. "I tried, sweet Grace, I tried. There was a fire!"

"You let me die, Daddy. I hate you! Mommy hates you! I hope you die too!"

And with that I watched a shimmer, and Deception disappeared as my destroyed young self broke down into sobs through strained breath, head buried in the sheets.

"You thought it was a dream," said Kay. "It was real."

I only stared.

"I'm sorry, baby. This is a lot, but you had to know. You will have your opportunity for revenge, William St. Denis. I will see to it."

I squeezed Kay's hand. She was frozen, but it was comforting. A Concept as old as time itself was giving me attention, care, and devotion. I felt such strength from her presence, and it was intense with her in form and not just as a hibernating Blackwood Blade. I loved her, not in a romantic way, but in a way far beyond anything I'd ever felt or experienced.

I understood, as she guided me through my tragic history, that she cared for me.

"Show me the end, Kay."

She nodded, fiddling with the Reality curio again until that familiar metallic clink echoed in my ears.

We were standing on the Crooked River railroad bridge.

"May 14, 1915," she said.

I watched as my former self stood on the edge of the bridge in the soft moonlight, moments away from ending my life. They'd destroyed me. Wife gone, daughter burned, son having never seen the light of the world. My house in ruins, my life destroyed.

All by the manipulations of Luck and Deception.

The sudden and unceremonious falling of my body through hundreds of feet of space below the bridge was surprising. I turned away when I let go and fell. I didn't need to see the impact. There was nothing to say. My entire inner monologue was only sadness. Kay and I sat upon the bridge, looking out over the canyon and river below. We were both comfortable in the space of our own thoughts and silence of the night sky. I had a thousand questions I didn't know how to ask.

"I'm sorry," she said.

"Why bring me back? Why pick me as your Caretaker?"

"It wasn't right, William. You were wronged. Manipulated. We were all used and manipulated, and for what? For a Concept to weight the world in his favor. You don't understand how many of us are furious that this happened. You're the key to righting this wrong. As long as I could ensure you were still connected to Dee, Luck wouldn't succeed. So I brought you back, kept it quiet, and chose you as my Caretaker."

"Kay, why didn't she say something to me?"

"Baby, Destiny suffered for a hundred years. She wanted to share everything with you but was unable to do so without altering everything and losing you to Luck again. So she soaked in every moment with you and enjoyed what she could. She made sure whenever you visited it was the farmhouse. Deep down she hoped you would remember on your own. She always wanted you back. She wanted you soothed and comforted until it was time for her to go. Ending her altered your path, mine too."

I shook my head.

"What is it, baby?"

I shrugged. "Doesn't matter. Right now Elise is dead at the end of a baseball bat. Power consolidated between Deception and Luck. The world is out of balance. Duncan dead. Destiny gone. In terms of disasters that affect the fabric of all life, this is high on the list."

The metallic clink of Reality's curio rang in my ears.

We were back in the white void. Destiny's body lay before us, bloodied and pale. I noticed some differences. She looked older than she'd been in the reality Kay and I had just visited. My heart felt heavy with the weight of the world at the sight of the wife I'd once had, dead by my hand. All those years visiting her and she couldn't say a thing because she was protecting me and enjoying what she could of me. My chest tightened thinking about the devastation of my life and what I'd done.

Kay rubbed her hands together.

I watched her. She sighed and turned to me.

"My Caretaker," she said, "we'll return you to your time. And when we do, I will be with you."

I didn't understand.

"We have a piece of reality, baby."

"So?"

"I'm going to put you back into reality, moments before you killed yourself on that stage. You'll notice some differences."

"What?"

"No knife." Kay smiled.

I looked at her with a question in my eyes.

"I'll be in you," she said, emphasizing the words and poking me in the chest with a frozen finger. "When you return, there will be no knife. I'll be inside of you. Elise will be alive. Duncan will be alive. The only difference is that you will be Death. You'll only have a moment before Faust swings that bat and kills Duncan."

"I will be Death?"

"Oh, yes." Kay winked.

"What does that mean?"

"Oh, baby," she cooed. "When you return, I will be in you. You will be in me. You will be Death incarnate. All of my power, yours to wield."

"What do I do?"

"You'll know what to do. Save the people who have been by your side, those who matter. Destroy everyone else, including Deception."

My head swiveled to her. "Luck?"

"No," Kay said. "Off-limits. Trap him, but he must live. Too many Concepts need him to face justice for his betrayals. Now go. Get your revenge. Do it for Grace. Do it for Dee. Do it for you. We don't have a lot of time. With Destiny gone, the world will come apart quickly."

I watched her take out the Reality curio for the last time.

"Oh, and William?"

"Yes?"

"Have fun, baby."

I closed my eyes and heard a familiar metallic clink.

CHAPTER 31

THE RAGE OF WILLIAM ST DENIS

I opened my eyes and heard the cheers of the crowd in the auditorium. I was on my knees, center stage. Elise to one side, Duncan to the other. Bats at the ready behind them. I remembered this moment. This was just after Deception had held the blade up to the crowd, then placed it back on the table before continuing to work them into a frenzy.

It was like replaying a movie I'd already seen. Kay was right. There was no blade before me.

She was in me. I felt her, connected.

I'd become Death. When I focused on the crowd, I didn't see people or colors. I saw souls ready for harvest and the detailed features of every being in the auditorium. Their very essence was laid before me. Every connection they had to one another or to anyone in the fabric of this world was in the same dimension as my eyes. I saw threads connecting them to others, to each other, to themselves, and to other souls across the world. I was a human in this reality, and a multidimensional being and Concept in the fabric of every reality.

Through the walls of the Dolos Casino I saw threads extending out thousands of miles to others. The web of humanity and fabric of interconnectedness was within my view, and I understood it all.

I would sever those threads, cut loose the bonds of these souls and send them to whatever ether they should return to.

I heard Deception speak.

"Tonight, my friends, you will witness something so unsettling that you may never be the same. Death will be in this room with you."

That shot of shock and gasps filled my ears once more. I smiled a wicked, delicious smile. Death was in this room.

"Do not worry," continued Deception, holding up a reassuring hand, "for she only comes for her Caretaker this evening. William will grace us with his exceptional talent. He will end his own life before you and travel to another existence right in front of your eyes."

Deception walked to the side of the stage and pointed to a balcony high above. This was where he gave Faust his tribute.

"Ladies and gentlemen," announced Deception, "let us also take a moment to recognize my guest of honor and personal friend, Faust. Without his influence, tonight would not be possible."

Without murdering my child.

Without snuffing out my son's life.

Without destroying me, my life, my marriage, and Destiny.

I craved revenge.

The audience rose to their feet, turned toward the balcony, and gave a rousing and long-lasting applause. "Though," continued Deception with a gleaming smile, "you know him by a different name." He laughed.

The ovation continued until Deception quieted them down.

It was almost time. I looked toward Duncan. He was staring at me with his good eye and his expression changed when my eyes met his. His mouth opened and a wash of realization appeared.

He mouthed the words, "Your eyes."

The reason I saw the fabric of connectedness between all life was because my eyes were swirling with eternity, just as Kay's had appeared when we were separate. It was a giveaway. She was me.

I felt different, cold, strong. Deception walked over to me, hushing the crowd.

My moment arrived.

He leaned down to me, holding the microphone away from his mouth to have a private word. "You will kill yourself now, and I will meet you there when you arrive. You know that, don't you, William?"

"I do," I answered, looking down to hide my eyes.

Deception gently stroked my cheek with the back of his hand, injecting my being with the desire to deceive everything and everyone for a moment. He leaned down to meet my eyes.

"And that will be your end. You know that, don't—"

I saw my eyes reflected in his own, the depth of swirling galaxies through all of space and time. His face went pale. I stared into his bright soul, taking an inventory of every connective luminescent web arcing out from his being into billions of souls in this world. I was witnessing all of it, all the interconnected lies and deception. Everyone affected showed up within my eyes as if there had been an x-ray of every soul who had ever been deceived, tethered to Deception himself.

My skin became ice-cold. I felt warmth pulling toward me, outside of my control. I was becoming Death's black hole, drawing the very nature of existence and life into my inescapable event horizon.

Light began draining from the auditorium. Everything darkened, but I could see it all with such clarity.

I heard gasps and murmurs in the distance.

I breathed in deep and watched the walls bow and bend, misshapen by my presence. They darkened as I breathed out. Panic began spreading, souls and their connected tethers vibrating and becoming agitated. It was as if I'd caught everyone in a massive web, and I was the spider. The predator.

I was hungry for harvest.

"You're right to be afraid," I said to Deception.

He stood and took a step back. "What? How? What has she done?"

I stood. My heart was still. There was no life within my body, yet I felt charged with power. My fists curled and transformed into the pure energy of entropy itself. I looked at my hands, only to see them become barbed tendrils, shifting and appearing glitched and out of focus in this reality. The soundtrack of screams filled my ears as everyone realized this was not the show they'd expected.

"Where is Death?" Deception screamed.

I made my heart beat a single beat and everything and everyone in the auditorium moved as if in slow motion. I watched expressions of horror creep across faces. Green-eyed Guardians climbed over one another to attempt escape or rushed toward me. I watched as luminescent souls shrieked in horror, recognizing their end, their panicked human vessels frantic and overrun by fear.

Deception was turning away. All sounds were muffled. I reached out and snatched him by the throat and he began moving at the normal pace of reality with me. Whereas time slowed in the grip of Death, I'd brought Deception in my literal grip into my timeless existence.

My barbed tendril squeezed his throat and there was no resistance. I held him inches above the ground and pulled him toward me. Thorns of night and shadow gripped him, piercing the flesh of his human form, causing his blood to drain under a tightening tentacle as I squeezed life from him and choked his soul into nothing.

He shimmered but could not change. I wasn't straining. I felt only power. No matter how hard he fought and flailed, my grip clenched harder and tighter. I held him in front of my face and watched his eyes bulge, bloodshot and frantic as I studied him.

"I will destroy you," I whispered, my voice low and intense, changed and altered by the shifting reality around me. My grip on his throat froze him, squeezing his soul from his body. I watched as his webs, luminescent cords stretching from his being to the billions he'd deceived, began vibrating and straining. They began snapping as if over-tightened strings on a guitar, each curling back and withering away as his light faded.

He clawed at my tentacled grip but could not touch me. Blood poured from the barbs slicing him apart and my swirling eyes stared at his shrieking soul.

I brought my other hand—formed into its own barbed tendril—to his chest.

"Give me your heart."

With a flash of pure energy, I tore open his chest, gripping his heart in the void of my grasp and dragging it from his body. I wasn't only destroying his form, I was ripping his heart from his soul. His existence drained as I emptied both his physical and abstract vessels.

With a snap, I removed his heart and consumed his foul soul. I dropped what looked like a burst-open balloon of bloodied flesh to the stage floor and looked up to the scene of chaos before me, frozen in time.

Faust was nowhere to be seen. The balcony was empty. He was preparing. He knew I was coming for him next.

My tendrils retracted back into my human form and I took a deep breath. I raised my hands and the walls of the auditorium turned into a slick black miasma of soul-consuming energy.

Time shifted back to normal. Screams of horror and panic echoed throughout the large hall. I had them all, every green-eyed accomplice, every agent of Luck and Deception frozen in fear, locked as insignificant insects within the web of the end.

Elise was on the ground staring up at me with her own terror. Duncan had scrambled backward, leaning against a wall to the side of the stage, his one eye wide and trying to make sense of everything going on.

I made my heart beat a single beat and all the darkness coating the walls began shooting out in spikes of entropy, piercing the hearts of hundreds of green-eyed Guardians. Strings of connections visible to my dimension-spanning eyes snapped and curled, withering away.

In an instant, I'd consumed every soul except for Elise and Duncan.

The auditorium was silent. The darkness receded. I was in normal form again.

I ran over to Elise, lifting her up from the stage floor.

"William, what the fuck are you? You're frozen. What just happened?"

"There's not much time," I said. "Faust. Faust is Luck. He's been the one making all of this happen. Elise, do you know where Knowledge is? The phone?"

She shook her head. "I-I don't know. Up in his suite, probably?"

"Caretaker, what the hell is going on?"

I turned and saw Duncan walking across the stage, stepping over bloodied and broken bodies.

"Your eyes."

I nodded. "Okay, you two. I'll give you the quick version."

There was a rumble deep underground, and a few sconces fell from the walls and crashed to the theater floor.

Elise looked around. "You killed Deception. Everything here is going to crumble. William, this is bad. Really fucking bad."

I pointed to the ground. "Duncan, give me that bat!"

He snatched it from the ground and handed it to me. I gripped it and watched as shadows in spider form crawled from my fingertips and soaked into the wood. The color of the bat darkened, and I handed it back to him.

"Hey! It's cold!"

"It's a curio now. Cursed. Death's power is within that bat. Take Elise, get to the suite. Find Knowledge. We can't let it disintegrate inside this place. Save Knowledge. If anyone fights you, hit them with that bat."

Elise looked back and forth between the two of us. "How did you know to do that?"

"I just can. It's weird."

"Where's the knife?"

"Death took human form; there is no Blackwood Blade. She showed me my history, and tonight I'm righting every wrong."

"Is Destiny safe?"

I shook my head. "No, dead by my hand. I had no choice."

Elise's face fell. "Oh no, William, I'm so sorry."

I nodded, but sadness and grief would have to wait.

Duncan walked around me and stood next to Elise, putting a hand across her shoulder. She reached around his waist and helped him stand. He was broken, but not done yet. "We should go. I know this place."

"Get the phone and get out. I'll track down Faust. It won't be difficult. He'll be waiting for me."

"Are you going to kill him?" asked Duncan.

I remembered what Kay had told me before she brought me back to this reality. Destroy Deception. Destroy everyone. But Faust must live. Now, though, I felt power, and I wanted to unleash it upon the Concept that destroyed every facet of my life.

"Yes. I am."

Duncan smiled. He respected me and he looked proud, as if things were in place. Duncan always craved order, and it was being restored. He patted my shoulder. "Good luck, Caretaker."

He wouldn't understand how relieved I was to hear him finish that sentence, and to know they were both alive. I watched them run off through a back door. With the floor rumbling beneath me, I left through the exit doors on the same side as Faust's balcony and into the halls of the casino until finding my way up a flight of stairs and through an access door to the casino floor.

There was another rumble. The fabric of reality shook. The casino floor was silent and unsettling. Machines still whirred and made noises, but no other person was in this space. I'd destroyed most of the Guardians back in the theater and Duncan and Elise should be able to handle the rest with the deadly curio I'd given them. I had singular focus now.

Faust.

I stood underneath the overhanging balcony above that stretched around the entire casino floor. I saw tethers, otherworldly webs of souls connected to the Concept of Luck. They stretched out through incomprehensible distances and other realities and times, focusing on a single point above the casino floor. Deception's cords of influence had been staggering in number, but witnessing Luck's influence was breathtaking. Every creature, every being, every event through all time reached him and his soul, shining bright and blinding.

I saw him standing on the second-floor balcony on the opposite side of the casino floor, staring at me.

"You're dead, Caretaker."

"I am Death, Concept."

I breathed deep as warmth and light drained from the expansive casino floor. Machines stopped and blinked out of power. Silence and ice gripped the room. The walls of the Dolos bowed and creaked with my breath. Darkness descended and crept down the walls, turning the bright colors of the room into monochromatic black and gray. All I could see were two emerald-green eyes staring at me from the balcony above.

I reached out with my arm and a shadowy spike of pure entropy extended from my hand, smashing into the balcony just beside Faust, causing it to shatter and crumble. I watched him tumble to the casino floor, then stand up and begin walking toward me.

"Missed. How unlucky."

With my other hand, another jet-black tendril shot out, smashing into a slot machine beside him, causing coins and electronics to fly across the room, clinking across the floor. A large piece of the machine flew off and toward Faust's face as he continued plodding toward me. Without diverting his gaze, he snatched it from midair and began running toward me.

"Missed again!" he shouted, leaping into the air and coming down at me with an enormous chunk of metal gripped in his huge hand. I felt it smash into my forehead and could feel my skull crack under the impact as I hit the floor and bounced backward into the wall.

I climbed to my feet, but before I could summon any strength, Faust's massive hand gripped my throat and he hurled me across the casino floor as if I was a rag doll. Flesh bruised and scraped as I tumbled my way through casino machines and tables. I fell to the ground as I felt ribs crack and flesh tear open.

"Guess even Death can crack," Faust spat. "Hit those machines in just the right spots to break things, didn't you? Luck will never be on your side, Caretaker."

He made his way toward me. I climbed to my feet, brought my hands together, and felt a surge of power welling up in my body. The casino walls froze, covered in glistening frost as the building seemed to be in a glacial grip. Blackened tendrils crept out from my body and across the floor, climbing Faust's legs like ivy, pulling him toward the ground. He fought it, plodding forward with his beastly body until he drew closer.

My swirling eyes saw his threads, the cords connecting Luck through space, time, and reality. It laid his influence bare. I knew everything about every tiny connection he'd ever had on any being.

However, one cord stood out.

Out from his back, a large thread charged with energy shot off into the distance through all of space and time, connecting him to a being outside of this reality.

It was his tether to the Concept of Power.

I was straining to hold him down, but he was too strong and kept moving forward, breaking my bonds. I turned my arm into the embodiment of the Blackwood Blade, devoid of all life and light, the sharpest honed edge in eternity, and a shade so dark, mortal eyes wouldn't be able to comprehend it. With a flick, I severed the connection between Faust's soul and the influence of Power. The conduit between them snapped and like a rubber band, he flew forward, crashing into me and sending us both tumbling out the shattered glass of the Dolos revolving door and onto the Boardwalk's wooden planks outside.

It was night. Dark. Bathed in moonlight with the expanse of the ocean a short distance away, we landed. I could see people standing around us, backing up and forming a circle that encompassed us.

Faust and I stood facing each other. I looked around. I saw Emmanuel, and holding on to his arm was a familiar blind bartender, a manicured handlebar mustache adorning his lip. Duncan and Elise were there. She had a phone in her hand. She was holding Duncan up with her arm around his waist and his arm draped over her shoulder. He was too tired to stand, but was leaning on a bloodied, splintered bat.

I saw Eric, the kid who'd given me a ride to Atlantic City after the crash, watching us while hiding a joint in his hand. The Concept Perspective. My intuition had been right.

Other Concepts were there, ones I'd seen through the last century. Pain and Pleasure, the ever-present bickering couple. Anger, appearing as an eight-year-old boy on the precipice of a tantrum at any moment.

Justice, raven-haired and elegant. Brutality, the leather-aproned butcher, masked and terrifying. Memory, that ever-familiar face I couldn't quite place. They were all here for Faust. Like me, they'd all felt his betrayal and had been used.

"What have you done, insect?" Faust growled.

My hand turned to a barbed tendril of shadow and entropy once more as I reached out and gripped his massive body.

"I ended your power."

"You ruined everything," he said, twisting and struggling under the constricting icy grip of my extended being.

I launched him into the air and slammed him into the boards below, hearing them crack and splinter under the force of impact. In a blink I was on top of him, pinning him down. Blackened shadow and the grip of Death's void held him to the ground, emanating out from my being like vapor from dry ice.

There wasn't a sound. Concepts stood and stared.

"My wife!" I shouted, drawing my fist high and slamming it down on his face, feeling my frozen power crackling against him.

"My children!" I screamed, pounding his face again as his strength waned under the force of my blow.

"My life!"

I put my palm on his face, squeezing him with my hand. The essence of Death began draining from my arm and worming its way into his eyes, mouth, nose, and ears.

I allowed my being to burrow into him, to reach in and rip his soul out of existence.

I wanted him dead. I wanted to tear his soul from his form and torture it for the rest of eternity with the full fury of Death realized. With the rage and power of the end of all existence, I raised my fist high in the air, only to feel my hand fall down and pound against his hulking body with a soft thump.

The shadows disappeared.

My power disappeared.

Beside me stood a figure. Kay. Death herself had split from me and returned to form.

I shook, staring at her, then I turned back to Faust, pounding on his face with my bare knuckles. Breaking my bones, cutting open his skin, beating him with my bare bloodied hands until Kay pulled me off.

She picked me up and held me in her frozen embrace while I sobbed in her arms.

"It's okay, baby. It's okay. You're done. I've got you now. And you've done everything you could. But I couldn't let you do that."

I held on to her, my arms wrapped around her, a century's worth of broken heart pouring out of me as I released all the pain I'd ever experienced. My tears fell to the boards below.

The Concepts, Stewards, and Guardians surrounding us stepped forward, encircling Faust as Death held me.

"I am so proud of you," she whispered as she gave me a gentle kiss on the cheek. "You will always be my Caretaker, William St. Denis."

CHAPTER 32

THE CARETAKER

The morning sun was peeking over the ocean, and soft amber light illuminated the sky, ushering the tragic night to sleep. The gentle hush of the sea touching the shore soothed my tired body. I felt strange. Being imbued with Death for that moment had changed me. I understood her as I understood myself. Everything she saw and felt. I'd seen the universe as she saw the universe, and I'd felt her power, though in the end I hadn't respected it.

Maybe I was human after all.

I sat on a bench outside the Dolos Casino. Duncan sat on my left, Elise to my right. Khali was discussing something with the bickering couple, Pain and Pleasure. Justice and Brutality stood and listened. I couldn't imagine what they had in store for Luck, but it wouldn't be pleasant. That was obvious, because Pain yelled at Pleasure and told him to go stand somewhere else.

Anger, the eight-year-old boy, was a little farther away at an arcade, raging at one of those claw machines that never seem to pick up the stuffed animal no matter how hard you try. Pleasure walked over to him, squatted down, reached into the door of the machine, and stole a small stuffed donkey from inside.

With a gigantic smile on his face, he handed it to little Anger, who twisted its head off, threw it at Pleasure, and stormed off to rage at something else.

Elise put her arm around me. "Is this even real?"

I didn't have the strength to react. I was still processing the events of the last few hours. My old life. Destiny.

Duncan turned and looked back at the Dolos Casino, which looked decrepit and ready to crumble and fall into the sea. "Do you think people will notice?"

Elise shook her head. "No. Reality changed everything from last night. To the people who live here, it's been like this for years. We kind of jumped into an alternate reality timeline."

"Is anything else different?" he asked.

"No. You're still an asshole."

That got me to chuckle. Duncan didn't find it as funny. He shook his head. "I still don't understand what happened. How did you end up becoming Death?"

"I know it's confusing. You were dead."

Duncan looked at me, confused.

"It's true. We were on the stage. The blade was there. I drew it. Faust grew impatient, walked over to you, and crushed you with the bat. One blow to the back of the head. You were dead."

"Well thanks for taking your time, then."

"He was about to do that to Elise, and I drove the blade into my heart. Visited Destiny. Deception was there. I tried our plan, but the Blackwood Blade had no power there. He was too strong."

Elise pulled me close and held me in a tight hug.

"I see," said Duncan. "And that's where you killed Destiny."

"It was the only way. She told me to trust her, grant her destiny. If I hadn't, everything would've failed. It would all be out of balance. She saved all of us."

"Then what?" he asked.

"The blade disappeared. Khali appeared, Death as herself. She showed me my history, how I'd been used, manipulated, wronged. Faust had destroyed the prior Destiny, made Dee into Destiny to take her place through some means I don't understand. He was obsessed with her and it was the only way he could keep her."

"Oh," said Elise.

Duncan and I both looked at her.

"I know some things," she said.

"Like what?" I asked.

"I can't say right now."

Duncan rolled his eye. "Fucking Concepts. Knowledge wants you to shut up?"

"Correct."

"Well," I continued, "Khali agreed to put me back moments before you died, Duncan. She was me, and I was her. It was weird."

Elise threw her hands up in the air. "It was fucking awesome! Terrifying, but awesome!"

Kay walked over to us, Justice by her side. Elise, Duncan, and I stood. Kay rolled her eyes.

Justice laughed. "Relax you three, no need to be too formal. We have some things to straighten out."

"Okay," I said.

"William, thank you. You've done a great service, and you've received a just ending to the torment and hardship they have put you through. I apologize for not being able to resolve this sooner."

"I understand. Thank you. I'm sorry I almost killed him. I got carried away."

"You did," she said with a nod. "For the record, I wouldn't have come down too hard on you for that either. But it's good this worked out the way it did. Faust will pay. Don't worry. You'll not see him again, and he'll hold no power or influence anymore."

"Elise," continued Justice, "you are Knowledge's new Caretaker. He's enigmatic. You've got quite the task ahead."

"Yeah," she said, "but he can tell me how to steal cars."

"I'll pretend I didn't hear that," Justice shot back with a smile. "You have friends to help you. Many Concepts will want to work with you, and many more will look to leverage you. Be careful. Knowing you and what happened, and how much William leaned on you when he was losing his way, I know you'll be fine."

We all turned our attention to Duncan.

Justice sighed.

"What?" he asked.

"Nobody knows what to do with you. You were Deception's right hand for so long. I wondered if we should just destroy you."

Duncan stepped back and everyone looked at Justice, trying to gauge if she was serious.

"You were also the exact friend William needed when he needed you. You were tough on him, and you made him realize his place and his ability."

Duncan nodded, his face torn to shreds and half-swollen. He was having a hard time staying on his feet.

"You need to heal. But when you do, there are options. You know this world and you respect the order of it. I can't make any promises, but you'd make a suitable replacement for Luck or Deception, if you'd be looking for a change of scenery."

His jaw dropped.

"Think about it," said Justice. "Certain Concepts will get in touch with you. Now if you'll excuse me, they need my attention elsewhere. There is a lot to do."

With that, Justice turned and walked away. She took Anger by the arm as he threw a tantrum, dragging him with her like a bratty son.

Kay turned to me. "We should go. There's a lot of work for you to do too, William. You killed Destiny, and while it's a forgivable act, there will be a target on you, and we will need to find at least two new Concepts depending on what Duncan decides. You were the instrument of their death. Tradition demands that you are a part of that process."

"Okay. There are some people I'd like to say goodbye to first."

"Of course, baby. Go talk to Perspective and Love. Those two chatterboxes need a break from each other, anyway."

I walked over to Emmanuel and Love. They were in some kind of discussion with Perspective, who was still smoking a joint and offering it to Emmanuel, who held up his hand in refusal. Elise and Duncan followed close behind.

"Thank you," I said. "All of you. I owe you all a lot."

Love smiled wide. "Ah, the fabulous William St. Denis! My wonderful friend, magnificent to hear your voice again amongst the expanse of the sea and the salted air!"

I laughed.

"I will leave soon, my dear man, but I think I may spend a little extra time here fostering a relationship or two."

"Oh? Getting some work done while you're in form?"

Emmanuel and Perspective laughed.

Love pointed toward Elise and Duncan, a mischievous smile crossing his face. "Can you just imagine what it would be like if I influenced these two?"

"No!" Elise shouted. "Not my type. Not my type!"

Love threw his head back and laughed. "You love who you love, you know?"

Duncan shook his head. "Well that's all the motivation I need to become a Concept and get the hell out of here."

I extended a hand to Emmanuel. "Thank you, my friend."

"You are welcome, William. Come see me again. We'll have a drink together. A normal one."

I turned to Perspective and held out a hand. He moved right past it and gave me a warm hug. He was wearing a worn Pulp Fiction T-shirt and smelled like weed and chocolate.

"You saved me when I needed it most. I appreciate you."

Perspective waved his hand. "It was nothin', chief! Good times! I have something for you."

I watched him reach into his pocket, fishing around for something. He pulled his hand out, and in it was a silver flip lighter. He handed it to me.

"What's this?"

"Curio, bro. Just in case you need a little extra perspective some time."

I smiled at him.

We said our goodbyes, turned, and walked back toward Kay. The four of us stood together facing one another.

"Well, what now?" I asked.

"Duncan and Elise, you two should stick together for the time being. Elise needs to get on her feet, and I can think of nobody better to help her with some aspects of this world than you. True, she has Knowledge, but you have the experience to help her. Plus, you may pick up a thing or two yourself. Elise, baby, be careful."

I watched as the two of them looked at each other and sighed. I detected a slight smile on both of them though. Maybe Love was serious about that pairing. I had my doubts.

"Caretaker?"

"Wait, am I still a Caretaker if you're here in form?"

Kay shrugged. "That's what I'm calling you. Pretend I'm a knife. But do me a favor and shut up from time to time. You wouldn't stop talking to that blade and I just might have to murder everyone if you do that to me for another hundred years. Also, no more putting me down your pants."

I blushed, unsure of how to react to that joke. "Um, noted."

"We need transportation. Elise?"

Elise took out the iKnow phone, tapped her thumbs against it, then smiled. "There's a car a block from here. Parking garage on Union Avenue. Third floor. It's a white Cadillac. Key is in the glove box and it's unlocked. The owner won't miss it."

Duncan laughed. "Deception's Caddy? That's amazing."

Elise stuck her tongue out and winked at him. "Thought you'd like that. If you like, I can ask him where to find a monocle for your stupid face."

Duncan scowled at her.

I reached out and hugged Elise. She held me tight in return.

"I don't know what to say that could possibly tell you how much you mean to me."

"You don't have to. I already know."

She gave me a sweet kiss on my cheek and touched my face with her hand. "I'll also always know where you are. Don't worry, we'll see each other soon. It's time for our paths to wind elsewhere, I guess."

I held out my hand to Duncan and he met it for a firm handshake.

"Caretaker," he said.

"Thank you."

He shrugged. "I knew you had it in you. You did well. Thanks for letting me die before you saved everyone. Jerk."

I laughed. "Thanks for driving a car into an airplane."

Elise and Duncan waved a last goodbye and walked off together, Elise buried in her phone. Kay and I walked down the Boardwalk. The Concepts had all returned to their places and realities. We were alone on a stroll, Death and her Caretaker soaking in the morning sun. We reached the parking garage, walked up the stairs, and found a pristine white Cadillac parked in the corner.

I opened the door and sat in the driver's seat. Kay sat in the passenger seat, snagged the keys from the glove compartment, and handed them to me. In moments, we were exiting the garage and turning down the street. We made our way onto the highway out of Atlantic City, the pain and destruction of what had just happened stretching into the background as we moved forward.

"Where to?" I asked.

"First thing's first, we need to get to Boston."

"Boston? Why?"

"That's where we'll find the new Destiny. You've got work to do."

I smiled. "I'll try not to lose you this time."

Kay put her boots up on the dash and moved her seat back to recline. She opened the window and stuck her hand out, moving it up and down against the force of the air.

"Always wanted to do that?" I asked.

"Yes, I have. You know what? I have an idea!"
"What's that?"
"We should go kill some people."

I shook my head and turned to look at her, shocked. "Wait, what?"

She stuck her tongue out and laughed.

"Oh, you've got jokes now. Okay."

She reached over and hugged me tight in her icy grip, resting her head on my shoulder. In the warm morning sun, hours after I'd lost everything and saved the relationships that had saved me from losing myself, I set forth on my path to Boston. In a white Cadillac with Khali in the passenger seat, songs on the radio, and a mending heart, I had her by my side.

"Caretaker?"
"Yeah?"
"You and I are going to be best friends."

Thanks for reading.

You can learn more about David here.

YouTube:
https://www.youtube.com/c/davidbadurina

Instagram:
https://www.instagram.com/dbadurina_author/

On the Web:
http://davidbadurina.com

For publicity requests, please email
infj@davidbadurina.com

ACKNOWLEDGEMENTS

Honestly, I'm at a loss for words. I'm not sure how this happened. If you know me at all, you know you were a part of this book. Whether our paths crossed in person, or on social media, or simply in thoughts of similar souls, you matter to me and inspire me to keep moving forward. Thank you for helping me and pushing me to become better.

All I can think to say is ...

I appreciate you.

Made in the USA
Monee, IL
03 December 2020